the other side of together

EMILY COX
&
NICOLE ALLEN

Cover design by Asombra Studios

Chapter heading images from Canva

DEDICATION

Emily:
To Nancy Takacs, who once asked a question that shined light on my unspoken dream which is now printed on these pages in black and white.

Nicole:
To the Real MeiLi – the imaginary one may have been born in my head, but you were born in my heart.

CHAPTER 1

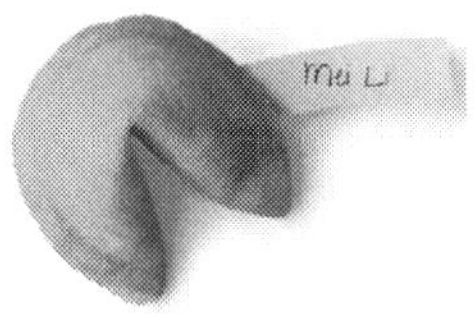

The cable car squeals to a stop, and I hurry up its steps to an outdoor seat facing the city, just as someone calls my name.

"Mei Li!" Chef Marco rushes up to the car and smiles, out of breath from running. "I just wanted to let you know…" He takes a quick breath. "You're going places. It has been a pleasure having you in my class."

My heart trips over itself and I manage a "thank you" as the car rocks forward. He waves and turns back toward the sidewalk. So much of my life has been dictated by others, but not this one thing. Mama and Baba don't even know I've been taking cooking classes, and I'll never tell them. I did it on my own. It's probably the last thing I'll be able to do on my own. No culinary school will accept me if they find out who I am. Or who I'm not.

But Nick told me he's sure I'll get an internship. Only eight more weeks and I could be in L.A. meeting famous chefs. Eight more weeks and my life will finally begin. Thanks to Nick. The more miracles he works in my life, the more I see us working. Someday. Eventually.

I settle into the corner of the bench and pull the elastic from my ponytail so my hair falls down my neck to block the breeze coming off the bay. The light rail clunks along the tracks and people dot the streets, headed into bars or nightclubs, some going home late from work. Laughter punctuates the crisp night, and car horns blare. My worries and fears slide toward me when the cable car climbs the hills toward Chinatown. Graduation. Possible internship with a top chef. Chance of culinary school in the fall. Nick's frequent mention of "our" future together. Getting out of a house that shrinks as Baba's anger grows.

Eight more weeks to figure this out.

The cable car grinds to a stop, and a group fills the spaces around me. Their chatter vibrates through the car and I wonder what it would be like to have so many friends you don't know which conversation to join. But I have Lin who talks enough for a hundred people. My world will be too quiet without her.

The cable car rocks forward again and the girl beside me talks to her friend about a guy she met in a club and thought he was *the one*, but he never called her back. Then she makes her friend promise she won't let her fall for someone new tonight since guys in clubs only want one thing.

I'll probably never step inside a club, and Baba wants me with Nick. But still. What would it be like to have options? I've kissed Nick maybe ten times, and he'll probably be my first and last. But I guess people marry friends they've known since childhood all the time. I'll think about it when I'm 25. Not 18.

The car stops and the group hops off, headed into the night that could hold someone new for that girl. I grab my bag and pull out my lip gloss when another passenger jumps on as the car lurches forward. My hand freezes, watermelon lip gloss hovering over my lips as Marcus Miller slips down the aisle, grabbing each pole along the way. His charter high school hoodie stretches across his shoulders and his overgrown, sun-streaked hair ripples in the wind. And the legs. Lin has worshipped them since Marcus hit puberty. I've always been more into his smile.

Nick is handsome in so many ways, but I've known him forever, and he's so predictable. Expected. Marcus Miller? Completely intriguing.

We've lived on the same block since I moved here ten years ago. He spends time in the same places I do, but rarely at the same time. Which is so, so unfortunate for me. Not that I'd ever have anything to say to him. Or dare. We have nothing in common but a trolley stop.

He shifts, his profile outlined by yellow streetlamps and neon lights, and I hope my thoughts don't float toward him on the breeze.

When he pulls his phone from his pocket, the screen lights his face. Whatever he's looking at makes him smile, and it spreads all the way up the car to me. For the love of all that's hot and holy. It's like the warm rain I used to run through in Taiwan, drenching every part of me. I squint into it, like the night exploded. If only the person who made him smile like that could see what they've done. It's probably a girl. An equally beautiful girl—tall and wispy and completely unaware of how lucky she is because she's used to getting guys like him.

I skim the lip gloss across my lips, then slip my phone from my bag and pull up Lin's last text, pretending to type as I angle the camera toward Marcus. I double check that the flash is off, then slide my finger over the button. He's still smiling, and I bite my lip as I send the picture to Lin. It needs no explanation.

Two seconds later, my phone chimes.

Lin: WHAT?????????????????

HOW?????????????????

YOU ARE BREATHING MARCUS MILLER AIR!!!!!!!!!!!!!!!

He leans his hip into the railing while he responds to a text, hair falling into his face as he looks at the screen. Dark eyebrows. Darker lashes. Golden skin. Smile lines like parentheses around his mouth. When he glances up, I jerk my focus to my phone, staring so hard at the screen my eyes burn. I shift sideways on the bench and pull my knees against my chest, texting Lin a real-time description of every move Marcus makes until the trolley rings for my stop. I grab my bag, hop off the car, and walk up the street, mentally rewinding the past ten minutes so I can tell Lin every detail from the beginning.

My phone buzzes and I sidestep construction cones on the sidewalk, glancing at the screen.

Lin: BE ON YOUR FIRE ESCAPE ASAP!

I shove my phone in my back pocket and take bigger strides up the hill, my calves burning. But as I glance over passing cars, my eyes collide with Marcus's across the street. I look away, narrowly missing someone stepping out of a shop. Apologizing, I hurry past them, my face and neck hot. Marcus caught me looking. But it's not like I'm stalking him. We live across the street from each other. He got on the cable car after me. I'm just walking home, scanning the street. If anyone's a stalker, it's him. Except I could only wish.

I'm focusing so hard on keeping my attention from leaping to the other side of the street that I don't notice the uneven section of sidewalk before my shoe does. I stumble and yelp, throwing my arms out for balance. When I'm steady on my feet, I straighten and grip my shoulder strap, cursing every earthquake that ever cracked the sidewalk. Marcus probably saw the whole thing. But my eyes aren't leaving this sidewalk to find out.

I round the corner onto my street, relieved to be out of his sight, but my fire escape is empty, and the restaurant's neon sign is off, so I veer toward Guo Mama's shop to wait for Lin and avoid Baba who's probably counting the till. But when I reach for the door, someone steps behind me and grabs it above my head. I look over my shoulder and my eyes climb a bulldog logo on a chest until they reach a face and my heart dives into my stomach.

"Looks like we had the same idea." Marcus smiles and I make a sound that's supposed to be a polite laugh but sounds gorilla-ish.

I hurry inside the shop, my ears practically relocating on my head to listen to Marcus behind me, his Adidas squeaking on the freshly mopped terra cotta. One footstep to every two of mine. My nose joins my overactive ears and catches the breeze coming off him, crisp and flowy. Fabric softener. Spearmint.

"Guo!" His voice rumbles over my head, through my limbs, and vibrates in my chest like I sucked it in and it's rattling my insides.

"Marcus Miller!" Her shrill voice skids around the corner before she shuffles into sight, her purple shirt billowing around the edges of her apron. Her gray hair is flat after a long day, the bobby pins giving up. "And Mei Li!" She stops when she sees me. "What luck!" She holds up the glass cleaner bottle like she's making a toast.

Marcus and I reach the counter at the same time, but he walks behind it like he's an employee and Guo Mama whips him with her cleaning rag before setting it on the counter. She grins as Marcus hauls her giant jar of fortune cookies from under the counter, glass clanking as he pulls off the lid.

"Hi, Guo Mama." I smile at her, my eyes slipping to

Marcus before I yank them back to her. "Just stopping by on my way home."

"How did your class go?" She sprays the counter and dries it with the rag.

"Really well. I think I'm ready."

"For what?" Marcus cracks open a fortune cookie, pulls out the paper, then pops both halves in his mouth and chomps while he waits for my answer. He tosses the paper in the garbage, his eyes never leaving mine, spreading blue heat on me like peanut butter.

Guo Mama turns to him and pats his shoulder, her eyes twinkling. "Miss Zhang is going to become a famous chef."

I roll my eyes. "Not famous."

"Wait!" Marcus's eyes widen, tinting everything blue. Think I might be floating. "Zhang? Like Zhang's across the street?" He jabs his finger toward the opposite wall.

Of course he doesn't know who I am. We haven't talked once in the ten years we've lived around the corner from each other. I nod. "My family's restaurant."

"Dude," he breathes, nodding slowly. "That is the best freaking Chinese food in the whole bay area. My dad and I are there every Tuesday night. No joke."

Yeah, I know.

"I order the same thing every single time. Also not a joke."

Yep. Sweet and sour pork.

"Sweet and sour pork." He rolls his eyes, then kisses his fingers and throws them into the air like an Italian chef.

I nod. "Good choice." My voice is thin and off balance, like it's still stunned to be in Marcus Miller's presence. *Talking* to him. Exchanging words. Standing in the blue heat of his eyes. Lin is going to stroke. Maybe I'm stroking.

He unwraps another fortune cookie and repeats the routine before popping it into his mouth, talking around it. "Maybe the owner's daughter could make a double order magically appear…"

I laugh. "Like right now?"

He nods, chews, swallows. "Yeah. Now, anytime. 24 hours a day. I could take it down in less than two minutes. Done it so many times." He unwraps another cookie.

"Too bad the restaurant's closed. Another time, maybe?"

Another time? Like this will ever happen again.

"How about this?" He chews and holds up his hand until he swallows. "I'm gonna write your fortune, and if it comes true tomorrow, you owe me a double order. You could leave it here and I'll pick it up after practice tomorrow night. Yeah? Deal?"

I tilt my head, pressing my lips together so my crazy-girl smile can't slip out. "Are you a fortune teller?"

He shrugs before holding out his hand for me to shake. "Guess you'll find out."

I glance at his hand, then shake it, stifling my inner squeal before looking back at him. "Deal." I let go and drop my hand, balling it into a fist so tightly, my nails cut into my palm. "But if the fortune doesn't come true, you owe me the biggest bag of sour Skittles in San Francisco."

Guo Mama cackles, and I remember there are three of us in the shop even if the world just shrunk to Marcus-sized.

"I'm not worried." He grins at me as he twists the lid back on the glass jar and puts it under the counter.

When my phone buzzes against my backside, I blink and pull my eyes from him, yanking it out of my pocket.

Lin: Where r u? Dying...

Marcus pulls a Sharpie from his pocket and snatches orange Post-It notes from beside the register, peeling one off and slapping it onto the counter. He leans over it, curling his arm around it so I can't see what he's writing. Left-handed. Explains the smudges up the side of his hand. He folds the note four times, then holds it toward me. I grab it, but he doesn't let go. "No looking until you get home."

I nod. "I won't, but maybe you should start researching where to buy gigantic bags of sour skittles. Just in case." I yank the fortune from his hand and slip it in my pocket, breathing through the realization that I have Marcus Miller's handwriting IN MY POCKET.

"Maybe," he says, shrugging and smiling, and Guo Mama chuckles.

I turn to her. "Lin's waiting. Talk to you tomorrow."

"I'm so proud of you, Mei Li. You are going places, I know." She reaches up to pat my cheek. "Many, many beautiful places."

I smile at her. Second time I've heard that tonight. I hope it's true. Glancing from her to Marcus, I squeeze one word through my tight throat. "Bye."

He holds up a hand in a wave and I turn to walk toward the door. "Can't wait for my after-practice sweet and sour pork tomorrow, Mei Li." His voice melts over me like warm honey, but I don't look back as I push through the door and step onto the sidewalk, the night glossy and buoyant like my thoughts. A guy with a dog walks past, no clue that the whole world just changed inside that shop. Or that Marcus just said my name.

My heart swells in my throat and I put my hand to my neck, smiling as I fast walk toward the alley, scaling my fire escape ladder before I dare to breathe.

Lin's head pops over the railing, her short, frenzied hair spiking toward me. "Where've you been? I've been here for seven excruciating minutes. Never do this to me again."

"I promise what I'm about to tell you will make your wait worth it." I drop to the landing and push open my window.

"Hurry, hurry!" she squeals, pushing me through the window from behind. "Baba doesn't know I left, so I don't have long and want every detail." She crawls through the window after me and flops onto my bed, kicks her legs up behind her, and wiggles her feet as she smooths her shimmery gold skirt over her backside. "Don't leave anything out."

I drop to my knees, elbows on my bed as I lean toward her and tell her every detail down to the neon green Sharpie Marcus used to write the fortune I'm afraid to read.

Her eyes widen and she squeezes my arm. "What does it say?"

I pull it out of my pocket, unfold it, and read out loud. "You will find another fortune waiting for you in Guo's shop after school tomorrow."

Her mouth falls open, and she stares at me before a smile takes over her face. "He plays dirty." She wiggles her eyebrows. "And smart. He knows how to get what he wants."

I squeeze my eyes shut, shaking my head. "He'll forget." I open my eyes. "I have to focus on real things like the internship Nick is lining up for me. Marcus is definitely not real."

"Uh, Marcus is *very* real. You just *talked to him* in all his glory. Don't you dare think about Nick at a time like this. You're officially the only one with a legitimate right to daydream about Marcus Miller. He is what dreams are made of. Nick's just gross." She wrinkles her nose. "Sorry. I know you and Nasty Nick have something brewing, but whatever it is stinks. Like an old man. Because seven years older makes him way too old for you. You can do way better. Like Marcus better." She pauses, then releases a breath and shrugs. "Sorry. Rant complete."

"You just don't know Nick well enough."

"Maybe not, but no amount of money can mask the weird vibe I get around him. And he better not mess with our plans to get on The Price is Right this summer because, so help me..." She waves her hand. "But whatever. All I'm saying is,

I'd rather date that homeless guy on the corner who walks his invisible dog. But…" She shakes her head and holds up her hands. "Let's just get back to Marcus Freaking Miller."

I pause, let my brain soak in a little more of the reality of ten minutes ago. "Think he's still at Guo Mama's?" I jump to my feet and sweep aside my curtains.

Lin follows and we lean against each other, faces almost pressed to the cool glass. I crane my neck and my breath makes a circle on the glass as I stare at Marcus in front of Guo Mama's shop, his hand on her shoulder as he leans way, way down to talk to her. His hoodie is slung around his waist now, showing off the muscle chiseled into his arms. Black, blocky words are written in Sharpie on his forearms and I squint to read what it says, but my breath fogs the glass again and I rub it away.

"Do you think all the girls at his school watch him like this?" Lin swipes a circle of fog off the window.

"Unless they're blind. I'm so jealous of all those girls. Super jealous of his girlfriend. You don't look like that and not have one."

"No, you don't," Lin agrees, squeezing my arm like she's taking my blood pressure, her eyes on the street below as she whisper-squeals. "Look at his legs."

My eyes move from the writing on his forearm to his legs, then to his face. "Yeah, but look at his smile."

Lin sighs and wipes away the window fog. "He has exceptionally white teeth."

Guo Mama grabs Marcus's arm, and he puts his hand over hers. My heart stutters at how gentle he is, even though he could pick her up with one hand. I swallow when thoughts of those fingers tangling with mine spread through my head.

He laughs to the sky again, sending a flash of light into the middle of Chinatown, and Lin gasps. "Whoa…did you see that? He *has* to be an amazing kisser." A beat passes between us, our eyes glued on him and Guo Mama. "I wonder what it would be like to kiss a guy like that."

"I'll never know."

"You could, though. You're gorgeous. He's gorgeous. The final moments of your senior year would be like being on The Price is Right, hosted by Marcus Miller and winning the whole Showcase Showdown."

"You know I can't." I shrug. "I can't even be a contestant on his show for 100 reasons."

Lin turns to me, grabbing my shoulders. "No way—you can absolutely choose door number two. You're only looking at door number one right now, which is some ugly, oak bedroom set from the 90s—complete with a waterbed—and not even considering door number two, which is an all-expenses paid trip around the world in a private yacht named Marcus Miller. Which would you rather have? You have choices, Mei Li. Stop being so worried about your parents and Gross Nick."

A moment squeezes between us. She doesn't understand just how much it matters to me and my parents that I'm with Nick.

"Anyway…" Lin takes a deep breath and smiles. "I have to go. But if I didn't, we'd make a plan to get Marcus to kiss you before graduation." She slides up the window, crawls out, and blows me a kiss as she smooths her skirt, then sticks her head back inside the room. "I'm going to walk right past door number two. All you've got to do is choose it and all that can be yours." She grins, then waves as she backs down the ladder.

The April air curls around me, pulling me out of my stuffy room and onto the landing. I lean against the railing, smiling and covering my mouth when Lin crosses the alley and walks past Guo Mama and Marcus. She turns around and blows me another kiss, calling into the night. "See you tomorrow, Mei Li."

Marcus looks up and our eyes slam into each other. I grab the railing and consider ducking, but he'll see me through the slats and I don't want to be weirder than I already have been, so I scramble back through my window, slam it shut, and yank the curtains closed.

CHAPTER 2

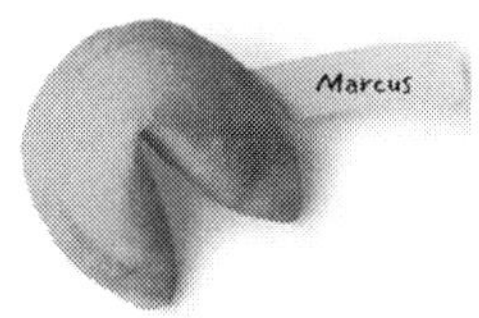

Two weeks later

Aww, yeah. Tuesday night Chinese food *plus* a view of Mei Li between Dad and Lex's shoulders. Dude… Zhang's has way more than the best Chinese food in San Francisco. Mei Li's way more interesting than Dad's and Lex's conversation about the new detective they're working with at the SFPD. And apparently more interesting than the sweet and sour pork I've been craving since biology. Which is a weird time to think about eating animals, but my stomach was threatening to eat itself. Only now, I can't think about pork because Mei Li's between our table and the next one.

She reaches for one of the customer's glass and a narrow strip of skin peeks out between her low-rise skinny jeans and her shirt. When she straightens, she drops a piece of paper on the floor next to me and I stare at it before leaning down to pick it up. I straighten in my chair and my eyes catch up with her as she walks away. Unfolding the note in my lap, I glance down at her loopy handwriting.

I didn't switch my shift just because I knew you'd be here tonight. But…I didn't say no either, so….

Biting back a smile, I shove the note in my pocket and scan the room, spotting her at another table. Contact #24 since we met at Guo's shop two weeks ago. The morning after our chance introduction, I'd stopped by Guo's on my way to school and left Mei Li another fortune so the first one would come true and win me the double order of sweet and sour pork. After practice, there was the biggest takeout box waiting for me. And a note—number three. I wonder how long it will take her to down the jumbo bag of sour Skittles I left for her just for fun.

She's at a table across the room again, and when she tilts her head and laughs along with the lady she's serving, my eyes get stuck in her pink lip gloss. Her smile is a circle of light in the dim, red restaurant. Her ponytail sways with every step, waving for me to follow her through the swinging door she bumps open with her hip.

"Marcus? Hello? Marcus Miller?" Dad's Southern drawl pulls me back to our table, a huge envelope in front of my face. "This came today. Thought you might be mildly interested." He flips his tie over his shoulder and slurps Lo Mein noodles, and Lex takes down his beef and broccoli. Way too much broccoli, not enough beef.

I set down my chopsticks, scanning the return address before looking at Dad, back to the envelope, back to Dad, like eye ping-pong. He doesn't know I'm gonna say no to what's inside that envelope. No way I'm telling him tonight, though.

"Open it!" he says around a mouthful of noodles, shoving it toward me. "Let's hear how much I don't have to pay for you to become a brain surgeon." His biceps strain impressively in his rolled shirt sleeves like he wants to rip it open himself. My leg bounces, my knee ramming the edge of the table and shaking the candle in the middle of it. My whole body knows what's inside, and my brain's trying to figure out how to say yes to it, even though there's no way I can.

I slip a finger under the flap and slide it through the seal, then pull out the official Stanford letterhead. The offer. Full scholarship. Stanford soccer jersey. All mine if I sign.

"Don't find offers like that in a fortune cookie!" Dad whoops, and Mei Li glances at us. I catch her eyes, but the guy she's waiting on grabs her arm, and she turns back to face him.

My gaze lingers on the guy's hand squeezing her arm until Lex leans across the table and slaps his palms against my chest like I'm a hand drum. "You know how to make your godfather look good." He sits back in his chair, beaming as he crosses his meaty arms over the radio strapped across his dress shirt. "No big surprise, though—Ray's raised the perfect kid."

Except perfect kids don't consider signing that Stanford offer and leaving their dad alone. It's always been the two of us. If I leave him alone, I'll be just like my mom.

Mei Li flows toward the kitchen, balancing dirty dishes on a tray she practically bear- hugs to hold. I think about her note. What I'll write back. The Sharpie in my pocket. The bowl of fortune cookies near the register. Getting away from this table so I don't accidentally tell Dad I accepted USF's offer so I can live at home. I could sign the line and lock in my dreams right now. But I can't. So I need to get far away from the temptation.

Lifting my cup, I let it slip through my hand so what's left of my Dr. Pepper sloshes down my practice jersey. Swearing, I dab at it while Dad and Lex throw napkins at me, but I scoot my chair back. "Gonna go clean up."

I weave away from our table toward the register, swiping a fortune cookie from the bowl on my way to the bathroom. Holding the hem of my jersey, I wave it dry as I push through the door and carefully open the wrapper, pull the fortune out of the cookie, then slide my Sharpie from my pocket. Yanking off the lid with my teeth, I use the wall as a writing surface and write my phone number on the back of the fortune before flipping it over to read it. I smile. No way. *Someone in your life needs a letter from you*. Maybe a text? A call? All of it.

Wedging the paper back inside the cookie, I drop it in its wrapper, then squat under the hand dryer, punching the button. I wave my shirt under it until I sweat, and when Stanford slips into my mind again, I push out of the bathroom, stopping to scan the restaurant. Mei Li's balancing her tray as she hands drinks to a new group, so I stride through the table and chair maze and drop the fortune cookie on her tray as I pass.

When I slide back into my seat, Stanford's offer stares up at me next to a fresh Dr. Pepper. She came to our table while I was gone. I pick up my soda and take a drag, even though coach will kill me for drinking it.

"Can't believe this is it, M.C." Dad grips his cup, swirling the soda inside before taking a few gulps. "Marcus Charleston Miller—Stanford's next big thing." He nods and Lex grins. "Always knew it." He rubs his chin, the stubble from his 18-hour shift rustling against his palm but then I intercept Mei Li's smile and pink spreads up her neck and settles on her cheeks and my stomach flips, trapping all the air I should be breathing.

Whoa.

Dad leans into my line of sight. "Off to Stanford on a brand spankin' new motorcycle, right, M.C.?" He raises his eyebrows.

I tear my gaze from Mei Li, and feeling rushes back into my limbs like carbonation as I jab my chopsticks into my food and nod. "Yeah—definitely." Somehow, she makes oxygen deprivation totally pleasant.

Dad picks up his chopsticks and attacks his noodles again. "Been thinking about sweetening that deal."

I frown and chew. "How's that?"

"Keep avoiding girls until graduation, motorcycle's still yours." He crosses his arms and rests them on the table, leaning toward me. "Avoid girls until you finish undergrad, you've got yourself a car."

I stare at him, then open my mouth, close it and ease back in my chair. "You serious?"

"Dead."

Lex whistles and shakes his head. "Why don't you make the boy a monk while you're at it, Ray?"

I glance at him, then back to Dad. "Like what kind of car?"

He shrugs. "Whatever you want. Think you can do it?"

"Thinking about it."

He frowns through a smile and tilts his head. "What's there to think about? Let a girl mess you up or get a car—easy choice."

It had been pretty easy so far. Sort of. There'd been a few times when long legs had momentarily blurred my focus, but…only six weeks until graduation. Mei Li and I have only talked in person once. But those 24 notes…and now my number…

"Deal's on the table. Know what I'd do." Dad goes back to his noodles as motorcycles and tricked-out cars race through my head. Black car—tinted windows. Nice rims, sweet system. So fast. No big deal. Right? I sneak a glance at Mei Li.

Maybe.

"Hey…uh…Marcus?" Dad interrupts my daydream of Mei Li sitting right next to me in my very fast car. He glances up from reading a text on the phone next to his plate, then holds it up for Lex to read. "Head back to The Clubhouse and get your homework done, how 'bout? Have a night at home." He pushes away from the table and Lex wipes his mouth and throws down his napkin, scooting his chair out.

"What's going on?" I pop another piece of pork into my

mouth and look from him to Lex, but Dad throws on his suit jacket, then talks to his wallet while he rifles through cash.

"Another woman disappeared. Number fourteen. Can't all be runaways." He shoves his wallet back into his suit pocket, and Lex pats me hard on the back as he passes. "Now, Marcus—home."

Before my eyes, Detective Ray Miller transforms into RoboCop, and Tuesday night Chinese is officially over. "Any chance of a ride along? I could do chemistry later and—"

"Not a chance. Don't want you anywhere near this stuff."

CHAPTER 3

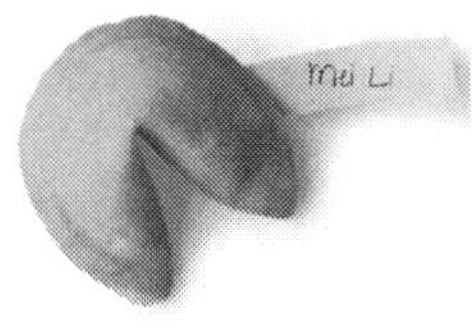

*Never had a conversation on the back of a takeout menu, but let's keep this up. Check every scrap of paper. Never know where I might leave the next note. BTW, looked up the meaning of Mei Li. 1 million points to your parents for their incredibly accurate choice.**[1]

—M

I grunt as I lift two bulging garbage sacks and use them to push open the back kitchen door. Light from Chinatown wanders down the alley and gathers in the corners like neon fog. Kind of like the inside of my head when Marcus Miller wanders into it and a fortune cookie wanders into my pocket.

I bite my lower lip and hurl the garbage bags into the dumpster. The sidewalk is dotted with people laughing and talking their way down the street. Guo Mama's shop window sign says open, but she's not outside in her bamboo chair or I'd hurry over and tell her all about who I waited on tonight. If she was younger—like sixty years younger—she'd be all over Marcus Miller. She *is* the only other female he talks to around here. At least in person. He talks to me on paper now.

I close my eyes and replay The Moment from tonight. The

way he kept his eyes on me as he walked to the bathroom. The breeze he left after he dropped the fortune cookie on my tray. Like a gust of wind that stole all the air around me.

Stepping into the shadows, I pull the fortune cookie from my pocket, its wrapper crinkling, the cookie all but dust. I shake the bits into my hand and let the dust fall between my fingers, leaving a white slip of paper behind. My very fortunate fortune.

Dark writing stares up at me when I flip the paper over in my palm. A phone number. Marcus's? Not possible. Except… it has to be.

Two weeks, twenty-four notes—he's never hinted that he wants to talk to me in any other way. But then he shows up tonight, looking so good, fresh off the soccer field. His usually shaggy hair pulled back into a tousled half pony. I tried not to look at him, but he didn't seem to try not looking at me, so I stopped trying. When our eyes met, his flushed face said things and mine responded in pink, all the way up my neck and into my cheeks. Between my pink cheeks and his blue eyes, there were purple streaks in the air throughout the restaurant. No wonder Nick kept giving me weird looks—I was a walking pink and blue tie-dye.

Now, my heart is attempting to leap from my chest and run through Chinatown, bragging to everyone that I am holding Marcus's phone number. That he gave it to me. But there's only one person that needs to know right away or she'll kill me for withholding.

I tug my phone from my back pocket and dial, wiggling my knees to shake off the chilly air and my nerves while I wait for Lin to pick up. But her ever-cheery voice welcomes me to her voicemail and invites me to stay as I glance at the time on my phone. 8:02. She's probably getting her brother ready for bed.

When the voicemail beeps, I whisper, "You will never guess whose number I have in my hand right now." I end the call, clench the phone in my fist, scan the alley and street, then text: re: an incredible pair of legs - and smile, face, eyes, hair, etc - Call me!

When the kitchen door scrapes open, my head snaps up and I shove my phone in my back pocket with Marcus's number as Nick steps outside. "There you are." He sways a little before reaching for the brick wall. A loud truck rattles up the street at the end of the alley before Nick speaks again. "I couldn't help but notice how beautiful you look tonight." His words slur on their way out and ripple in my stomach. I knew he was drunk when he came in tonight. A cloud of booze hung over his usual corner table. "Especially in that apron."

I take a quick breath to whisk away the Marcus cloud in my head and flip the dumpster lid closed. "Are you making fun of my apron?" I hurry toward him so he can't sense the excitement I'm leaving in the shadow under my fire escape. I smile at him and take the steps two at a time, reaching for the kitchen door, but he reaches out and tugs on the front of my apron, pulling me to him.

"Not making fun. It's hot."

I recoil when the rancid tang of alcohol sweeps across my face. "I think you've had a little too much to drink."

"Not too drunk to see. Care to know what I saw?" He points at one cloudy eye, the sharpness edging his voice digging into my stomach. "Anyone would have noticed." He steps closer. "You were noticing someone else. And he was noticing you." His eyes skitter across me as I swallow metallic guilt and shake my head.

"I'm not sure what you're talking about." I step back and reach behind me for the kitchen door but he pushes it closed as I press my back against the brick. "I was too busy to notice anything."

His voice is like tumbling gravel between us. "I know what I saw, Mei Li. The detective's son. He watched your every move. And he liked what he saw." Nick reaches out, his fingers sliding down my cheek, heavy and listless. I hold perfectly still, hoping to dissolve into the brick. "Of course he was watching you. You were the most beautiful thing in the restaurant. But…he doesn't know that I really…*really*…don't like anyone who wants what I want." He steps closer, his nose on my ear, and I tense. "I'm protective, that's all." His hand smooths down my bare arm, goose bumps rising like a warning. "Is that wrong of me? We don't want the detective to know too much, do we?"

My throat burns and I swallow, shaking my head. He's right. Detective Miller can't know about my family.

My phone chimes in my pocket, but I meet Nick's eyes and try to hold them as they circle. Is it wrong for him to be protective? Since his baba died three years ago, he's always been here for me and my family, keeping us and our secrets safe. Opening doors for me I could never open on my own. It doesn't seem wrong, but it doesn't feel right either. But why? I've loved having him in every detail of my life because he makes all the big, scary decisions so I don't have to. He makes sure everything runs smoothly. We would have been deported long ago if it wasn't for him. I know he cares. But since I turned eighteen last month, he's cared a little too much about everything I do. He's suggested things that feel too permanent between us. A few months ago, I liked the idea of something permanent since everything else about my life felt so fragile. But I'm not sure I want Nick to be the permanent part.

---

1. **Mei Li in Mandarin means "beautiful"*

CHAPTER 4

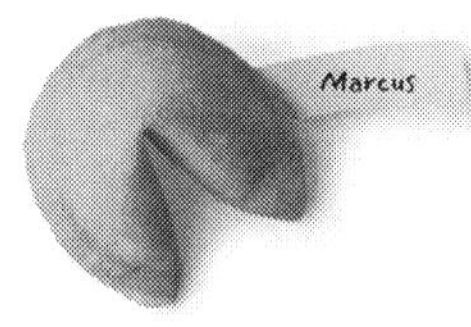

I shove the Stanford envelope in my backpack and throw it and my soccer bag over my shoulder. Heading for the back exit, I scan the restaurant for Mei Li. This back and forth is harmless. I'm not gonna lose my motorcycle by looking. I've checked out plenty of girls. Kissed one at a party in ninth grade, before the bet. If a touch-and-go counts as a kiss. Plenty of girls have looked at me, and I'm still intact. Dad doesn't need to know I pictured kissing Mei Li tonight.

She must be in the kitchen. Gotta find out the nights she works so I can see her again. Yanking my phone out, I text Johnny:

Marcus: Meet me at The Clubhouse.

If I can't go round up the bad guys with Dad, Johnny might as well come to the apartment so we can start our final AP history project. Dad just loaded the fridge with Mountain Dew so that'll get him there fast.

I duck out the door and turn down the alley toward home, stopping when a deep voice growls "I didn't like it" and my head snaps around.

Mei Li's outside the kitchen door, spotlighted by a yellow-orange floodlight, the high-maintenance Asian guy that grabbed her arm in the restaurant up in her face.

I crouch behind the dumpster as he says something in her ear. She hasn't mentioned a boyfriend, but the way he grips her arm makes me squirm, and when he pins her against the wall with his hips, he looks more rapist than boyfriend.

His back's to me, but his words ooze through the air like slime. "You're just so beautiful. He was watching you all night. Tonight, I realized how jealous I can be."

Dude strokes Mei Li's cheek and leans closer. "I hope we don't have to talk about this again."

She searches his eyes but shakes her head and he kisses her. And she kisses him back. Like, full-on kisses him, and I want out of this alley because my stomach's on the ground, writhing in alley grime. Something's off with this dude. Like really off, but while he gets busy on her neck, she opens her eyes and they collide with mine, almost knocking me backward.

I shake my head and hold up my hands, apologizing with my eyes.

Hers widen, and she shakes her head once, barely visible. *"This isn't what it looks like."*

Whoa. Apparently, our eyes speak the same language 'cause I got that, loud and clear.

Her palms press against the brick wall behind her and she closes her eyes again, squeezing them tighter when the guy whispers in her ear. He straightens, then takes her chin between his thumb and fingers, forcing her to look at him.

Doesn't matter who this guy is—he needs a cold shower. A kick to the groin from a pair of cleats. But she kissed him. Even though…kinda looks like she wants him off her. Should I throw something? I look around. I have a backpack full of binders, not an arsenal. The soccer ball in my bag to the back of his head could distract him, but—

He kisses her again, and all thinking grinds to a stop because he's eating her face. I focus on her until her eyes snap to mine again, looking at me over his shoulder.

I'm no expert, but this guy's moves border pornographic. *"Do you care about your lower lip, because I think he's gnawing it off."*

I'm pretty sure her wide eyes are begging me to stay, but maybe I'm getting it all wrong. If I stick around, I can't watch anymore of this. I'll throw my soccer ball at him, so he bites off his tongue instead of shoving it down her throat, or—

I lean down and unzip my bag as quietly as I can, palming my soccer ball, but her eyes go wider when I pop back up over the dumpster.

"No!"

"He's gonna rip out your esophagus and I—"

Two cop cars roll up outside the restaurant, blocking the alley, and the guy's a blur—down the alley and through a door in the building behind the restaurant. Mei Li's flat against the wall, hands gripping the brick behind her. She's completely still for a few seconds—and so am I—but then she pushes from the wall and bolts through the kitchen door. I'm still palming the soccer ball at my side when the door scrapes shut.

Not sure what just went down. Not sure why Face Eater took off when the cops pulled up. Still wondering if I'm the guy he saw watching her. I definitely was, but why does he care? And how did we have a full-on, silent conversation with our eyes? I have n*o idea* why I feel like I should apologize to her if he's not going to. Maybe that grimace on her face meant she liked whatever he was doing to her. I mean, I'd never wanna see that look on a girl's face, but what would I know?

When a lamp turns on in a second-story window above the restaurant, my eyes are all over it and the outline of a girl yanking her curtains closed, a mini-Buddha statue perched on the windowsill. It's the same window by the same fire escape where Mei Li and her friend were the night we met, and when a ponytail shadow sways behind the curtains, it's confirmed: definitely her. Buddha has exceptional taste in women. That fat, happy statue knows everything that's going on between her and Face Eater. And everything else in her life.

I keep my eyes on the window and diagram a mental pie chart: WHY I'M STANDING IN THE ALLEY STARING AT MEI LI'S WINDOW EVEN THOUGH I'M PRETTY SURE SHE HAS A BOYFRIEND:

47 percent adrenaline mixed with anger toward Face Eater; 43 percent eye convo; 11 percent something I haven't felt since I saw Jake's older sister in her bra a couple months ago. On accident—only on accident. Not like she left her door open on purpose, knowing I'd walk by.

I wanna talk to Mei Li again. Then again, why work to get to know her if she has a boyfriend? Even though I really wanna ask her what a girl like her is doing with a guy like Face Eater. Don't know him, but have a pretty decent read on his MO from watching him in action. I don't know her after passing a few notes, either, but like the smart, funny stuff she's said in them. What I've seen of her, I like. A lot. If I stare at this window much longer, and it's really hers, I might see more than I'm prepared for, though.

"Marcus Miller! I see you, boy!" Guo's thick accent calls from her shop door and I snap my head toward it like I've been caught doing something I shouldn't, but grateful for a distraction, though a wrinkled old woman probably won't be enough.

"Guo!" I throw my bags over my shoulder and walk toward her, arms open. "Hello, beautiful." I bend and pull her into a hug. She pats my back and when we pull apart, she reaches up and jabs her pointer finger in my face.

"Why didn't you stop Ugly Chao from bothering Mei Li?"

I squint. "Ugly Chao?"

"Why didn't you punch him?" She points toward the door down the alley and motions for me to lean closer. "He's a bad man." She shakes her head. "Mei Li needs a nice boy. Like you. No matter what Mr. Ray says about girls or what Baba Zhang wants." She flutters her eyes at me and I laugh, putting my arm around her and steering her toward her shop.

"Ah, Guo, you flatter me."

"I'm serious." She ducks from under my arm and steps in front of me. "She needs a nice boy. Like you." She reaches up and pats my face then pushes her palms against my chest. "I see you stare at her like this." Her mouth falls open, and she clasps her hands, swooning. But really, mocking. She grabs my arm and points. "Go back now. Give Mei Li a happy face."

"Sorry. She's inside—I have no way to talk to her. Plus, Dad wants me home for safety reasons." I jerk my head toward the growing collection of cop cars. "You know—young, innocent boy, neighbor ladies bothering me in dark alleys."

She slaps my arm and shakes a finger at me. "You have big muscles. You'll be fine."

I lay my hand on her shoulder. "I got a friend coming over. And Mei Li has a boyfriend, so I—"

"No. No. No." Guo shakes her head and stomps her foot, waving the idea away. "Not her boyfriend. And we want to keep it that way. Is your friend more beautiful than Mei Li?" She throws her head back and laughs. "Not possible, Marcus Miller."

I smile and shake my head. "Uh…definitely not. It's Johnny."

"Oh! Johnny will understand, then! He loves all the girls. You need girl and I'm a Love Hunter. Mei Li is the one for you, Marcus Miller." She nods, confident in her theory. "She's the one." She pokes my chest and I smile down at her.

"Pretty sure after watching that whole scene she's into

Chinese guys, not white guys twice her size. And he's pretty into her. Don't think I can compete with his possessiveness. But you keep hunting for love for me and let me know what you find after I graduate college."

"You teasing me?" She squints up at me. "I'll tell your fortune without a cookie." She steps closer and grabs my arm. "You and Mei Li will be together someday. You will see. Guo Mama knows. Guo Mama definitely knows."

CHAPTER 5

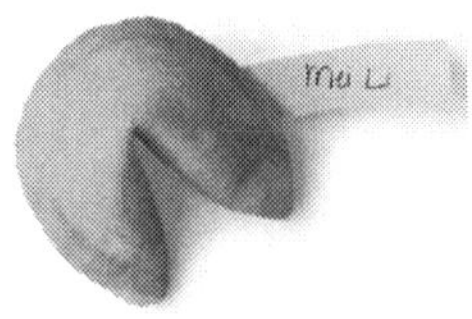

My phone rings for the fourth time from where I threw it in the pile of pillows on my bed but I'm mid-teeth brushing and can't answer. Or maybe I just don't want to. It's Nick again, no doubt. He's not used to being ignored, but I don't want to hear his excuses. His drinking has become a bigger problem than he realizes. And the way he ran away when police cars pulled up across the street…?

Whatever happened with him tonight scratches through my mind. He'd obviously been drinking before he ever came to the restaurant. It was practically seeping out of his pores, and I hate the bitter taste it left. Hate how possessive he was. I hate the way he kissed me like he was punishing me. That I kissed him back, even if it was to distract him from Marcus. But mostly, I hate that Marcus saw the whole thing.

Hot, coiling embarrassment and heavy shame fill my room until it's so tight around me, it squeezes me out the window and onto my fire escape. I take a deep, shaky breath, the crisp air sharp against my lungs as I grip the railing. But when I look down on the street, I hold the breath I just hauled into my lungs because Marcus is still outside with Guo Mama.

I step backward, my palm sliding along the windowsill as I duck to crawl back inside, but I bump Buddha and he clatters to the metal landing.

Bending to pick him up, I stare at the black spot on his belly where I've rubbed off the gold paint with my wishing, but my eyes are pulled toward Marcus and my heart leaps up my throat like it's the one who's been caught peeking. Marcus stares up at me and Guo Mama cackles before shuffling into her shop.

He holds the straps of his backpack while he walks toward my fire escape two stories below, then smiles and waves once as his eyes say, *"Hey."*

I straighten, bite my lip, and trap Buddha in my balled fist. *"Hi."*

He squints, holding my gaze. *"You okay?"*

I nod and shrug. *"Fine."*

He looks around before crossing the alley and I circle my fingers around my neck. It's so much easier writing to him. Saying things with my mouth or my eyes and watching him react in real life is emotional chaos, but I stand in the middle of it as he smiles up at me, head thrown back, black words covering his arm like a sloppy sleeve tattoo.

"That thing that happened earlier..." he calls.

I grip the railing tighter. "What thing?"

"With that guy." He makes a V with each hand and brings them close together, opening and closing them like two kissing alligators. "I think it was meant to be affection, maybe?" He shoves his hands in his hoodie pockets. "But not sure. Don't see that every day."

His voice rumbles up to me, onto the landing, vibrates through me, and digs up embarrassment and shame. But he doesn't know me. What if Nick kisses me like that every day?

What if I like it? I tighten my fists. Except I don't. Anybody would have noticed that.

"It isn't every day someone watches, either." The words wobble out of me and his teeth blare in the dark as he smiles.

"You were sorta busy, so you probably didn't notice, but I was kinda trapped behind a dumpster watching Face Eater gnaw off your lips."

"I didn't ask you to stay."

"Well, your eyes did, so maybe you should have a little chat with them about saying what they really mean. All I know is they didn't like whatever was happening as much as I didn't." He grips his backpack straps. "But wait—hold up! Just thought of something." His eyes widen. "If our eyes speak the same language, does that mean we're eye-lingual?" He grins up at me. "Like bilingual, but you know—eyes."

I press my lips together and curl my toes against a smile but when it slips out, I send it into the sky before looking down at him again. "I guess so."

Marcus rolls his neck, rubbing the back of it as he looks up. "It's kinda uneventful down here now. And my neck's killing me. Care if I come up?" When I don't answer, he steps to the ladder and pulls himself up the rungs and over the railing, dropping to the landing.

His eyes are glossy in the lamp light pooling around my window, starting a fire in my stomach that spreads up into my cheeks. His skin glows as he leans back against the railing and stretches his arms along it on either side of him. He's easily twice my size. If he steps closer, he'll pull me into his gravity and—

"So, you usually don't work Tuesdays?" He tilts his head, his long fingers wrapped around the railing.

I blink out of my thoughts and squeeze Buddha in my fist. "I covered for a friend. I'm in the kitchen on Tuesdays."

"Maybe I should switch nights."

I smile as the air between us settles and calms but shake my head. "You should probably stick with Tuesdays."

"Since you have a boyfriend but didn't wanna tell me because my notes are so poetic?"

My eyes snap to his and I inhale, shaking my head. *"He's not…I don't…"*

His left eyebrow arches. "Do I need to ask Buddha who Face Eater is?" He watches me pass the statue between my hands, nervous energy exiting my body through my fingers. "He'll tell me everything you forgot to mention in your notes. Or I could just ask Guo. She said, and I quote: 'Ugly Chao is the worst. As a dude and a kisser.' From what I saw, I'd have to agree. No offense, but…" He shakes his head.

"It's amazing how much you sounded like Guo Mama. You two must have had a long conversation about me." I swallow hot, itchy shame and look down at Guo Mama's shop where she's scrubbing her front window. Scrubbing the same spot, over and over. Because she's watching us out of the corner of her eye. "Should've known she's involved in this."

"This…?" He raises his eyebrows.

"You. Being here." I wave one hand between us, the other gripping Buddha as I take a deep breath. "She bribed you, didn't she?"

He grips his backpack straps and leans back against the railing, crossing his ankles. "To do what?"

"I don't know. Talk to me? Write notes?" I bite my lip and hold my breath, waiting.

He looks at the sky, then back to me. "Uh, no, thank you very much. Did this all on my own. I'm offended you didn't consider that I had to gather all my available guts just to talk to you two weeks ago."

My heart stutters in surprise, but I crush Buddha in my fist and roll my eyes so I won't squeeze them shut and squeal. "She bribed you to talk to me because she doesn't like Nick."

He frowns and scratches his temple. "Okay, so…first, why would she think me talking to you would make a difference, and second, I'm guessing "Nick" is Face Eater?"

I stare at him.

"He almost ate your face after yelling at it. So…Face Eater. Didn't say it was a creative nickname, but he definitely earned it. Am I wrong?"

Shame pushes up my neck in a hot rush and I talk to the landing. "He wasn't eating my face."

"All about perspective, Mei." He stops, raising his eyebrows. "Wait—can I call you Mei?"

"Umm…sure?"

"I mean, you know, since we're the only people who happen to talk with our eyes, we should be on a nickname basis." He smiles and when he shoves his fingers through his messy hair, nicknames for him flood my mind. All of them will stay safely inside my head.

Heat prickles my cheeks and I meet his eyes across the landing. Silence ripples between us before Marcus straightens and clears his throat. "So, back to that whole bribe thing and why Guo would care if I talk to you and—"

Mama calls from inside and I tense, my eyes darting to my window then back to him. "You have to go," I whisper, dive-crawling back into my room. I set Buddha on the windowsill and reach to pull the window down but Marcus ducks through the opening, his face inches from mine.

"When can I see you again? Besides at the restaurant."

He has a few, faint freckles on the bridge of his nose. His dark eyebrows are perfectly arched over blue, blue eyes, the left brow interrupted by a tiny scar slashed through its middle. I grip the window for dear life. "Notes are probably best." I'm not giving them up yet. His notes exploded into twenty-four bright spots in the last two weeks.

"Then I'm taking Buddha with me." He snatches the statue, still looking at me, still washing away the darkness with waves of sky blue. "He'll tell me everything you won't."

"He doesn't talk to strangers," I whisper.

"Please." Marcus rolls his eyes. "Buddha speaks to all peace-loving individuals. Plus, we're neighbors. If you lean over your fire escape far enough…" He throws his thumb in the direction of his building. "You can almost see my window. So…not strangers."

Mama calls again and I grip the window like it will help me win the tug of war between Marcus and her. "I have to go," I rush, pulling the window down a little.

"Wait!" He grabs it. "Buddha wants to tell me something." He holds him to his ear and pretends to listen. His eyes slide to my lips then he shakes his head and talks to Buddha again. "Sorry, man, what'd you say? I was distracted." He glances at me and grins, then nods, Buddha still at his ear. "Yeah, I totally agree. I don't get it either, and I'll tell her, but you're crazy for thinking she'll listen to me." He rolls his eyes and drops Buddha in his jacket pocket, sighing loudly. "So…he says you should stop making out with Face Eater if he's not your boyfriend. And if he is your boyfriend, you should break up with him."

I narrow my eyes and he holds up his hands. "Just the messenger." Grabbing the ladder handles, he backs down it, disappearing into the alley.

I close my eyes. My heart's still beating. I'm awake. That really happened. Marcus Miller was here and wants to see me again. Even after the whole Nick thing.

A smile stretches my face to new limits, but I press my lips together and take a deep breath through my nose, shaking off feelings I shouldn't have, especially about a moment that should never have happened and can never happen again. Unless I ask Su Ling to permanently switch shifts.

My phone buzzes from the pillows again and Nick shoves back into my thoughts and spreads guilt all over my head.

No. Never mind. I'll make sure I'm in the kitchen every Tuesday night from now on. It's the only way I'll be able to resist Marcus Miller and his smile.

My thoughts run wild in the empty dining room, swinging from pendant lights and jumping from table to table like Marcus-faced monkeys that have been caged since seeing him last night. I smile at the table as pots clang in the kitchen where the staff are prepping for breakfast.

I spray cleaner on tables and chairs, then scrub, hoping all thoughts of Marcus and last night's fire escape moment will slip out my fingers and leave me in peace. I'd barely slept because when I closed my eyes, Marcus's smile had flashed in my head and made it glow.

My phone buzzes and I set my cleaning rag in the bucket and pull it from my pocket.

Everything okay? Why aren't you answering?

The smell of Drunk Nick seeps from my memory but I spray the table and scrub, like I can erase last night from my mind. Truthfully, there's no room for bad memories with so much Marcus in my head. That's how I want to keep it, even if I'm torturing myself because no matter what he says, he can't be interested in someone like me. We're too different. And then there's Nick. Who's opened every door I've walked through since coming to America. In a few weeks, we'll be in L.A. meeting celebrity chefs, and if I'm lucky, I'll intern with one of them, all thanks to him. I want the future he's helping me create. Flirting with another guy could ruin everything.

Especially if that guy has the gravitational pull of Marcus Miller.

I pull the fortune he gave me during my shift last night from my pocket and stare at the phone number. All I have to do is dial and...Marcus. I shouldn't be thrilled Su Ling called in sick, but it was a Tuesday, and instead of hearing Detective Miller's booming laughter above clanging pots and hissing grills in the kitchen, I was in the same room. Thank you, Su Ling.

The door chimes and I glance up, blinded by the rising sun pouring in with a man in a suit. My eyes adjust to Detective Miller striding across the empty dining room, his smile reaching me before he does. It's an incredibly familiar smile, and I swallow, afraid he knows I was thinking about his son and is here to arrest me for thoughts I shouldn't have.

"Hi, Mei Li." He sticks out his hand, and I give him a shaky smile and wipe my hand on my apron before shaking his, then focus on the glossy black chair I'm scooting under the table. What if my eyes say something to him they shouldn't?

"Hello, Detective Miller."

"How can you work with those delicious smells? I'd be 400 pounds if I worked here. Noodles for every meal including breakfast." He pats his flat stomach, his hand resting over his pink tie.

I laugh, spraying the table and wiping it, glancing at him as I work. "Breakfast doesn't start for another half hour, but Wong will make an exception for you, I'm sure."

He smiles. "Tempting, but I need my brain to function today, and noodles won't help. I'd actually love to talk with you, if you have a minute." His Southern accent rolls toward me and my throat goes dry. "Just a few questions. I'll make sure you make your bus, promise. Mind if we sit?"

"Um...okay." I set down the bottle and ease into the chair across from him, folding my hands in my lap and squeezing my fingers together because this is Marcus's dad. He's a detective. He detects lies for a living. He will detect mine.

He shrugs off his suit coat, throws it over the back of the chair, and sits. My nerves spark under my skin because

Marcus strolls through my head in his soccer shorts while I stare at his dad.

"I'm sure you're aware there've been multiple women who've vanished from this neighborhood in the last year or so." He leans forward and rubs his chin, scruff rustling against his palm. "We're busting our tails to find them."

My body relaxes and I sit back in the chair, nodding. "Is there some way I can help?"

"Actually, yes." Detective Miller leans his forearms on the table's edge and the seams of his shirt strain while he studies the paper in his hand. He shifts in his chair and looks from it to me. Green eyes, not blue. "Su Ling was reported missing this morning."

My heart drops and I lean forward, hand on my throat, my voice barely squeezing out. "Baba said she called in sick…"

"Detective Miller, good morning." Baba's voice echoes through the dining room from behind me and Detective Miller glances over my head before I twist in my chair, looking over my shoulder. Baba weaves around tables and Detective Miller stands to greet him. They shake hands but Baba's smile is tight, like it might snap into a snarl any minute.

"Mei Li." He speaks down to me where I still sit in my chair. "Better get going. Don't want to miss the bus." His words are like a clenched fist.

I grab the spray bottle and rags, leaving my chair scooted out for Baba but he stays standing. I nod at Detective Miller, then dart toward the kitchen, the news about Su Ling holding onto my ankles and dragging behind me as I grab my backpack and push through the back door.

CHAPTER 6

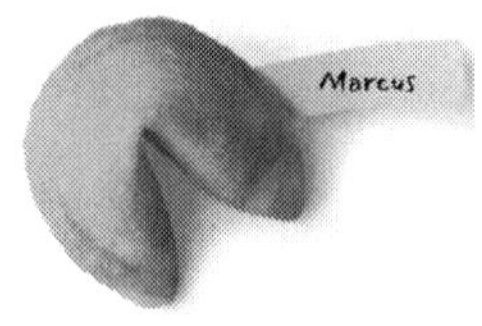

On the subject of time travel. If you could choose one day to revisit, what would it be?

I think I'd choose…hmmm…something from my recent past. Like…last night, maybe? Skip right past the alley part and start at the fire escape conversation. That was a first. A good first.

Mei

Didn't know that girl has purple contacts. Or that girl who's always in crop tops wears blue eye makeup. Too distracted by her five belly button rings. I make eye contact with every girl walking toward me in the hall between AP chem and AP History. That girl's smiling but I can't remember her name. I give her a chin nod and look over the crowd, catching any girl's eye to see if hers say anything. So far, big zero percent.

I turn into the science room and weave toward my table. Tavah looks up from digging in her backpack as I slide into my seat, throwing my backpack on the table. I glance at her and she smiles. Green eyes. Silent green eyes. But they kinda sparkle even in florescent lighting.

I unzip my backpack and search through it for my science folder.

"How's it going, Marcus?"

I hold her gaze for a solid three seconds. Nope. This eye language is solidly a Mei thing. "Hey. Good." I smile at my binder as I slide it out and slap it on the table. "How's it going with you?"

Her eyebrows jump and her smile spreads across her face, bright and shiny. Sparkly eyes, sparkly smile. "A little ready to get this AP test over with." She taps her pen on her binder and leans her elbow on the table, turning toward me. "Six weeks and high school's officially in our past. Kind of weird, right?"

Oh yeah. Graduation. College. But first, AP test. Chemistry homework I don't care about unless it's about the chemistry between me and Mei.

"Yeah. Crazy." I pull out my phone and check my messages. Still nothing from Mei. She has my number. She could text any time. Not that she would. She has a boyfriend. Or not. She wasn't totally clear about that.

Mr. Lomax sails into the room, apologizing for being late because his wife had to bring his laptop. "Phone away, Miller," Lomax says, plugging his laptop into the projector.

I shove it in my bag and flip open my notebook, copying what's on the screen but not absorbing any of it because Mei's smiling in my head. My pen hovers over my notebook. I wonder what class she's in right now. What guy's lucky enough to sit next to her. If she's seen Face Eater again. If her lips are still intact. I drum my pen against my notebook. What's she doing with him? Is that what girls like her go for? Like I'd even know.

I side-glance Tavah who's staring at the screen and remember what Johnny's said about her and the other girls screaming at our games. Is there a guy who's jealous I'm sitting next to Tavah like I'm jealous of whoever's sitting next to Mei? I've had at least two classes with Tavah every year since seventh grade, and we've never had a full conversation. She's definitely pretty. Like all bright and shiny and always smiling. Glossy lips. Shiny brown hair to her shoulders. What would she look like if she wore it in a ponytail like Mei? She's actually opposite of Mei in most ways—tall, athletic. Volleyball player, maybe. Green eyes that don't say anything except that she's pure energy. Totally different from Mei's that have layers I still haven't reached. Freckles on her arms. Mei doesn't have any freckles.

Tavah shifts and kicks me. "Sorry," she whispers, and I meet her eyes again. Still nothing.

Lomax writes some chemical reaction I should know but I've got my own chemical reactions going on from thoughts about Mei.

My leg bounces beneath the table, trying to burn off my Mei rush, but I'm skipping all the barriers and what ifs and I'm at the first kiss. In some crazy cool place. Kinda dark but not too dark so I can see her reaction. Nowhere cliché like Golden Gate or Muir Woods. Somewhere like…Mile Rock Beach. Yeah—paddle board to the rock at sunset. With a blanket. Don't want either of us to be shivering or her lips to be too numb to feel anything.

"See you tomorrow." Tavah smiles as she stands and throws her backpack over her shoulder, and I snap back to chemistry class which wrapped up while I was mentally paddling toward my first kiss with Mei.

———

"So?" Aunt Audrey stabs her fork into the baklava sitting between us on the café table and I scoot in my chair so people can pass on the sidewalk behind me.

I slide the plate toward me when violent hunger claws at my stomach.

"Still winning the motorcycle?" She raises her eyebrows and chews.

"Still winning, like I do most things," I say before taking down half our double order and picturing my promised motorcycle. Probability:100 percent.

"Still worth it?" She tilts her head and wiggles her brows this time. Digging.

"Definitely." Unless Mei's an option. Then, maybe not.

Audrey's shoulders drop and she yanks the plate back toward her, taking the rest of my beloved baklava hostage. "Seriously? Not even a hot girl in your math class or one of your friends' sisters? Are you blind, maybe?"

I lean into the table, eyeing the dessert before offering her the blank stare that drives her crazy. She doesn't need to know that thoughts of Mei blazed a hot trail through my head all day.

She stabs the helpless lump on the plate again, watching her vicious act. "Ah. Still letting your dad's past be your future. Even if you don't want it."

I jab the straw into my shake. "You finished? 'Cause I need to feed the angry beast in my stomach and get to practice."

Her eyes snap to mine. "I love my brother, but his whole women hatred thing is getting old. He and your mom were eighteen. They made a choice. It's done." She takes a deep breath, holds it before releasing it with a sigh.

I roll my eyes and scan the café's stained-glass window but can't help smiling. For an aunt, she's the coolest kind available. Kinda has the crazy thing going for her and likes to stir the pot with Dad and his campaign to keep me safe from anything with boobs, but she's cool.

"Actually, one more thing." She holds up a finger. "Your mom wasn't a bad person, Marcus. She was scared, and so was Ray. But you don't have to be. About girls or leaving your dad." She takes another bite, staring at me. Waiting.

When I don't respond she tilts her head. "You like girls, right?"

"Okay, seriously?" I throw up my hands and shake my head, then sling one arm on the table, the other across my stomach. "I look at girls. All the time. But girls didn't get my 4.0 or my starter position on the team. Pretty sure they won't help me keep either of them. That's it. I just want my freakin' motorcycle." With Mei on the back of it. I tip my cup for the last piece of ice to chomp.

"How about a friendly wager? I know how much you like a challenge." She leans forward. "A date. One date with a girl before our next dessert date and I buy you baklava for a year. I'll even ship it to you at Stanford."

I ignore the Stanford comment. Haven't told her I accepted at USF, and not ready to have that conversation with her yet. Instead, I cross my arms over my chest. "What's in it for you?"

"Don't want you to be the only guy on the Stanford soccer team who hasn't kissed someone, Baby Marcus. Just doing my auntly duties."

"Don't give me that—you're five years older than me. But you're on. And I'm gonna add a little juice to this deal. Whoever gets a date first wins baklava for a year. Haven't seen you with anyone since the last dude who looked like he'd been locked in a closet for fifteen years."

She snatches a piece of baklava and throws it at me. It bounces off my cheek and I laugh, then throw my napkin at her and stand, slinging my bag over my shoulder. "We have a deal?"

"Deal." She meets my eyes in her best tough-girl attempt, but the red glasses throw it off.

"Thought you'd see it my way." I scoot in my chair. "And even if I do ask a girl out, the only thing I'll be riding graduation night is a motorcycle."

"Don't be gross," she calls as I smile and wave over my shoulder.

Neon signs and car headlights blare on my walk home from the train stop after practice, but Guo's sitting outside her shop on her rickety bamboo chair, eating dried mangoes.

I yank out my earbuds and call to her. "Any good fortunes for me tonight? Maybe a note? Or three?"

"Ah! Marcus Miller!! Hello, hot stuff!"

I laugh and stop in front of her. "Where you picking up your slang these days?"

"I say what I see," she says, flapping her hand. "And I'd like to see you closer. Come here." She pats the chair beside her and I drop my bags and sit.

"You've got me nervous..."

"You afraid I'll kiss you and make all the girls jealous?" I laugh and she takes my shoulders, turning me toward her. "Look at me."

Old women scare me, so I do as I'm told, and she puts her hands on my cheeks, squinting. "I see," she mutters as she pokes my cheeks and measures my forehead.

I shift in my chair. "What are you doing?"

"Reading your face. It tells me all the good stuff." She smiles, her eyes disappearing into her cheeks. "About your love life. You'll be so happy about what I see. But first, I'll get some tea and an important note I think you'll like. Then I'll tell you. You need your strength." She chuckles and shuffles into the shop, her sandals slapping the tile.

I scan the street, anticipating what Mei's note will say. Hoping for some honesty about Face Eater, but also kinda not.

My apartment's dark; Dad's working all night on the missing girls case, so there's no rush to get home. Except maybe a shower. But Guo makes me laugh and lets me raid her fortune cookies. Teaches me dirty Chinese phrases. Plus… note from Mei. Not a bad way to spend a Wednesday night.

I wipe my palms on my shorts and settle back into the chair as Guo shuffles back outside and hands me a teacup which I sniff, then raise my eyebrows. "Is this more of those weird herbs that will get me high like last time?"

She waves her hand. "One cannot get high on Love Potion. Especially not you."

"Ouch. What's that supposed to mean? What's wrong with me?"

"Nothing's wrong. You just need lots and lots. You're never with girl. You always walk down the street, keep your eyes straight ahead. I'm the only girl you talk to."

I choke on my tea as I laugh, wiping my chin with my palm. "Nice try, Guo. I know you were watching me talk to Mei last night while you scrubbed invisible spots on your window."

She studies me, then grabs my chin between her fingers and sizes it up. I'm not sure if I should stare into her eyes or close mine. I don't want my first real kiss from a woman who's practically my grandma. "Something on my face?"

"Yes—all your secrets. Many great things." She hunches her shoulders and laughs.

"Like?"

"That you will be a great lover."

"Oh, wow. Alright." I push myself up, pick up my bags and teacup, then walk into her shop, weaving through racks of Chinese robes and waving Good Fortune cats toward her kitchenette in the back room. No way I'm talking about this with Guo. I set my empty teacup on the counter, but miss because it's like I'm floating. The cup shatters against the tile and when I look down, my feet are still on the ground, surrounded by glass shards. My head hovers somewhere above my body and there's a halo around my vision, but

I'm…warm. Relaxed. A little fearless.

Guo scurries in and grabs a broom which I take from her, mesmerized by its bristles sweeping against the terra cotta. I sweep and sweep, swirly patterns circling my feet until the room tilts. She totally laced my tea. Gripping the broom, I lean it against the wall and slowly turn to Guo who's holding out her huge glass jar.

"Fortune cookie?"

"You drugged me."

She waves her hand. "You're a silly boy. Fortune cookie?"

I fumble for the jar and pull one out, sliding out the fortune and popping the cookie in my mouth then reading the fortune out loud. "'The best year-round temperature is a warm heart and a cool head.' So wise," I drop it in the garbage can.

"Oh, please. I'll do better than that."

"Yeah?" I take another fortune cookie and toss the slip of paper in the garbage.

"Yes. I saw how you looked at Mei Li's house before you came in my shop. You like her." Guo smirks and nods, folding her arms. "Mm-hmm. You will find love with Mei Li. She will make you smile every day. I know." She points to her head. "You will love Miss Zhang deeply."

She's staring at me, and I'm supposed to say something but all I can get out is, "Dude, Guo, why does it feel like I'm floating? Am I?"

"She steps behind the register, bends down, and holds up a Magic 8 ball. "You ask Magic 8 if you will fall in love with Miss Zhang." She demonstrates how to ask it a question, then shakes it and holds it toward me.

I fumble it out of her hand and glance at her. How did she know that during practice, Coach yelled at me because my head was back on Mei's fire escape, my imagination making my eyes say a whole lot they would—hopefully—never actually say to her. But what if they do? That whole thing was so weird. But so cool. I wanna try it again, though I'll definitely have to censor my eyes.

Guo pats my arm and I drag myself out of my surprisingly vivid imagination, though my head's still floating somewhere above me. Beside me? Doesn't matter—not screwed on right if I'm having this conversation with Guo and a Magic 8 ball.

I laugh as I ask the question, the air around me tinted purple. "Is Face Eater Mei Li's boyfriend?" I shake the ball, turn it over. Squint to read the answer. *My sources say no.*

Okay. So far, so good. Kinda like this thing. I glance at Guo, then ask Magic 8 another question. "Does Mei Li Zhang think I'm the hottest guy she's ever seen?"

It is decidedly so.

I roll my eyes and shake the ball again. "Will I fall madly in love with Mei Li?"

You may rely on it.

Guo crosses her arms and grins. "You see?"

"You don't even know what it said."

"I saw your face. A light went on in your eyes."

"That's whatever you put in that tea." I slip the Magic 8 ball into my backpack and reach for more fortune cookies to calm my violent craving.

"No more for YOU!" She snatches the jar from the counter, holding it protectively.

"What did you put in my tea? For real, Guo. Why do I feel like I just took down a cup of weed?"

"Ah, you got the munchies?" She giggles, her teeth looking a little like a rabid squirrel's.

"Little bit. Would probably do anything right now for that whole jar."

"Anything...?"

"Likely."

"I have a job for you, then." She shuffles up to me. "Mei Li isn't home right now." She grabs a dusty blue silk rose from the vase by the register and shoves it at me. "Leave this on her windowsill. So romantic. Go. Now."

"Uh. Not a chance. If I had a style, that wouldn't be it, Guo. Besides—gotta go raid the Oreo aisle right now."

"No." She tightens her hold on the jar when I eye it. "You do it. It will make her night."

"Nope. She has my number but hasn't used it. She's probably with her boyfriend. Wishing she still had her lips."

"No boyfriend. Go. I'll give you all my cookies and buy you a week's supply of Oreos."

I raise my eyebrows, tempted. "Dude...Guo—do you know how many Oreos I can consume in one sitting?"

She nods like she's having a seizure. "It doesn't matter when love is at stake."

"Love? Ease up, Guo—we just met."

She slides the jar under the counter and straightens. "Guo Mama sees and knows everything."

"Everything?"

She nods. "Everything."

"You talk to her since last night?"

She shrugs.

"Know something I don't?"

Guo hands me a note, then pats my butt. "I know many things you don't, baby Marcus."

CHAPTER 7

Buddha doesn't like to pry, but we're both wondering what you're doing right now. I'm thinking about your time travel question. Before meeting you, I would've said 1966 World Cup. England v. West Germany. But now, I choose two weeks ago. Guo's shop. But not telling you why. So don't ask. These lips are sealed. Unless I have an unfortunate encounter with Face Eater and he gnaws them off. Kidding. He's not my type. Hoping he's not yours either. Gotta go. Buddha has a juicy secret he wants to tell me about you and your boyfriend.

—M

I shove Marcus's note deep inside my pocket and wish I was with him and Buddha instead of at Nick's gate which shrieks when I push it open, then slams behind me. It's probably best I'm not with Marcus, though, because I'd be tempted to tell him what's happening with Nick and never hear from him again.

I hesitate before taking the seventeen steps to the towering metal door, but the sooner I get in, the sooner I get out. My plan was to ignore Nick for a day or two while I figure out how to talk to him about the alley, but Baba insisted I run this package to him.

My finger hovers over the doorbell, but the lock clicks and the door swings open.

Holden's a giant shadow in the doorway, his shirt half tucked in, blond hair plastered to his forehead. His eyes graze my body, lingering on my chest. I fold my arms and he laughs before motioning with his head for me to follow him.

I pause in the marble foyer under a chandelier big enough to pull the roof down on all the shiny things lining the foyer. When Holden brushes against me as he shuts the door, I tense, but follow him down the hallway.

Men's laughter echoes from the living room ahead, the edges harsh and uncontrolled. I grip my bag strap as I step into Nick's living room where a white cloud curls above the table and the smell of liquor burns my nose, like breathing gasoline. Poker night.

I pull the envelope from my bag and set it on a table, then turn to leave, but a chair scrapes the floor as Nick's voice scrapes the air. "There she is. My girl!"

I glance over my shoulder as he sways around the table, stumbles, and reaches for the wall. He weaves toward me, a nauseating wave of alcohol reaching me before he does, but his smile is steady. "Want us to deal you in so you can destroy me like usual?"

My eyes roam towers of poker chips that remind me of my sophomore year when Nick taught me how to play. He brought all my favorite candy instead of money. His eyes were bright and clear back then, shocked when I won every round. They're cloudy and dull tonight and it's not even seven.

"I can't stay." I shake my head. "Brought something from Baba." I point to the envelope then turn toward the glossy black door so far down the marble hallway, but Nick grabs the same arm he left his mark on last night, and I wince.

"Wait! Sorry." He lets go and rubs the spot. "I've been out of my mind waiting for you to respond to my calls and texts. Can we talk?"

"I have to go—"

"Please." His black eyes swirl, unsteady.

Talking to Drunk Nick's not part of my errand tonight, but I'm afraid of his reaction if I say no, so I nod, rubbing my arm and following him through the room. Chaz is at the table dealing cards, a joint dangling from his lips. His eyes skim mine, and I wish cousins could speak eye language so he'd get my message and distract Nick, but Chaz looks away and Nick grabs my hand, tugging me upstairs.

When he trips on a step, he reaches for the railing, yanking me down with him. My hands land on his back and he twists toward me with a sloppy smile and laughs while his hands fumble around my waist.

"Don't." I fling his hands away and if he wasn't blocking my way, I'd be back down the stairs and out of here. My mind circles back to last night and how he fumbled with me before the police scared him off. What did he think I was going to let him do in the alley? Or tonight?

He regains his balance, pulling me upstairs behind him, and I swear he's sweating alcohol. I hold my breath.

"Close your eyes," he slurs when we reach the landing, and even though I'm terrified he'll try to kiss me again, I close them, my body stiff and jerky. I put my hand out in front of me as Nick pulls me forward until a doorknob twists and I snap my eyes open to see whatever I'm stepping into.

He flips a light switch and a chandelier drips from the ceiling over a giant bed draped in fur and silk and layers of velvety pillows. His arm wraps around my waist from behind. "It's yours." His breath in my ear is hot and sticky as my eyes jump around the room. "Ours. You'll live here during culinary school. Just like we discussed."

His words stun me, and my mind circles around them

until I understand what he's implying. A month ago, he mentioned that I could move into one of his three houses. I thought that meant one he wasn't occupying. "I haven't decided where I'm going to live yet."

"We've known each other forever, Mei Li. It's time to take the next step."

"After last night, I'm not sure there is one."

He takes a step back and looks at the floor, rubbing his neck. "Listen. I'm sorry. I don't know where that came from and—"

"I do. This…" I wave my hand in front of him. "The drinking. It's changed you."

He nods. "I know. I've just been under a lot of pressure." He reaches for me, pulling me to him. "I'll do better, I swear. I'll give it up if that's what you need." He leans in, his nose tracing my cheek and down my neck, his arms wrapping around me, pulling me tight against him. When his lips press against my neck, I stiffen.

"Stop." I twist out of his arms. "You're drunk."

"Come on. It's you and me, Mei Li. It's always been that way. So why not make it official?" He pauses, his eyes meeting mine. "Unless there's someone else."

Marcus's face drifts across my mind, and I mentally sweep it away so Nick won't see it in my eyes. Or so, if we ever talk again, Marcus won't see how Nick has my future in his grip, and that if he finds out I've been talking to Marcus, he could crush it all. No one gets an internship before they get accepted to culinary school. I'm lucky, no matter how I feel right now. Maybe taking this step is the only way to show him how grateful I am.

When his arms wrap around me from behind, I close my eyes and swallow. I have to forget Marcus, focus on Nick. But when his hand fumbles with the button on my pants, I grab it.

"I'm not ready." My words strain against my throat, my heart thumping like it's pushing me up and toward the door.

His teeth nip at my neck, and I squirm away and turn to face him. "Stop, Nick."

He growls a curse. "What's your problem?" Fire burns away any softness in his eyes.

"I have to go. My parents will wonder."

"Wonder what? You're eighteen. I've waited long enough." He grabs me again, backing me against the bed until I fall backward onto the mattress. He hovers above me, pinning my arms to the bed as his lips scratch along my neck.

"I said stop." I thrash under him, but he jerks me closer, and a sound launches from the hard panic in my chest and out my throat. His lips smother it, but I twist my head away, pressing my lips together.

"I'm tired of your teasing," he growls, and I strain my neck away from him, adrenaline hurling through me. His fingers scrape under my shirt. "I give you everything you want. It's my turn."

I drive my knee into his groin, and he roars and rolls to the side of me. Scrambling to my feet, I dart toward the door, but he grabs me, spinning me around until he trips, and we fall, my cheek smacking the nightstand before we hit the rug.

All sound is muffled as he pins me face down on the rug, red and orange flowers bleeding together as I cup my face, catching up to the moment. Heat swells under my palm and tears burn my eyes as I will the spinning room to steady, my breath rattling out of me. Nick flips me to my back, hovering over me, eyes and hands greedy.

"Nick!" A voice rises and when it breaks into the room, my heart leaps toward it, and my eyes land on Chaz who looks from Nick to me.

"Get out," Nick snaps, his voice gravel, but Chaz shakes his head and motions over his shoulder, his eyes darting to mine.

"There's something you need to handle downtown."

"Take care of it," Nick snarls, but Chaz stays in the doorway.

"Above my head. It's gotta be you."

Nick curses and pushes himself up, stumbling out of the room. My chest heaves, heart pounding in my throat while I lie still, like any movement will remind him I'm here.

Chaz's hard eyes pin me to the floor before he disappears, and my muscles surrender, shoulder blades sinking into the rug. My body shakes and I pull my knees to my chest, tears slicing my swollen throat.

A door slams downstairs, rattling the crystals dangling so far above me. There are hundreds of them, but even together, they're not bright enough to shove away the darkness spreading through me. Nick has never hurt me. He's brought me gifts. Offered to pay for culinary school and to let me stay in one of his houses. I've let him. Almost let him take something I didn't want to give him.

My palm rests on the screaming welt on my face like I can hide from what just happened on this bleeding flower rug. Feeling comes back into my fingers, and when chairs scrape downstairs, I scramble to my feet, grabbing the duvet for balance.

Scanning the open door, I swipe the back of my hand over my neck where Nick's mouth left wet spots. I smooth my shirt. My fingers tremble over the button on my jeans and fasten it. I'm in one piece. Everything's where it should be. Except for my insides.

I snatch my bag off the floor and dart out of the room, gripping the railing as I skim the stairs, jerking to a stop at the bottom where Chaz lounges on a sofa, smoking another joint. A girl wearing next to nothing is curled next to him, her sunken eyes on me while her fingertips trail his stomach. I dart toward the front door, and Chaz's voice echoes behind me.

"Family or not, I can't keep bailing you out."

I glance over my shoulder, my eyes skimming the girl before meeting Chaz's. "You've never had to. He's never been like this."

"Doesn't matter. He'll take what he wants, however he wants, because he can. He owns you, me, your parents, the restaurant, our existence in this country. Some of us would like to keep it that way." He takes a drag and tilts his head back, blowing smoke into the air above the girl. "If you and your parents want to stay here, you'll do what you gotta do."

My throat burns as I rush to the front door and hurl myself outside. Towering bougainvillea vines swallow the lights on Nick's house, and I dart around the corner, promising myself I will never step near him again. I will move out after graduation and tell no one where I'm going. Chef Marco said I'm going places. I can make that happen. Somehow. I can figure it out.

I don't want the oak bedroom set. I can choose another door.

Hot, swirling anger seeps from under the rock of panic in my stomach, and I clench my jaw and cross my arms, shoving my hands into my armpits to bring feeling back into my fingers. His generosity is not out of the goodness of his heart; it comes with thick, strangling ropes.

A homeless man slumped against a building whistles at me, but I glare at him as I pass, my anger and hatred toward Drunk Nick shooting out of my eyes and striking this innocent person. I turn corners and cross streets, wishing my feet could move faster down steps, across Union Square, and into Chinatown where the smell of chòu dòufu clings to the air. Laughter from a passing group of teenagers stings my ears; it's the sound of freedom. I don't care that Baba and Nick's baba were best friends, or that when Nick's baba died, he left all his money to Nick who promised to use some of it to help Baba with the restaurant. Nick's baba snuck us into America, and since Nick helped us stay, he has the power to hold me hostage. I bet that wasn't part of his baba's dying wish. Or that Nick should become a monster.

A shiver ripples up my spine, and cold shame creeps through me. I was so afraid of losing my future, I was willing to let him be part of it. And then last night. I kissed him to stop the accusations about Marcus.

I touch the welt on my cheek. Chaz says Nick owns me, but I can't lose myself to him or the promises he dangles over me.

A hazy neon light blinks TATTOOS, PIERCINGS, READINGS in Mandarin and English and I stop in the orange light puddle under the sign. The haze inside the dingy shop matches the inside of my head and wraps around me, pulling me inside.

A group of people sit cross-legged in a circle around a giant bong, swaying to a song a Chinese guy with dreads is plunking on his guitar. I envy their relaxation. I've never done drugs, but I hear they take people away. I'd like to be far, far away.

A bulky, bearded man with crooked teeth smiles at me from behind the front counter which is slathered in stickers. I turn to leave but notice words inscribed on a wooden sign above the door: *I hear and I forget; I see and I remember; I do and I understand. Confucius.*

"You okay?"

The bearded guy points to my cheek, and I cover it with my hand and nod. "Yes. Fine. I ran into a door. Walking and texting." I give him a shaky smile.

He grimaces, then motions over his shoulder. "I can get you some ice if you want. Looks pretty swollen."

"No, I'm close to home."

"Anything you came in for tonight? It's kind of slow. Perfect time to get some ink." He grabs a book on the counter and opens to a page of designs.

I shake my head. "I don't think so. Thanks."

He nods and smiles. "I was scared my first time too. But look at me now." He pulls up his shirt sleeves to show arms completely hidden by colorful ink.

The same determination and pride I felt taking the culinary class by myself rises in me. Chef Marco said I was going places. Me. Mei Li Zhang. "Can I get my name tattooed?" I look at my wrist, my ankle, then remember the birds tattooed on that street performer's neck outside our restaurant a few months ago. No matter how she moved, the birds didn't budge. I lift my hair, exposing the back of my neck. "Maybe here?"

The guy rubs his hands together. "Absolutely. Show me what you want." He ducks behind the counter and slides a pen and notepad across the counter toward me.

I clench the pen and draw the characters of my name:

張

美

麗

My name, not Nick's. A forever reminder that he may be in control of my life, but he'll never own me.

I slip through the kitchen entrance and tiptoe toward the staircase that smells like trapped fried noodles and fish, hesitating when Baba's voice murmurs behind the closed office door.

"But where is she?" Mama replies, her voice timid as usual. "Do you know?"

I grip the railing. I should have been home an hour ago, and Baba's going to—

"That's not our concern," Baba hisses. "Tell anyone who asks that Su Ling found a better job. Detective Miller's come in already."

The floorboard I'm standing on squeaks, and I race up the

stairs and fling myself inside my room, closing the door softly behind me and backing against it. Su Ling didn't quit, she's missing. And Baba knows more than he's saying.

I step to my window and shove it open, cool air swirling in around my frantic thoughts while I wait for my world to steady. But my eyes fall on a Magic 8 ball propped face up on the window ledge beside a note written in black Sharpie and familiar handwriting: *Should Mei call Marcus?*

My eyes skid to the Magic 8 ball's answer and I suck in a breath: *Signs Point To Yes!*

CHAPTER 8

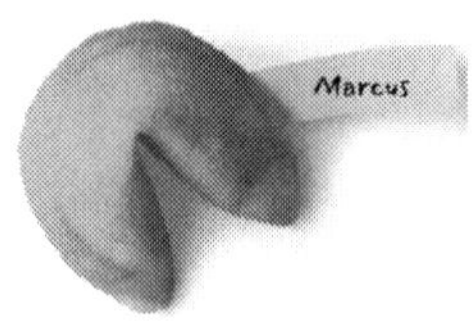

"Tavah Riggs was at the game for you tonight, Miller. Again."

I finish my text to Meemaw about our insane win, slouched low, knees pressed into the train seat in front of me.

Johnny leans his head back and swivels it toward me. "'*Yay, Magic Miller*'," he whisper-screams in falsetto, waving his hands to imitate the girls at our game.

I laugh once and shake my head, still texting when Johnny goes on.

"Should've seen your dad's face, dude. Had a pretty good view from my usual spot on the bench and, every time those girls yelled your name, he had his hand on his gun."

I shrug, my mind replaying the game, wishing I'd scored one more goal as the train wobbles toward Chinatown.

"You blind and deaf, maybe? 'Cause ain't no one comes to our games but girls screaming your freaking name." Johnny looks at his phone and laughs to himself, then responds to a text before swiveling his head back toward me, but my phone beeps and I read Meemaw's response:

YOU'RE MY CHAMPION. Love you, my big ol' grandbaby.

"You into guys?" Johnny asks, and when I don't respond, he straightens in his seat and turns fully toward me.

I glance at him, clicking off my phone.

"Or maybe you aren't into either. It's cool. You can tell me anything."

I toss him a weary glance, then pull out my Sharpie and write the final game score on my arm. "I like girls." Especially when there are girls like Mei anywhere in this universe. Haven't told Johnny or any of the guys about her 'cause I don't want Dad to find out, and they have oversized mouths.

"Good to know, since there's a whole stadium full of them who want you." He shakes his head. "And Tavah, man. She's fine. And Savvy's best friend, so…best friends dating best friends…"

I pull up a picture of my future motorcycle on my phone, flashing it at Johnny. "Meet my girl—she's Asian. I like Asians." Huh. Yeah. True. But I can't really *like* like the real-life Asian girl until after I get my two-wheeled Asian girl.

"No wonder you tear it up on the field. All that pent up frustration."

I laugh again. "Maybe you should stop scoring with Savvy and you'd score on the field more often." I smirk at my phone screen as it lights up with a call from an unknown number. Usually, I wouldn't answer but Johnny's not gonna drop the girl thing. I accept the call and hold it to my ear. "Hello?"

"Magic 8 is kind of bossy."

My entire body stiffens, down to my sore calves, and I shoot up in my seat. Girl. Phone number. Magic 8 ball. No freakin' way.

"Hello? Can I talk to Buddha, maybe?"

I swipe my arm across my forehead, glad she can't smell through the phone.

"Who is it?" Johnny mouths.

He'll tell the guys and there'll be no mercy. Then, when they're all over some night, Dad will hear the jokes and—

"Hello?" Mei's voice is in my ear and the reality gets me to my feet.

I grab the overhead rail and walk down the aisle away from Johnny and his curiosity. "Uh…sorry—hey. Buddha's… in the shower. And then he has meditations and a whole bunch of other stuff before bed. Can I give him a message?" I put my fist to my mouth where my lips aren't sure whether to smile or let out a scream.

"It must be time-consuming being a hostage."

"I've got him doing all my chores in his free time. Organizing drawers, returning emails, folding my socks. Which is really hard for someone his size."

"Mmm. Important stuff." She's smiling. She. Is. Smiling.

I grip the rail tighter, the metal burning against my sweaty palm. "Don't sound so sad. I'm sure we can work out visitation rights or something."

"Isn't he afraid of losing his place to a Magic 8 ball?"

"Uh, no." I smile to the black tunnel outside the window. "He and Magic 8 are working together, and turns out they're pretty effective. Also, he told me he prefers the view from my windowsill. You know, street versus alley. He's grateful for the guy time too 'cause he said you talk about embarrassing girl stuff, and he needs sports talk and bad language. But he did tell me in total confidence that he misses you." I curl my toes in my Adidas.

"Sounds like a lot of late nights for someone so old. He should probably come home and rest. I'm afraid he might pick up some bad habits."

"Oooh." I sigh. "Too late, but…" I lower my voice. "Maybe we could schedule a visit? I'll give you two some time, and we'll let him decide if joint custody is possible."

"I'm listening…"

Should've thought before I spoke. "Um, okay, so..." Where do I meet her? Can't meet at The Clubhouse; Dad will come home and sense all the girl voodoo in our apartment. My mind flicks through locations, but the train lady announces my stop and I'm out of thinking time. The only thing on my mind besides Mei is Oreos. "Meet me at Phil's Big Deal."

"Umm...where?"

"You know—Phil. The market guy around the corner from our apartments. Big orange sign? Next to the new boba place?" Silence. "He's bald? White goatee? Wears purple pants way too short for him? Not sure what the store's actually called—can't speak Chinese. I just call it Phil's Big Deal 'cause he holds mahjong tournaments in his basement."

"Where Guo Mama goes on Sunday nights?"

"That's the place! Meet me there in five? In front of the Oreos? Aisle three."

"Okay." Her voice curls at the end.

I end the call, then stare at my phone, my stomach wrapped around itself like a mass of cold, jittery noodles. The moment I daydreamed about all day is about to happen in real time. Me and Mei...alone. If only I already had my motorcycle. If only I knew what's going on between her and Face Eater. Also, if only I was as smooth in real life as I am in my head. Oh, the things we've done in my head.

Johnny's still watching me as I grab pole after pole, walking back to my seat to grab my bag. "Don't even try to lie to me, Miller. That was a girl on the phone."

"Catch you later, man." I move toward the train door and when it finally opens, I take a deep breath and rush out.

Taking the escalator steps two at a time, I hit the sidewalk at a jog, my bags bouncing against my back until I slow under Phil's bright orange sign and take a deep breath. Anticipation shoved me here. I wanna see her, but I'm throwing gas on a raging bonfire. Am I willing to let my motorcycle dreams explode for this moment? This is girl contact—the stuff I told Dad was no problem to avoid. But it's a huge problem. I wanna see Mei. Bad. Dad didn't say I couldn't talk to a girl. We're just two humans about to have a conversation at a convenience store. It could happen with anyone, anytime. Talking doesn't make babies.

Pushing the door open, I slow way down, roll my neck, and pop my knuckles. Phil's not behind the counter, which is probably best. He's a cool guy, but hat's waiting for me on aisle three is way cooler.

I turn the corner past the Chinese candy, and my eyes skid to a stop on skinny jeans that outline surprisingly long legs, and hair draped over her shoulder in a black, shiny waterfall. Surrounded by glossy packages of Oreos. One stop shop for God's most beautiful creations.

I talk myself into cool as I stop in front of Mei, meeting her eyes. "Hey."

Her head's tilted and she gives me a shaky side smile, her eyes darting away. "This seemed like a good place to run into you."

Is it the fluorescent lighting, or is her face bruised? "Think I'll hang out on aisle three even more often than I already do." I smile, then squint, looking at her cheekbone that's casting a bigger shadow than it should be. Definitely swollen.

I resist the urge to hold her head between my hands to get a closer look. "You've got a little somethin' on your face and…I'd offer to wipe it off, but it doesn't look like it's coming off anytime soon."

She tightens her jacket around her and turns to face the shelves.

"Was it Face Eater?"

She shakes her head. "I ran into my closet door."

I squeeze between the shelf and her, looking down at her. "Does your closet door have a fist?" She watches her feet, so I press a little harder. "Everything okay at home?"

"Yes. I'd just rather not talk about it."

Confirmed—Face Eater. "Uh, okay. Well…I'm not really cool with the way your closet treats you, and there's a 95 percent chance I'll bring it up again, but I'll drop it for now."

"I'm okay, really."

"Maybe you are, but your eye's not." I pull out my phone. "And your closet's gonna have a close encounter with the cops."

"No." She puts her hand on my phone, fingers on mine. I look at them, then her. "Please. It was an accident. Completely my fault. It's embarrassing."

I search her eyes, looking for hints. "I don't believe you."

"You don't have to." She presses her lips together and turns to walk away.

"Fine—okay." I sidestep and cut in front of her, holding up my hands. "Sorry. Let's get something for your cheek. Then we can go for a walk and not talk about it."

"Can we maybe go somewhere not outside?"

"Uh, sure." But where? We could go to Guo's but I wanna talk to Mei without a pair of old but surprisingly good ears listening. I could *slowly* walk her home through dark alleys, but I'm not ready to say goodnight, and Face Eater might be hiding in his ninja clothes. He obviously already practiced on her tonight, which makes me wanna bust his ugly face. I swallow anger. I could take her to The Clubhouse. Dad's working late. He hasn't gotten home any night this week before 4 AM. After she leaves, I'll scrub it clean, so nothing smells like Girl.

But I could lose the motorcycle if we're in my apartment alone. But no. I won't. No. Just…ice for her cheek and talking. That's it.

———

A few minutes and a grocery bag full of milk and Oreos later, Mei steps inside The Clubhouse and I freeze in the doorway. No girl besides Aunt Audrey and Meemaw has ever stepped inside this apartment and this is the first time I've ever spent time with a girl my own age besides the girls in my Sunday school class who guilt me into helping them bake cookies for old people. They're on Dad's approved list 'cause they love Jesus and service. But I *am* doing service. And with cookies. Just not for old people. No big deal. Bet still on.

Mei follows me inside and I lock the door behind us. There's a girl IN THE CLUBHOUSE. Where are the sirens and blaring lights? Where's my brain? I was mentally capable before Mei called. But it's also kinda like I don't need to be. Like I'm on autopilot. Didn't know I came equipped with autopilot.

"Do I get to see Buddha now?" Mei's voice pulls me from my thoughts, and I snap into motion, setting the bags on the counter and snatching a bag of peas from the freezer and wrapping it in a towel.

"First this." I hold it out to her. "I'll go tell him you're here, but he's not gonna be happy about your closet's aggression."

I walk into my room, stop, close my eyes, and take a deep breath. In...out...calm. Cool. All the freaked-out parts of me collected. I roll my neck like I'm warming up for a game and let out a shaky breath as I snatch Buddha from my windowsill and walk back to the kitchen.

Mei's checking out the bookshelf in the corner and I'm just glad I picked up the pile of dirty socks by the ottoman and vacuumed the rug yesterday. Glad there are no jock straps lying around.

Mei glances up. "Someone likes history." She gestures toward the bookshelf, and I nod, setting Buddha in the center of the table before grabbing two bowls. "My dad. Huge reader. By candlelight, actually so…candles." I wave my hand around the room.

"He reads by candlelight?"

I shrug and nod. "Yeah. Kind of his thing. And collecting weird, abstract photos." I nod toward a few pictures hanging above the table. A tree made of bike chains and a river made of wire and rope.

"That's…unexpected for a detective." She smiles and walks to the table, grabs Buddha, and sits across from me while I pour milk over the mound of Oreos in each bowl and stare at Buddha in Mei's hand. Kinda wish I was him right now, Mei's hands all over me, her fingers on—

I slide my bowl over a shriveled piece of cereal I missed wiping off this morning and jerk my eyes to her face.

"So, what you do," I explain as Mei watches, "is pile Oreos in the biggest bowl you can find. Then you drown them in milk, and when I say drown, I mean, like a Pacific Ocean of milk. Then, you wait four and a half minutes exactly. They'll be perfectly soaked and show your mouth a whole new world. Guaranteed."

She holds the peas over her left cheek and eye, but her right eyebrow arches.

"And while we wait, you can tell me what the Buddhist said to the hot-dog vendor." *[1]

She rests her elbow on the table. "What?"

I pop the lid back on the milk with my palm. "If we're gonna hang out, you should know I tell stupid jokes. Done it forever, no matter how obnoxious."

"I'm fine with that."

"The hanging out part or the stupid jokes?"

She shrugs. "Both."

"Yeah?"

"Yes."

"Cool." I swirl my Oreos in the milk with a spoon.

"So, are you going to tell me the answer?" she asks.

"Was kinda hoping you're a guesser."

"I'm not."

"But you like me to guess." I look at the peas she's still holding to her face.

She stares at me until her eyes talk. *"Hi."*

I smile and lean forward, forearms on the table, and respond silently. *"Hey."*

Her one eye blinks.

Both of mine hold it and say, *"So…Face Eater…"*

Her solo eye responds, *"I still don't want to talk about him."*

"I don't wanna talk about him ever but…Face Eater is…" I push an Oreo into its milky grave with the back of my spoon. "This is where you fill in the blank." My heart goes for a jog when I meet her eye again and I wanna fill in the blank by introducing our lips.

She presses hers together, but her eye tells me she understood my silent thoughts, loud and clear. Like a megaphone next to her ear.

I swear through a smile and hold up my hands. "Sorry! Just discovered a big problem with Eye Language. Can't hide my thoughts from you. Even with your obvious disadvantage."

"I like that."

"I'd like it better if it went both ways."

"We'll see."

I bark a laugh. "Is that, like, some obnoxious pun?"

She shrugs and smiles.

"Could you *be* any more cryptic?"

She shrugs again.

"Ah—you can. Awesome." I dig into my Oreos. It hasn't been four and a half minutes, but I need a distraction.

"Are you going to tell me the answer to your joke?"

I look up, shaking my head, my mouth stuffed with Oreos. "Nope. You have to earn it."

"How?"

"Let me consult Buddha." I slide my hand across the table, palm up, and she places him in my hand. "He knows how to work things out peaceably. He's a great listener; I've told him everything. And he told me some pretty interesting things about you."

"Like?"

"Nope. Confidentiality, you know? He's totally trustworthy—something about religious convictions."

She eases back in her chair. "How exactly do you talk to him? Just curious."

"Hold on." I hold up my finger and lean toward him. "He needs to tell me something. It'll only take a minute." I rub his belly and put my ear near him, laughing and shaking my head like he said something hilarious. I whisper in his ear, then listen to his reply. "I know, man, I know, but since you're a statue, guess you'll have to be okay with it."

Mei tilts her head. "Okay with what?"

"You know…eating Oreos. Together. You. Me." I wag my finger between us. "Hangin'."

She stares at me while sirens blare outside, then smiles. "Tell me more about what 'hangin' with you requires so I can make the decision for myself."

I roll my eyes. "It's pretty grueling, actually." Slouching in my chair, I lean my head back. "No one's ever survived it. Then again, no girl's attempted."

"No one?" Her eye darts away, but not before I read it loud and clear. *"How is that possible?"*

"Ha!" I jump out of my seat, leaning across the table. "I saw it. Dude—I'm getting good at this Eye Language translation thing, and it's only been twenty minutes. And you're only talking with one eye." I settle back into my seat and sigh. "Ahead of the curve, right where I like to be." I devour another Oreo. "I'm flattered, but I've made it possible for eighteen years."

"Why? There are a million girls who like you."

I frown at her. "Uh…I think your estimations are a little high, and even if they were accurate, there are approximately zero that I've liked back. Except…" I play with my spoon, lift it, twist it, watch it. "I don't know…" I stare at my Oreos, then glance up at her. "Think I might like you." The words run out of my mouth like prisoners set free, not looking back.

A smile lights her face, and she sets down the peas. "You don't even know me."

I rub my palms on my shorts and lean into the table. "I know I like your smile. Really like it, actually. And your notes. Especially your extremely symmetrical handwriting." I glance at her, gripping my knees under the table. "You have big, gorgeous mostly brown eyes with a shimmer of green. It's like…" I scan the living room behind her, remembering a day in Astoria, Oregon. "It's kinda like sitting in a forest, looking up."

She presses her lips together, trapping a smile and pink floods her cheeks.

I hold on to her gaze as the words swing out of me. "Reminds me of one of my favorite places. Like…you're kinda a favorite place. And…I like you. And…everything else. Including your choice of Wednesday night company."

She grins but looks past me to the framed artwork above the table. "You're not brave enough to like me."

"Why's that?"

She shrugs, smiling at the table again before looking back at me. *"So…what if I think I might like you, too? What are my chances?"*

I hold her eyes, then lean forward and pull the Sharpie from my pocket, grabbing her wrist. I pull her arm toward me across the table and write *100%,* snap the lid on the Sharpie, and sit back. Dad just can't know. Betrayal and guilt tango through my chest and leave a trail of hot lava no amount of Tums could touch. But I don't wanna fix it if it means resisting Mei. Why can't I have my motorcycle *and* her? If she's even available. We can like each other. Just can't do anything until I graduate. Forget the car. Motorcycle's barely worth it now.

She reads the number. "Really?"

"Yeah." I tap the Sharpie against the table's edge. "As long as Face Eater doesn't want in on this. Like I said—not my type. And we're the only people who speak Eye Language. He might feel left out."

"We're also the most unlikely people to be together."

"Why?"

"Because." She talks to the crumpled bag of peas on the table. "You're you and I'm me."

I frown into the air. "How 'bout a real reason?"

She tilts her head. "For someone who's never done this, you seem to know exactly what you're doing."

"Or you make it feel like I don't have to worry about what I'm doing."

Her eyes drop back to the table.

"I think I've got a lead on Face Eater since I won't beat you, but give me a percentage. If I were to guess just by reading your eyes, I'd say I have a solid… 75 percent chance."

She looks at me. "You're a terrible translator."

"Lower?"

"It's complicated."

"Ah." My fingers drum the table. "Don't know enough about this whole liking each other thing to understand complications."

She bites her lip and looks away, stirring her Oreos.

When she lifts her eyes again, I ask, *"Am I being stupid?"* She shakes her head, I swallow. "'Cause I wanna get a 4.0 in this liking you thing."

"I'll bring down your GPA."

Footsteps clomp up the stairs outside and my heart plummets. Dad footsteps. I grab Buddha and both bowls and bolt toward my room, motioning for Mei to follow, whirling my bedroom door shut behind us. "My dad's home," I whisper. "He can't know you're here."

"Should I go out the window?"

I shake my head, my eyes on the door, head lit up with visions of Dad finding her here. "No. Stay here. I'll be right back."

Mei's eyes go wide. "But my jacket's still out there."

---

1. *Answer: Make me one with everything.

CHAPTER 9

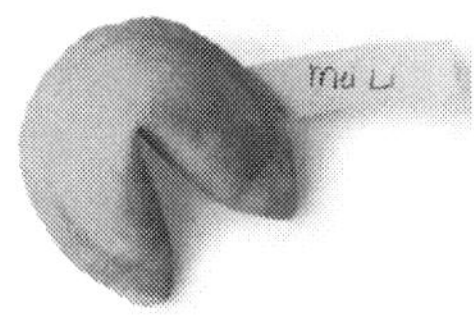

Oh. My.

Soggy Oreos bob in the bowls I'm still holding, the milk shivering from my shaking hands. I set the bowl on the dresser beside a framed picture of Marcus and his dad standing next to mountain bikes, beaming and sweaty.

I drag my eyes away so I don't leave eye-prints all over things I can't have when Detective Miller's voice rumbles from the living room and through the closed door.

"No movie tonight?"

Marcus's response is closer. "Nah, sorry. Can't stay up late."

"Understood. Maybe tomorrow night."

"Perfect. Night, Dad."

I spin around, scanning the room. I should sit and look comfortable somehow. My eyes skip over shelves of signed soccer balls and trophies. Stacks of books on the nightstand. A chalkboard wall covered in pie charts, diagrams, percentages. Navy down comforter on the bed, orange blanket balled near a pile of pillows…Nope. Not there. I jerk my eyes away. Desk chair?

I tiptoe-run to his desk beside the window and drop into the chair. When the door opens, I spin to face him, the room streaking around me before solidifying into lean, bare arms and shoulders in a tank top on a Marcus who closes the door behind him.

"Whoa," he whispers, leaning his head back against the door, clutching a bundle of clothes and closing his eyes. He crosses to the hamper and tosses in the bundle. "Rescued your jacket. No evidence," he whispers, "but I'll wash it 'cause I had to hide it in my hoodie and now it smells like fear. That was way too close." He runs his hands through his hair.

"Am I not supposed to be here?"

"So…about that…" He lets out a long breath before pulling a fresh shirt out of his drawer and yanking it over his head. It feels like I'm watching him dress, so I shoot off the chair, eyes on the chalkboard wall. My ears stay behind to listen to every rustle he makes, my tattoo throbbing.

The floorboards creak as Marcus steps beside me, his arm brushing against mine. "To answer your question…" he whispers, "my dad doesn't want girls here. Or anywhere near me." His words land heavily on my head, then drop like rocks on my shoulders.

"Did something happen or…?"

"Yeah." He nods and stares at the chalkboard wall. "My mom. She wrecked him and he's…" Marcus pops his knuckles and rolls his neck. "He's trying to protect me."

"From girls."

"Yep. My meemaw and my aunt are the only two girls allowed near me or in The Clubhouse."

"I don't want you to get in trouble, so I'm going to leave." Don't want myself and my family in trouble, either.

"One big, fat problem," he whispers. "There's only one way out and Dad's right by it. We're in here until he goes to bed which could be awhile. He's used to late nights. Plus..." He looks down at me. *"I don't want you to go."*

I think I swallowed a sparkler.

Pulling out my phone, I text Lin:

Mei: Cover for me.

I don't have to wait for her reply to know she will. I move to Marcus's closet, facing it to muffle my voice before dialing Mama's number, and she answers on the third ring.

"Wéi?"

"May I have a later curfew? Lin and I are working on our final chemistry project that's due tomorrow." The lie pours out of me, pushed out by the thought of hanging out with Marcus a bit longer.

There's a shuffle on the other side, a door clicks shut, and when Mama speaks again, her voice is hushed. "That is fine but be quiet when you get home. Understand?"

"Yes. Thank you." I end the call and turn to Marcus. "I can stay for a bit."

He grins. "Guess I'll give you a very quiet tour of my world, then. This eye language thing is gonna come in handy, I think."

He looks back to the chalkboard wall. "You should probably know that I draw on everything. Arms, legs...walls." He motions toward the chalkboard. "My dad installed this after I drew all over the wall with Sharpie in Kindergarten," he whispers.

I smile at the pie charts and diagrams scrawled across it, my pulse thumping in my neck. "What was your specialty?" I whisper back.

"Army guys. Koalas in hot-air balloons."

"Wait—it's on my bucket list to see a koala in a hot-air balloon, and you're telling me there's one just behind this chalkboard?" I frown-smile up at him, then look back to the board. "All I see is math."

He smiles at the wall and rubs the back of his neck. "Probability."

I point to a blank space. "Are you saving that for a really big koala?"

He tilts his head, squinting at the wall, then down at me. "I was," he whispers, "but I've got a better idea." Stepping to his nightstand, he pulls out a piece of chalk, then points to the empty space. "You should stand right there. And wave."

I hesitate, then turn and press my back to it and hold my hand up. "Like this?"

His smile shoots light at me. "*Exactly like that.*"

He squats in front of me, tracing around my left foot, up the side of my leg which tenses, tingling when his hand brushes it. The chalk pauses at my hips before moving up my torso, but he hesitates at my chest and catches my eye.

"Didn't think about how awkward this could get. Never had this issue in kindergarten."

"What issue?"

He straightens and steps back, smiles at the floor, taps the chalk against his thigh. "Girl in my room. Close proximity. All the…" His face flushes. "Hormones."

My twisting stomach wrings a nervous whisper-laugh out of me when he steps closer, his eyes mock serious. "Don't laugh," he whispers down to me, the air warming. "95 percent of guys twelve through twenty-one wrestle with them every second."

I smile and roll my eyes while he continues tracing.

"Is this too weird for a first date?" he asks the chalkboard under my elbow.

I press my lips together to keep my somersaulting insides inside. "No."

"If this is considered a date, I mean." He takes a step back and jerks into motion, continuing his outline.

I squeeze my eyes shut to trap the thought. "Depends on your definition, I guess?"

He rounds my shoulder and traces my neck, his face so close, the heat of it washes over my cheek, and I swallow, pressing my lips together as he responds. "Don't have a definition, but…" He stops, erases with his fingertip, then continues. "If we're voting," I say definitely. As long as you're down."

My chest tightens to stifle an inner squeal and I nod. "I'm down."

"Yesssssss," he says through a smile, then moves my hair and goosebumps play tag across my skin.

I drag in a breath through my nose and wiggle my toes against his rug when the line he's drawing swerves outward.

"I don't think my leg bends like that," I whisper to the ceiling.

He snatches the eraser from his nightstand. "Got distracted."

"By…?"

"Thought about kissing you." He tosses the eraser to the floor and focuses on his drawing again. "But I won't. Promise."

A swallow lodges in the middle of my tight throat. This is only a daydream or I'm unconscious. I'm actually in math class right now, wishing I was here, that's all. If he really tries to kiss me, it's only me hallucinating.

Marcus speed-draws the rest of me then steps away, holding his hands up. "Done."

I meet his eyes but am too afraid of what mine might say so I step away from the chalkboard and turn around, hand circling my neck as I nod. "An excellent, 2-D me," I whisper, smiling at my waving outline on his wall. In his room. Drawn by him. I'm still passed out.

"Whoa." Marcus hovers behind me and I glance over my

shoulder at him. "The tat on your neck wasn't there the other night."

Feeling plummets from my face, pools in my toes, and I turn back to the chalkboard because I don't want to talk about the reason behind the tattoo. But Marcus's fingers smooth my hair over my shoulder and all feeling that left me five seconds ago surges back into me, hot and tingly.

"What's it say?"

I press my lips together and close my eyes, breathing in heat. "My name."

A moment of silence throbs before he speaks again. "So…" He steps around me to the chalkboard and draws a heart in the middle of my chalk chest. "It's kinda stating the obvious, then."

"What do you mean?"

"You know…meaning of your name." He rubs the back of his neck. "Beautiful. Obvious." He focuses on the chalkboard and swallows. "Did it hurt?"

I smile at my feet, wiggling my toes to distribute the heat from his comment, then look at him and shrug. "Kind of."

He sections my chalk heart into two halves, the veins in his forearm shifting beneath his skin as he writes *50% Buddha* in one half and *50% Face Eater* in the other.

My stomach lurches and I grab the chalk from his hand, erasing *Face Eater* with my palm before drawing a question mark. Then I turn to him and shove the chalk against his chest, patting my hand over it, my fingertips flexing to get closer to him.

He stares at the board, a smile stretching across his face. "I can totally take that question mark."

My eyes flutter open when the crack in my curtain sends a laser of sunlight into my room. I fell asleep in the hoodie

Marcus gave me on our walk home at 3 AM, and when I pull it off, my skin refuses to let go of his smell the same way my mind won't let go of last night. Actually…I glance at the time on my phone. Seven hours ago. When he walked me to my fire escape, and I figured that would be the last time I'd see him. But then he'd said "see you tomorrow."

I snatch my phone from the nightstand and find a screen full of Marcus texts beaming up at me. Clutching it, I flop back on my pillows with a squeal and open to his most recent message.

> Marcus: Good morning sleepy head! Just me again, hoping you're finally awake and I'm not still talking to myself. How's your eye? Your head? School? I have zero focus but am oddly energized after only two hours of sleep. Magical.

I bite my lip and smile, my stomach flipping around as I scroll to the first text in the very long chain he sent while I was sleeping and he should have been.

> Marcus: Can't sleep after tonight.

> Now you probably can't either. Sorry. Shh. Go back to sleep. I'll tiptoe back to my side of the phone. Sorry. So sorry. Being quiet now. Very, very quiet…

> But one more thing before I go…just gotta say…we should be hanging out right now. Yeah, I get the only ones awake at this hour are cats and people forced to work night shifts but sleep is such a waste of perfectly good hang out time, IMO.

Okay. Well...sounds like you're sleeping. I can hear you snoring from here, so this is coming a little late but good night. Actually... good morning. Good 4:11 AM. But really. Bye. Sleep tight. Sweet dreams. See you later. Night night. Buh-bye. Signing off...

(Unless you're awake now and have nothing better to do than text....)

Dude. My head won't shut up. It keeps very loudly wondering how we talked for so long at my apartment. I've never done that. Ever with anyone, not even my dad who, you know, I live with. And how did he not hear us laughing? Especially that one time when you snorted? He's a detective. Are we that stealth?! That was wild. The most excellent kind of wild. Love to be stealth with you again. Very, very soon? Yes, please—100% times a billion or so.

How's your eye? Hopefully closed. Sleeping. Or staring at your phone while you're texting me back any minute now...

Waiting...

So patiently...

Ok so you must really be asleep. Guess I'll try. Here goes...

I laugh to the ceiling before texting:

Mei: I'm here! I'm awake! But I wasn't at 4:11 AM. Now I wish I was though. I was completely exhausted from being so stealth I guess but I'd love to get exhausted being stealth again...100% times two billion...or so.

I press my phone to my chest and picture Marcus lying in his bed all night, sprawled out, thinking of me while he wrestled his sheets and waited for a text. My insides bubble and I whisper-squeal into my pillows.

The dull buzz of conversation and the smell of coffee sneaks upstairs from the restaurant and under my closed door. Which means Mama and Baba are busy and distracted and I'm free to figure out how to navigate this day. I've never skipped school, but the bus rumbled by hours ago, and I'm not walking through the halls with this advertisement from Nick on my face.

My phone buzzes in my hand and I flip it over while my stomach does the same, but it drops when Nick's name slides onto the screen with a message that makes me want to throw my phone at the wall:

Nick: Sorry about last night. Can't wait to see you again so I can show you just how sorry I am. Promise I will make it up to you.

I clench the phone in my hand, like I can squeeze his words from it. I don't want to hear his excuses or his big plans for us that he thinks will somehow make up for his actions. I never want to see him again. But that's impossible if I want any kind of future for myself.

I release a frustrated breath and turn onto my side, hating that nothing in my future will work without Nick, even angrier that he barged into this perfect morning. I hesitate, then force my fingers to type a single word response to his text so he doesn't suspect anything:

Mei: Okay.

As I hit send, a text from Marcus slides onto the screen:

Marcus: FINALLY. You definitely know how to make a guy wait in agony. I survived the long night and now I'm trying to survive history by thinking about my most recent history. Specifically last night. This morning? It was way better than anything Napoleon's army could have pulled off. Napoleon could only wish. And—sidenote—apparently he was a very short dude with a raging case of narcissism.

What class are you in right now? How you feeling?

I'm feeling so, so good, especially if his texts keep coming and crowd out Nick's. I smile as I respond.

Mei: Fully smiling from your sleepless night of texting. Just caught up. Also...skipping school.

His response pops up seconds later:

Marcus: Seriously?! Arrrgghh!!!! Ask Magic 8 if I should skip with you.

But I don't need to ask Magic 8 because everything about Marcus is a yes. Exclamation point, exclamation point.

Marcus: Magic 8 said, and I quote, WHY ARE YOU ASKING ME THIS STUPID QUESTION?! So weird. I've never seen that response before.

A selfie of him slumped in a desk chair slides onto the screen and I can't stop smiling.

Marcus: Obviously, I don't know how to properly navigate my life without Magic 8. Totally made the wrong choice and came to school. A whole day wasted in foolishness. Regrets are taking me down. Looking for the nearest exit.

I take a selfie of me in my bed, my head turned to the side to hide my bruised cheek and send it to him.

Mei: Rough day for me too. :)

We text for ten more minutes, the grin stretching my face making my jaw ache until Marcus sends an audio clip of the bell ringing, then a hurried, whispered message. "Just gonna say, you look way too cozy in my most favorite hoodie as I go off to face the consequences of my poor life choices in chemistry. But you look way wayyyyyyyyyyy better in it than I ever could so keep wearing it. Also! I might have left something for you at Guo's. Hint: it's not me, no matter how bad I wish it was. Later, my favorite delinquent student."

The audio clip ends, and I hesitate, soaking in the moment and staring at the selfie he sent, memorizing the way his tousled hair sweeps across his forehead, his dark lashes reaching out and drawing me into deep blue. The smirk on the edge of his lips and the symmetrical lines of his face, confidently set into perfection. My eyes blur from staring and I blink and click off my phone, then ease off my bed toward my closet, my whole body sore like it was slammed against a wall. Or a bleeding flower rug.

Shaking my head, I focus on my row of sweaters but catch my reflection in the mirror—bad memories smeared across my face in black and blue, casting a shadow over the morning. I turn away; Nick isn't going to be part of this day.

I reluctantly slip out of Marcus's hoodie, his smell refusing to let go of my skin like my head clings to his voice and smile, and I pull on a sweater before sliding his hoodie under my pillow and stepping into my bathroom to brush my teeth and hair. Grabbing a scarf, I wrap it around my neck, wincing when the threads pull at raw skin around my tattoo.

I hurry downstairs and edge through the kitchen where the chefs are a blur of white against stainless steel and clouds of steam hiss from the grills. Servers dart in and out through the swinging door with trays and coffee pots as I slip behind shelves of stacked cans. I push open the back door and smack into a guy holding a sprawling bouquet of red roses.

"Sorry!" I call as I hurry down the chipped steps.

"Mei Li, wait!"

I glance over my shoulder as he takes off his hat.

Xander's teeth glint in the morning sun slicing through the alley as he holds out the bouquet. "From Nick."

I stare at the flowers, then turn toward the street again. Flowers won't fix my eye or Nick's drinking problem.

"He wanted to deliver these himself but had last-minute business in L.A. and won't be back for a week or so."

I dig my nails into my palms and look over my shoulder as he pulls a pink card from between the rose stems. "At least read the note."

I hesitate before taking a few steps back toward him and snatching the envelope, not breathing as I pull the card out.

Mei Li,

I am so sorry for how I acted last night. I have work to do to become the man you deserve. Please let me try.

Yours, Nick

His name stamps cold spots through my chest, and I press my lips together to stop their quivering. Does he really think flowers will erase last night? Xander holds out the flowers and I take them, choking the stems as I walk toward Guo Mama's.

I don't want Nick as "my man." Not anymore. Alcohol makes people do things they normally wouldn't. Baba was an alcoholic for years and ruined our life in Taiwan. If Nick keeps drinking, what will he ruin?

I put my palm over the welt on my face and clench my jaw against the memory of last night as I push through Guo Mama's door. I drop the flowers and card in the garbage before swerving through racks, into the back room, and falling into a chair at the table. Three days ago, Nick was nice. Flirty but harmless. Baba wasn't hiding something. Marcus was just words on paper and a Tuesday night spark in the restaurant. Now everything's flipped. And Marcus is throwing sparks all over my life. Sparks I have to keep stomping on so they don't turn into a wildfire.

Murmuring floats around the corner from the storage room and I turn in my chair to intercept the sound. I catch Mama's voice and squint, listening to Guo Mama scoff at whatever she said.

"She is not a child any more Jia Li. She can handle the truth."

"She already hates me. If I tell her, I lose her forever. I should have told her years ago, but I was afraid she'd run away, and I'd never see her again."

The voices quiet and a door shuts. I stand, ready to bolt, but Mama rounds the corner.

Her eyes triple in size, and on the one place I'm trying to hide. "What are you doing here?"

I clench my fist at my side like it can squeeze words out of me and a moment swirls between us, gathering all the tension into a ball in my throat before Guo Mama shuffles to Mama's side, hands clasped behind her back.

"I asked for help with boxes after school, but thank you for coming early, Xiao Mei." Guo Mama's eyes sweep over my bruised face, her jaw tightening.

My eyes dart after Mama's so I can catch them and say, "You know who did this." Instead, I nod and talk to the air, hoping Mama gets the hint to leave, "I'll be home before my shift."

She stares at the floor, then nods and ducks her head as she walks through the shop and out the front door.

"Ah! Beautiful Mei Li..." Guo Mama's wrinkles droop as she studies my face. "I can either guess what happened," she says, motioning to her own cheek, "or you can tell me. I'm not your Mama or Baba. I don't need to protect Ugly Chao and neither should you." She stares me down while shame leaks through me. "It was Ugly Chao, yes?"

I hesitate, then nod and she purses her lips, shakes her head, pivots toward the counter.

"He will wish I never saw this." She drops the heavy words between us like an anchor then shuffles to a drawer, opens it, and pulls out a Tupperware container. She pries off the lid with her gnarled fingers before pulling out a folded piece of paper and giving it to me. "This will make everything better. And I mean everything."

I stare at the note, and all thoughts of asking Guo Mama about the "she" from her and Mama's conversation disappears. Mama can hide whatever she wants, and so can I.

I smile at Marcus's precise creases and my name written on one side in his blocky, sloped handwriting I've memorized.

I look at Guo Mama and she waves her hand toward the note. "Read! It's so very good!"

"You *read* it?"

"Of course. I can't pass notes without knowing what they

say." She claps her hands, then brings them to prayer. "Everything's going to be splendid, as I predict." Humming, she shuffles off and pushes a rattly cart into her storage room.

I swallow and unfold the note's corner flap, my fingertips pressing into the paper as I read the short message scrawled at the bottom corner in Sharpie instead of pen:

How would you feel about a second date? Saturday, 10 AM, maybe? Unless work and homework can tell better jokes than I can.

Guo Mama's slippers flap against the terra cotta, and I straighten, balling my hands into fists at my side to keep all this energy inside. I don't want to lose a particle of this feeling. She pats my shoulder as she passes, and I turn to her. "You can't tell anyone, Guo Mama. Promise? I know it's a stupid idea and I can't have him but…I just…" I scan the letter again, my smile spreading. "I really like him and just want to pretend for one date longer."

She cackles to the dragon lanterns hanging from the ceiling, then blinks at me. "You know I am good at keeping secrets. This one is special, and the gods are already helping you. Check your work schedule. You will see."

CHAPTER 10

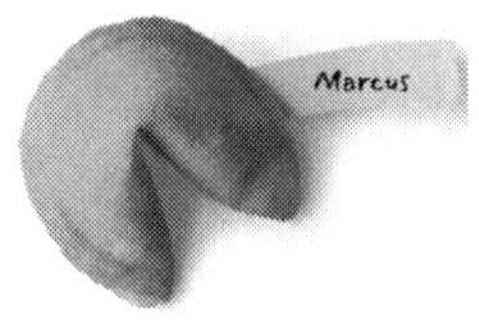

Mei: To answer your question from last night, I'd rather go without sugar for one week than not shave my legs. As for American names, I would choose Stella. Or Violet since it's my favorite color. What do you think? If I had to choose a different name for you, it would be...maybe Bruno? Elwood? Or—I know—Alistair, Ali for short. You do go to that rich kid charter school, so...you should stop wearing hot boy t-shirts and jeans and switch to chinos and loafers. And a sweater around your neck. Maybe carry around a tennis racket.

I laugh at my phone, then shove it in my pocket and cross the street to the park where the boys are at the table under Ellie, the naked, red elephant-lady sculpture.

Johnny tosses an orange in the air and knee dribbles it while the other guys count. I walk by and snatch it, then throw it over his head to Ty. Johnny does a roundhouse and barely misses me, so I grab his leg until he falls. The guys laugh and I slide onto the bench, then destroy the triple decker turkey sandwich I made before school.

"Where's your head been lately, Miller? Coach almost ripped you apart after you missed that pass during the game last night."

I take a huge bite, chew. Shake my head.

"I'm tellin' you." Johnny leans around Jeff, pointing at me. "Miller has a girl, and he's not spillin'. Last night on the train, he was talking to someone on the phone all secret. Must've been someone good, too, 'cause his face was doing this." Johnny stares at the sky, his mouth open in a stupid smile.

Jeff barks a laugh and Ty slaps the table. "Yeah, okay. Hilarious. It was probably his grandma telling him how much money she's giving him for graduation."

Ty leans across the table and pats my face with both hands. "Miller's got girls trying to get his attention all the time, so unless she's a super model, no girl's gonna get him."

I shove him away and Johnny slides onto the bench next to me. He wraps his arm around my neck and forces my head onto his shoulder, patting it. I jerk away from him, shove him off the bench, then finish my sandwich before ripping open a bag of Cheetos.

A week ago, soccer was my girlfriend, and I was a devoted boyfriend. It'll always be my first love, but soccer doesn't have a smile that shoots lasers and explodes my heart, or curve a pair of skinny jeans like Mei does. Soccer doesn't have a voice that makes me shiver or turn my brain into neon cotton candy.

The guys move on to another topic and I pull out my phone, my heart tripping over itself when there's a response from *a-MEI-zing*:

> Mei: Having a hard time focusing on anything but last night...

I glance at the guys, leave the table, and slip around Ellie into some trees before dialing Mei's number. I hold my breath.

"Hey."

My heart jumps toward her voice. "What are you doing tonight?"

"Make your wildest guess."

"If the answer's working, we should change that."

"Wish I had a good reason to take it off."

"Or…maybe someone will come into the restaurant tonight." I turn toward Chinatown and Mei's school full of guys who look nothing like me. I turn a circle, scanning the girls sitting in clumps around the park and along the curb, hunched over their phones. None even compare to Mei. They're not even in the same game.

"Twice in one week?" she asks through a smile that spreads through the phone to me. "Impressive."

Jeff yells at me and I glance over my shoulder, then rush, "Gotta go."

"Me, too, sadly."

"Don't be surprised if you see me tonight."

"I like surprises."

"Reason 362 why I like you. See you later." I end the call and walk back to the table and grab my backpack. "Anyone craving Chinese food after practice?"

Johnny pops a fortune cookie into his mouth and reads the paper, then waves it in the air above our table, chewing as he talks. "I love this place! Fortune cookies before dinner, not after, and then, this fortune." He throws the paper in the middle of the table like a touchdown. "Luck? I'll take it. Maybe I'll become the guy all the girls want instead of Miller."

I snatch it and read, rolling my eyes at Johnny before

glancing over to where Mei's washing a table. When she turns around, she catches my eye and smiles, then looks away, scrubbing the life out of that table. I wanna see that smile as much as possible as close as possible as soon as possible. But not too close. Four more weeks. I can do this.

She glides toward the kitchen door, and my eyes get caught in the movement. Maybe I can't do this.

I snatch Johnny's fortune and hand him mine. "Nah, man. You got the wrong fortune. This one's yours."

He takes it and reads it out loud. "Being alone will bring perspective." He tosses it on his empty plate and swears.

"Looks like loneliness is in your future. But perspective's nice."

He flips me off, then takes a drag on his Mountain Dew. "We'll see 'bout that, Miller. I'll work some magic with our waitress. Watch and learn, boys…watch and learn."

He leans around Ty and waves his arm at Mei who weaves between tables toward us. She'd be killer on the soccer field.

She tucks her hair behind her ear when she's close, avoiding my eyes. I'm freaking losing it over the way she moves. She's wearing makeup tonight. First time I've seen her with stuff all over her face and I prefer her without. But she did a decent job of hiding the bruise. Totally prefer her without that, too. Still wanna rip Face Eater apart. Or have Dad do it. Dad would destroy him. Not sure why she's protecting him.

She smiles at every guy but me. "Ready to order?"

"Yeah, but quick question." Johnny lounges in his chair and tilts his head back as he talks to her. "If you were to take your shot at any of us here, which black guy would you choose?"

Mei glances at me and her cheeks are either reflecting the red tabletop or she's blushing, and my leg bounces under the table. "Since you're the only black guy at this table, you've got a pretty good chance."

"Told you who's what." Johnny slaps his chest.

"But," Mei continues, "if you want to know who I'd take to the back pantry…I'll just say…" Her eyes dart directly to mine before wandering back to Johnny. "It's not you." Mei turns and her curves move in all the right ways, blowing me completely apart like they're sending shockwaves across the room.

"Ohh…dude!" Ty laughs to the light above our table. "You should see your face right now. That girl just got all my maddest respect."

I try to focus on the guys and not how to get to the pantry and what could happen in it, then send her a text, pretending it's to Dad: Which way to the pantry.

I keep my phone in my lap and Mei in my peripheral vision as she moves around the restaurant, and when every noodle and grain of rice disappears from our plates, she skims toward the table. Without looking at me, she leans across it to hand everyone their bills, and I have an eye level shot of her chest. I swallow and avert my eyes, opening my bill to slide my card inside but instead of a bill, there's a note:

> *I went to the pantry. Guess we missed each other. But good news! My work schedule changed. Not sure why or how, but I didn't ask questions. So, if there's still an offer for a second date….*

I glance up, my stomach doing a couple flips. She's at the next table, holding a pitcher as she talks to a few old ladies, her long fingers wrapped around the handle, and I picture them all tangled in my hair, then take a drag on my Dr. Pepper to cool down the vitals.

I slip the folded note I wrote during class inside the bill sleeve, then use the pen to add:

Saturday = you + me + all day. See you at 10 AM.

I lie flat in my bed, watching my fan spin. Kinda like my brain. It's so incredibly heavy because I didn't ask The Question weighing it down when Dad and I went for a run along the bay after I got home from Zhang's. Today was the first time in two weeks he had longer than two hours off work. Didn't wanna add my brain junk to his night. Even though he's wide-awake right now, painting his room since he can't sleep like a normal person anymore, and I'm over here pretending to sleep because I pansied out and couldn't think of a way to bring up my burning question. It's 2 AM. I've been wrestling that burning question and equally hot thoughts about Mei for two hours. Tomorrow cannot come fast enough. Neither can graduation. Unless I can find a loophole in The Bet. Gotta talk to Dad.

I throw off my comforter and hurl myself out of my room and across the hall into Dad's.

He stops singing to his music and glances over his shoulder. "Did I keep you awake? Sorry, man—can't paint without Zeppelin."

"Nah." I run my fingers through my hair. "Just…too wired, and thought you could use some help."

He smiles, then turns back to his painting. "I won't turn down the company. Brushes are in the box."

I rub my eye then snatch a brush, focusing really hard on taking off the plastic while I figure out how to bring up my question.

Dad gave me The Talk in third grade when I asked him what sex was while we were standing in the aisle of the train headed to a Giants game. He'd told me we'd talk about it when we got home and, during the game, he'd stared silently at his Dr Pepper. Wish he had one to stare at now because he's probably not gonna like this question, either.

I dip my paint brush in the can, then swipe it across the door jamb to the beat of Led Zeppelin squealing from the speaker. This song always brings out Dad's falsetto and I smile, then realize the song's almost over. After tonight's pantry talk, I have so many questions about the motorcycle. If I don't ask, the guilt will rip me into confetti. I should just avoid Mei. But I can't. Also can't lie to Dad.

I step off the ladder and wipe my hands on a towel tossed over the paint bucket as the song ends. "So, Dad…"

He watches his roller smooth gray paint over his white bedroom wall. "Yeah?"

"About the bet…"

"Yeah?"

I twist the rag around my fingers. "I have a few clarifying questions."

"Shoot." He stands and steps back to admire his work.

"What exactly are the requirements for getting the motorcycle? Like…you know…" I scan the polka-dotted plastic sheet on the floor and blue tape strips around the open window, hoping for all the right words to fly through it. Or maybe if I sniff these paint fumes a little longer, the question will just slip out. "Like I just wanna make sure I understand what you mean by staying away from girls. Prom's coming up and since I'm a senior…just wanna know what's off limits." He glances over his shoulder and his eyes leave a streak of panic in the air, so I rush, "Just checking. You know…don't wanna lose the motorcycle over a technicality."

His knuckles are white on the roller handle, so I pick paint off my fingernails. He sighs and turns to me, sets the roller in the tin, and runs his hand through his hair, leaving a gray streak through the brown. He inspects his fingers and bends to snatch a rag.

Flipping an empty bucket upside down, he drops onto it,

forearms on his knees. "Look, M.C.…if you want to go to prom, that's fine. I get it." He rubs the rag so violently on his hand, his skin's gonna peel off.

"Here's the thing…" He tosses the rag in the corner, the gray streak still in his hair. "You've got goals. Big dreams. Girls get in the way, I promise. They're fun to look at, but they're…" He scans the room. "Like candy, maybe? Something that's so good, you can't help yourself, and then, you're sick and kind of hate yourself for not taking it easy. Stopping sooner."

Okay. So…my mom was too much sugar. Dad didn't stop, and it messed him up. Kind of nasty to think about, but I also get how it can happen. Too many times to count, I've taken down a package of Oreos, then felt the effects. And Mei's way better than Oreos, so…

"If you keep your distance, you'll get what you want and avoid all the aches girls can cause. That being said, you can take a girl to prom, sure. You can even dance with said girl. Just don't do any of the after-prom kind of stuff and you have nothing to worry about." He waves his hand. "If you find some girl you can't resist, great—finish med school then marry her. Commit. Prove you mean it and do it. Just save all the other "doing" until after you're married, if you know what I mean." He turns back to the wall. "Trust me—I didn't listen to that old-fashioned advice, and it detoured my life." He stands and picks up the roller. "I'd never take it back because I got you, but…" He shakes his head. "It messed with me, so just…save it for someone who's worthy of all your big ol' feelings. You know I know, and I don't want you to know in the same way."

My existence is a result of two people who obviously had 'big ol' feelings' for each other but didn't know they came with a kid. So weird to think Dad once had the same crazy, out-of-control feelings for my mom that I'm starting to have for Mei. I haven't even kissed Mei, so there's a zero percent chance of a Baby Marcus. But man…I kinda get how things could get to a Baby Marcus Warning level. A few weeks ago, I was thinking about state championships, college, finding a job, tacos, and avoiding Prom. Then Mei. Now my brain's swimming in girl thoughts that spill over into other parts of me. Dad obviously wasn't able to stop with my mom, so will I be able to stop if I start with Mei?

"So basically," Dad says, his eyes back on his roller moving up and down the wall, "keep your hands to yourself, keep your pants all nice and zipped until you've graduated med school. That's it. Motorcycle, car. Happy life, done."

Hands to myself. Pants zipped. Uh…okay, but what about that feeling when my whole body wants to be as close to Mei's as possible? What about wanting to be on a machine that pumps Mei-infused air into my lungs? Or when my eyes wanna trap her smile so every time I blink, it flashes? What do I do with my fingers when they wanna touch her like I'm a blind person identifying her in a girl lineup? Or with my brain that plays her laugh on repeat?

I find the end of a piece of tape and pull it off the wall. Mei's definitely my weakness, and I'm gonna have to watch my intake very, very closely.

CHAPTER 11

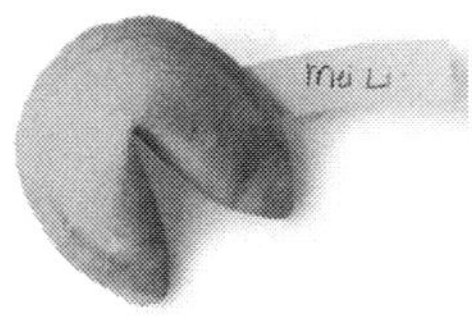

*Hey Mei. Sitting in AP Bio. Population ecology's fascinating and all, but I'm wondering what class you're in right now. Wondering if you're ever gonna answer my stupid joke from last night.**[1] *It's a classic. Also wondering if we could hang sooner than Saturday . Midnight-3 AM seems perfect. You get loopy around 2 so that adds to the appeal. My teacher's pacing the room so I'm gonna write actual notes.*

Even dispersion: individuals are separated by a fairly even distance, yada yada yada, blah blah, blah. Etc. etc.

Okay. He's gone. And that definition seems true. My school's on the east side, you're on the south, a whole lot in between. I don't like any distance between us, even or not. It'd be way more fun if you were here. I can't go to yours since, you know, don't speak Chinese. Think there's an eye-language school? It'd be small.

Anyway…if you were at my school right now, I'd be staring at you pretty hard from across the room. You wouldn't find it creepy or annoying or anything. I'd be thinking of ways to ask you out and trashing all of them because they're all stupid ideas since I don't even know what you like to do. Major disadvantage. Gonna change that. Teacher's coming again. MC out.

I slide Marcus's note in the folder labeled "CALC" and shove it back in my bottom desk drawer before walking into the bathroom and pulling out my makeup bag.

There's no way I'm walking through school with a greenish-purple cheek like the one in the mirror. I thought it would've faded at least a little by now. It hasn't, a lot like my anger toward Nick. I still haven't responded to any of his texts or calls from the past two days, but sooner or later I'll have to. I don't even want to speculate what ignoring him might mean for me or my family. So, I'll just pretend a little longer. Wish I could pretend I didn't have a calculus test today and stay home.

Grabbing my backpack off my bed, I hurry downstairs and out the front door to avoid Baba or Mama. I fast walk down the street and turn the corner, glancing up at Marcus's window. Where I was two nights ago. With Marcus, whisper-laughing and talking about everything like we've known each other way longer than three weeks.

When the bus hisses to a stop and the door swishes open, I steal one last look at Buddha on Marcus's windowsill before hauling myself onto the bus and dropping into my seat. I lean my head against the window while laughter and shouts ricochet off the metal roof, pelting me like hail. Traffic blurs past, and Lin darts through a break between cars, running for the bus like usual. A few seconds later, she drops beside me, adjusting the straps on her orange wedge sandals.

"Got stuck with dishes again."

"Shocking." I smile, keeping my bruised cheek toward the window.

"Seriously." She rolls her eyes then squints and shoves her head into my space.

"Where were you yesterday?" Lin's stare is like a laser on my face, hitting layers beneath the surface. "Did it have anything to do with all this makeup you've got going on today?" Lin frowns, her gold eyeshadow glinting. Her gaze is heavy, so I shift in my seat to push it away. "Marcus doesn't even go to our school. And I know you aren't doing it for Sean no matter how bad he wishes you were."

I swallow and take another deep breath, let it out slowly to calm my heart, then talk to the green leather in front of us where someone has carved a misspelled swear word. "Just thought I'd give it a try." I stretch my arm and put my fingertip over the slice in the leather seat, pretending it's smooth like I wish my face was right now.

Lin drops her shoulders and rolls her eyes. "Makeup is wasted on your face. Let me know when you want to tell me the real reason you're wearing it. And confirm what I already know about Gross Nick." Her eyes flick to my bruised cheek. "What happened?"

Last time Lin asked probing questions, she found out about my family, so I'm surprised she's digging. But I'm not saying a word this time. I can't risk it.

"Okay..." Lin mutters under her breath. "Well, since you're not talking," she gestures to my cheek, "tell me what's new with your boy toy."

I stare at the rows of heads in front of us. I want to tell her every detail of two nights ago and how Marcus makes me feel invincible, and wherever he is, there's light. But I also want to keep it all to myself because as soon as I release it, reality will suck the life out of it.

"He's not mine, but he and his friends came to the restaurant last night. So, I guess there's that!"

"And why do you think he'd do that?" Lin raises her eyebrows.

"They were hungry?"

"Sure. Let's go with that. Except we know Marcus is madly into you, like every other guy that exists." Lin chatters, asking if it's okay if she has a crush on my boyfriend, but my mind is stuck on the "madly into you" part. No matter how that idea lights up my mind, Marcus Miller will never be mine. Even if two nights ago really happened, he's not an option for me. Detective Miller will find out about my family, and we'll be on the next plane out. Still…If these are my last days in America, I'd choose to spend them on Date #2 with Marcus.

My eyes roam the bus and land on Harvey a few rows ahead. He's laughing with his friends, and still has the same smile my fifth-grade heart couldn't get over. We constantly played kissing tag, and I caught him more than once. He's funny. And nice. And wasn't a bad kisser when he was ten.

James says something in Harvey's ear, and he swats the back of James's head. Maybe I should stick with what I know. Harvey would understand my family situation since he's first-generation American, too. But his smile doesn't make lines around his mouth like Marcus's, and while Harvey's hair falls into his eyes, it doesn't wave like Marcus's.

I close my eyes and dig my nails into my palms, but Marcus's laugh rumbles through my memories and echoes off every cold, brittle thing inside me like it can shake me open. And his body. I dig my nails deeper into my palm. His legs are the perfect mix of lean and muscly. His shoulders stretch under his shirt until his back is an upside-down triangle pointing to his shorts hanging low on his waist leading to his backside.

My cheeks burn, and I slide low in my seat, grateful for make-up to cover my thoughts from giving themselves away on my cheeks. But as intriguing as all the lines of his chest and the ridges of his abs and back must be, I always come back to his eyes on me when we talk. Like he's absorbing everything I say and storing it somewhere deep inside for safekeeping.

I sit up a little taller, watching Harvey while Lin chats with Shuney across the aisle. If I stare long enough, he'll look over. Maybe I've never given his eyes a chance to talk to mine, but when he glances my way, he smiles and waves. I wave back and attempt a silent conversation, but his eyes are quiet. I try it with James whose eyes skim mine a few times, but he raises his eyebrows and winks. He's definitely not reading my thoughts. Maybe I'll try Sean in first period.

My phone buzzes and I blink myself back onto the rattling bus and pull it out of my bag. A message pops up on the screen.

Nick: Have dinner with me when I get back? There's a new place in the Mission you'll love.

Nicks message is a reminder: I can't have Harvey or James or Sean and I definitely can't have Marcus.

I stare at the message while thoughts of what almost happened in Nick's stupid room sneer back at me. He was drunk. He's been drunk a lot lately. It's making him do things he normally wouldn't. And if I keep ignoring him, I won't be able to ignore the consequences. I have to pretend to care enough about him so I can keep pretending about Marcus.

My cheek throbs, and I take a deep breath and type a text:

Mei: Sure.

As if he's reading my thoughts from across San Francisco, a text from Mmm slides onto my screen:

Marcus: Today is not close enough to tomorrow.

The rattling bus, the ringing voices, and the cars outside the window screech to a halt. The world rolls together, my throat goes dry, and feeling drains from my fingers.

"Who's that?" Lin leans against me, craning her neck to

read the screen and I bolt up in my seat and turn toward her, my phone facing away from her. "Nick."

She crosses her arms. "Tell him to keep his gross off your phone. You don't want to get whatever he's got."

Another buzz.

Marcus: You there?

Thoughts blow around my head, and I try to catch a clever one so I can respond, but my fingers are impatient and type Yes! I pause before sending, shake my head at myself, and delete it before texting:

Mei: If by there you mean on a bus headed to school, yes. Very present unfortunately. Where are you?

Marcus sends me a gif of a kid at a desk, eyes rolled back in his head.

Marcus: Mentally? Not on the train to school. Let's hang tonight. You, me, Buddha, Oreos, movie of your choice.

The wind in my head stops, and the blustery, swirling thoughts drop. Everything is silent until Lin blurts, "Woah!" Her eyes leap at me. "What did Nasty Nick say? You actually squealed. Or actually, maybe I don't want to know. Never mind."

Frantic, giddy Marcus thoughts squeeze out all rational ones, battling the fact that there is absolutely no way I can hang out with him tonight.

The bus veers into the school parking lot and everyone stands. My hands shake, disappointment tugging at me as I huddle in my seat and respond to Marcus.

Mei: Can't. Work. ☹ But we can hang out mentally.

A GIF of a cartoon cat with tears spraying from its eyes pops onto the screen. I cover my smile with my hand and let hope flutter through me like a butterfly on crack, then type:

Mei: Can't wait until tomorrow, though.

His response is immediate:

Marcus: 27 hours, 24 minutes. Or more precisely, 1640 minutes. Wanna guess how many of those I'll spend thinking about tomorrow? Oh, that's right, you're not a guesser.

---

1. *Joke: Why won't monsters eat ghosts?
   *Answer: Because they taste like sheet.

CHAPTER 12

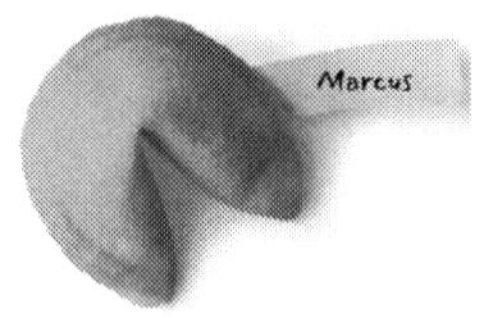

Marcus: 7 eternal hours til Date #2. Capital D. Actually, in my head, it looks like this: DATE #2!!!!!!!!!!!!!*@#$*##@#!!!!! TMINUS7HOURS!!!! But all I can do is text cuz it would be weird to lay in bed and yell it. Texting's better than nothing, but...texts don't smile at me.

Mei: Why are you awake at 3 AM?

Marcus: Probably the same reason you are. P.S. Is it weird I was kinda jealous of Johnny *trying* to flirt with you the other night?

Mei: I'm using you to get to your friends.

Marcus: I'd just hate to lose the girl before she becomes my girlfriend.

Marcus: Not that you are.

Marcus: My girlfriend

Marcus: Yet

Mei walks down the alley toward me, staying close to her building. When she spots me, I put my hand over my heart and shoot a smile over lines of cars riding their brakes down the hill and clumps of tourists blocking my view. When they pass, I catch her eye again and dial her number.

She answers on the first ring. "Hey."

"Whatcha doing today?"

Her smile spreads and takes mine with it. "Knitting. Lots of knitting."

"Oh. I'd love to see your work. You should bring your yarn and meet me at the dragon gate."

"There's a lot of yarn. Think I'll leave it home. But I'll be there." She ends the call and grips her bag strap, smiles, and walks down the street. I shove my phone into my pocket and do the same but can't keep my eyes off her as she dodges fruit stands and people, and I barely miss slamming into a fire hydrant.

At the crosswalk, I stay outside the crowd. I catch Mei's eye across the intersection, put my hand over my heart and pat my chest like a heartbeat. She bites her lower lip and looks down, touches her tattoo. Really wish I could touch it, too.

We continue walking on opposite sides of the street until we pass under Dragon's Gate and out of Dad's jurisdiction, and hopefully out of Face Eater's sight.

She crosses the street toward me, smooth, like she's gliding around people, hips swiveling as she steps over cracks, onto the curb. My eyes are overwhelmed, and it takes me way too long to haul words up my throat to say, "Hey."

She smiles up at me, her knuckles white on her bag strap, cheeks a shade of pink. And it's no sunburn. "Hi."

I hold out my hand and she takes it, watching our fingers

weave together while I watch her. Too soon? I squeeze her hand and she squeezes back. Nope.

Her hand's half the size of mine, but our fingers fit together like finger soul mates. I pull her into my side, and she wraps her other hand around my bicep which flexes under her touch, but she smiles at the sidewalk and keeps it there. I could probably fly right now.

We follow side streets and back roads until the Palace of Fine Arts rises at the end.

"This is the best spot to knit." She laughs and I drop my backpack and yank out my favorite blanket, spread it on the ground, then flop onto it. Lying on my side, I prop myself up with my elbow and pat the blanket beside me. She pulls her bag over her head and slips off her Vans before lying on her side, facing me.

"I've never been here." She picks at a thread on the blanket. "Especially on a blanket with orange dinosaurs all over it." She smiles, smoothing her hand over two T-Rexes sharing a bowl of ice cream.

"That's because Meemaw made this one-of-a-kind masterpiece for me when I was eight, and it's been somewhere on my bed ever since. I wash it with this certain kind of fabric softener so it always smells like her house, and it'll be with me until I die. Even though I'm sure it's probably happy for the change of scenery and doing something different with its life today. But can we go back to you never being here before?" I frown. "How long have you lived here?"

"Ten years. I don't leave Chinatown very often."

Her eyes are all shimmery, like melted chocolate, and her lip gloss outlines her mouth in light pink. I think about outlining it with my finger.

"We're changing that today." And I have a feeling a lot of other things are gonna change today, too. This close to her, my priorities dissolve. I don't feel so bad about lying to Dad when I'm with her. All I gotta do is keep my hands to myself and everything's cool. Or hold her hand and only her hand. "Where'd you move from?" A leaf falls on the blanket and I pick it up, keeping my eyes on hers.

"Taiwan. I was eight."

"Whoa." My eyebrows shoot up. "So, when I was getting a dino blankie for my eighth birthday, you were moving to a foreign country. You still remember Taiwan?"

She nods. "Kind of. The smells mostly. And my Nai Nai's house. She liked yellow."

"Grandma, I assume?"

She nods. "She was the best. She gave me Buddha before we moved here. She sculpted him herself and said to keep him with me for good luck."

I watch the leaf twirl between my fingers. "Is she still alive?"

Mei shakes her head. "She died three years ago."

"I vow to take extra special care of Buddha, then, 'cause your grandma was right about the good luck thing—I've been feeling pretty lucky about a lot of things since I met him." I jiggle my foot when the urge to lean toward her plows through me. "But hold up." I widen my eyes. "What if your grandma reincarnated into the Buddha and she's spying on me?"

She tilts her head. "If I believed in reincarnation, I'd hope she'd be a little more alive."

I laugh to the blanket and cross and uncross my toes. "Sorry. Just assumed Buddhist…"

"It's more about tradition than religion in my family. I want something different."

"I get that." She watches me, waiting, so I let the words fly that have been circling in my head. "I like God. Feel like we get along pretty well." I lift a shoulder. "But I have lots of questions. About him. Religion. And other stuff, more recently."

She raises her eyebrows. "What kind of stuff?"

"You. Lots and lots of questions about you."

"Like…?"

"Like…how we've lived this close for ten years and never met." I flick a fly off my wrist.

"Oh, I've known about you for a long time." She rolls her eyes at the tree above us. "You've just never noticed me. You're way too cool."

I shake my head. "No way. If I'd met you before, this thing would've happened a long time ago." I wave a hand between us. "You just don't wanna admit you've been locked in a closet for the last ten years and just escaped."

Mei laughs, her smile splitting the air with light before she rolls her eyes. "My baba's probably thought about it. Can't wait to get away from here."

"Won't miss your parents?"

"No."

I nod and practically hear her inner doors slam shut on that conversation. "So…I'm guessing if they knew you were out with me, you really would be locked in a closet."

"Good thing they don't know." Her smile is lightning on a sunny day. I'm singed inside.

"But they're cool with Face Eater?"

"He's practically family. And he's Taiwanese, so…" she says to the blanket, the light going out of her face, but I want it back, so I duck my head and catch her eye.

"What do you think about boys who aren't Taiwanese?"

She smiles at the blanket, then the sky before dropping her eyes to mine again. "I think…I like tall ones who play soccer and get a 4.0 and write funny notes and have dino blankies from their meemaws and tell stupid jokes and—"

"Stupid?!"

She nods. "The stupidest."

I shrug and adjust my elbow. "Like what do you call a fish wearing a bowtie?"*[1]

"Exactly like that."

"Guess the answer and you've got yourself another date with a tall white boy who plays soccer and writes notes and has a 4.0 *and* a blankie. Although...the 4.0 is in danger because of a short Taiwanese girl with killer eyes and an assassin smile who makes me laugh until it's an ab workout."

"If the short-according-to-your-standards Taiwanese girl doesn't guess the answer, does she not get the date?"

"Nah." I shake my head. "She'll just be in charge of date number two."

Her eyes flick to mine. "So either way, I win. Buddha's tossing around the good luck."

I inch my fingers across the blanket toward hers, then lace them together until our palms meet like our hands are sending a thank you prayer to God. Our eyes crash into each other as my fingers explore hers, and I ask her a million questions until my stomach rumbles.

She raises her eyebrows and laughs while I untangle our hands and slap my stomach, then pull out my phone. "No way. 1:00 already." I swear and drop my forehead to the blanket, groaning into it before popping back up, meeting her eyes. "Why do the perfect days go so fast and the days between drag?" I push myself up and offer my hand to help her up, then stuff the blanket in my backpack and take her hand like this is what we do every Saturday. Like I'm supposed to be touching her instead of avoiding her because she's my personal, life-sized Oreo and could be the death of my motorcycle.

"You don't have to be back in your closet anytime soon, right?" I smile and glance down at her, shrugging my backpack on.

She smiles up at me. "No. My parents think I'm at Lin's."

"Any chance you could stay at Lin's until, like, 10 PM, maybe? That's when I have to be home to act all studied out so my dad doesn't guess what I've really been doing all day."

She laughs and we cross the street. "I'm sure Lin won't

mind my imaginary company until then but…I'm guessing your dad doesn't know you're with a girl today."

I glance down at our tangled hands, watching them swing as we walk. My arm's twice as long as hers, but somehow, our arms and hands fit perfectly. Bet there are some other things that might fit perfectly, too. Lips. Only lips. Geez. I mentally shake myself and clear my throat. "Uh, nope—definitely not, but I haven't even kissed you yet, so I think I'm pretty safe." I grin into the afternoon as she raises her eyebrows and laughs, just as shocked as I am that a piece of my thoughts slipped out. "Also glad you didn't answer my stupid joke earlier 'cause now you owe me a date. Mei Li Zhang style."

The rain goes from drops to downpour, so we stand under a tree, soaked and downing Starbursts we bought along the way. My blanket's wrapped around us, and Mei's so close, my body cranks up the heat until my palms sweat and my face flushes. I pray the rain never stops so I can stand here all day and absorb her. Or kiss her. She'll taste like lemon Starbursts. But if I do, I'll drop the blanket around us, and she'll move away and…moment ruined. Also, I want my hands free to go wherever they wanna go. Which is pretty much everywhere they shouldn't. So…motorcycle. MOTORCYCLE. I've always known girls could mess me up, but this is next-level internal chaos. So glad my head isn't see-through.

When the rain lets up, we saunter out of The Presidio toward Golden Gate Bridge and Mei smiles at her feet.

"What?" I ask, trying to meet her eyes.

"Nothing."

"Your smile says you're a liar."

"I was just wondering what you're thinking. I can't see your eyes from down here."

I smile into the air ahead of us. "Uh…I'm thinking a whole

lot about kissing you." She presses her lips together and I hurry and add, "But I won't. 'Cause I know how pathetic my self-control is with things like Oreos and soccer and you're way harder to resist than those. So..." I pop a Starburst into my mouth to keep it busy.

She frown-smiles. "What does that mean?"

I shrug. "Oreos are my weakness. Used to be my biggest." I take the wet blanket, stuff it in my backpack, then walk backward, unwrapping another Starburst, watching her smile at me. I pop it into my mouth and wiggle my eyebrows, then glance over my shoulder to make sure I won't back into anything. "Keep hanging out with me and kissing will happen, Mei Z. Fair warning. Just gotta keep things chill until graduation."

She plays with her necklace, bites her lip. "Why's that?"

"A little bet I made with my dad in ninth grade," I call to her, the sound of traffic on the bridge swelling around us. "Avoid excessive girl contact until after graduation, get a motorcycle." She nods, so I go on. "I really want it, but I also really want you, so...it's gonna be hard if we keep this up."

"Not sure I can compete with a motorcycle."

My Adidas shriek against the wet grass as I continue walking backward, and Mei walks slowly toward me. "I already know you're *way* better than any motorcycle. I just want both."

Her smile cuts through the mist, making me squint as I smile, and she runs toward me. I switch my backpack to my chest so I can pick her up and swing her onto my back. She squeals and I grip her thighs as I run across the field, down the road, and through a tunnel. Laughter squishes out of her every time she bounces against my back. The sound echoes off the cement walls and into me as I run up the ramp, laughing at her laughing.

Slowing to catch my breath, I walk along the bridge railing. Her chest presses against my wet back, her arms wrapped around my shoulders, hands on my chest like she's locking us together. My fingertips flex against her thighs and I slow, way, way down. Her hair tickles my neck, and I wanna flip her around and press her against the chain-link fence. Make out with her while cars whiz past and shake the bridge beneath us. But if I want my motorcycle, I won't. And if I don't wanna scare myself or her, I can't. Even though I should be scared and running 'cause now I understand why people jump off this bridge when their feelings get too big. Mine wanna burst out of me, climb the bridge, and paraglide out to the ocean.

She rests her chin on top of my head and I suck in too much air, coughing a few times. About halfway across the bridge, I stop and let her slide off my back. We stand next to each other, pinkies hooked around each other as we look out over the bay.

She takes a deep breath and lets it out in a sigh. "This has been one of the best days ever."

I smile into the breeze. "Top ten, at least?"

"Top two." She glances at me out of the corner of her eye, and I turn toward her, my elbow on the rail.

"What's number one?"

"It hasn't happened yet. I'll tell you when it does." She watches a seagull float on the breeze.

I wanna be the biggest part of her number one day. I wanna be part of all her days.

"What are you doing after graduation?" I swallow and curl my toes in my shoes.

She pauses, watches the ship below us, then talks to the bay. "I've got an internship in L.A. Hopefully culinary school in the fall."

"Where?" My stomach tries to hide behind my other organs.

She shrugs and swallows like whatever she's gonna say

hurts. "I'm waiting to hear." She shifts, looking through the fencing and over the bay. "What are your plans?"

I wanna ask more questions but she's locked that inner door again and I shouldn't have asked the "future" question at all 'cause I don't wanna talk about mine. I slide my fingers through hers, the answer scraping up my throat as I pull her away from the railing and off the bridge, down the ramp, back through the tunnel.

When she looks at me and raises her eyebrows, I look straight ahead, my eyes scanning the tunnel's opening so far away. "Verbally committed to USF." It's too loud in here to talk. Traffic rumbling above us, wind, the silence of unsaid words I wanna suffocate.

When we reach the end of the tunnel, I pull her into my side "Still good with being out for a few more hours?"

She nods. "I'm fine with never going back. As long as you're okay."

"I'm so good." I shove away college and internships and what-ifs and pull her closer so we bump into each other as we walk. "What if I'm a kidnapper?"

"You're my top pick for kidnappers."

I stop walking and pull her toward me, wrapping my arms around her. "That's the nicest thing anyone has ever said to me."

She laughs into my chest then looks up at me. "On the topic of kidnapping. My very favorite movie ever is showing in Dolores Park on Monday night, and I was thinking since I owe you a date, maybe you'd go with me? Hopefully willingly so I don't have to throw you in the back of my white van."

"Does your van have candy and puppies in it?" I smile and hold her tight until her smile melts through my shirt. "Don't promise if you can't deliver."

She laughs to the sky, her chin jabbing into my chest. "Candy, definitely."

"I'll tie myself up and be ready on Monday."

Her smile lights the space between us and now, I wanna think about the future. The rest of this day. Monday. Whatever days I'll spend with her after that.

"So…" I sweep away hair that blows across her face. "When you said your best day hasn't happened yet, I decided I wanna take that spot. And just…stay there." The ocean breeze whips our hair around, and I smooth hers against the back of her head. "But only if my chances are at least 50 percent."

A motorcycle speeds past, its rumble shaking the ground and my guilt, and I almost let go of her until she talks against my chest.

"At least 50 percent."

I take a deep breath, fill my lungs with mist. Tonight, when I can't sleep because there's too much Mei in my head, I'll figure out how I'm gonna get the girl and the motorcycle.

I unwrap myself from her. "Challenge accepted." Pulling out my Sharpie, I write #1 on my arm, then cap it and slide it back in my pocket.

---

1. *Answer: Sofishticated

CHAPTER 13

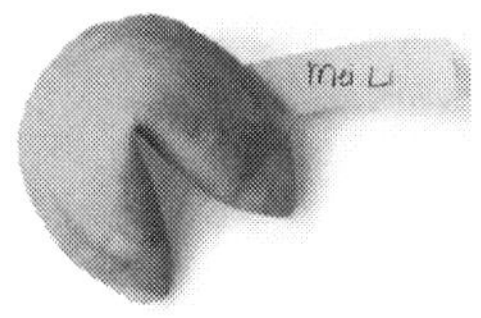

Marcus: Mei Day, Mei Day, going down. Sooo tired. FaceTiming until 2 AM takes it out of a guy. Know that guy we saw in Union Station yesterday with the fedora who was sleeping standing up? I'm that tired. 429% Worth it, though. Church isn't helping. I legit head bobbed and got an elbow to the rib. What are you doing?

Mei: Thinking about you.

Marcus: I approve of this. We're in 2 different places doing the same thing even when I'm supposed to be thinking about Jesus. Jesus and I are cool though. Got a text from him just now that says you and I should hang out again. Sooner than soon. Quicker than ASAP. Muy rapido. And whatever "fast" is in Chinese. That. Don't know if I can wait until tomorrow night.

Mei: I love that hint from Jesus. He and Buddha probably talked. But bad news—I have to go. ☹ Thanks for the note. Still smiling.

Marcus: NOOOOOOOOO..........

Mei: I'll text after my shift.

Marcus: We should hang after your shift. Maybe we can stay...by the bay...catch some rays...the rest of the day. Yay?

Mei: If I could, it would...be so, so good. It would be my tres favorite day...says Mei... but I have to work at 2...Boo...rather be with you...

Marcus: Guess it's just me and Jesus until tomorrow night. Then? You and me, #Dos Date...of Fate...don't be late...

If only Marcus knew the truth about me.

I almost told him so many times yesterday. We'd texted the entire day. Marcus counted 1353 texts. Plenty of chances to tell him the truth, but I got scared. So...maybe tonight.

People stream past me, carrying blankets and pillows, lawn chairs and wine bottles. I scan the faces of the couples holding hands and laughing as they disappear down the grassy hill toward the movie screen. Two guys in glow-in-the-dark footie pajamas dart through the crowd holding hands as a group of old ladies flutters past in Audrey Hepburn hats, robes, and slippers. Marcus texted saying he was on his way and my nerves are swirling in gusts of excitement and a bit of adrenaline, sparky and jittery.

I scan the park and spot him coming down the steps in

straight-leg jeans rolled at the ankle, a black hoodie, backwards baseball cap, and his gray Adidas. I swallow and clench my fists at my side, digging my nails into my palm because it's Marcus Miller, and he's here with me.

When he sees me, his smile bursts in the dim backdrop and he jogs toward me where I stand by the Mexican Liberty Bell. All thoughts of dimming that smile with my reality evaporate into the cloudy sky.

"Hey." He bends and wraps his arms around me, picking me off my feet. Which is perfect since he makes my legs wobbly every time I see him. I wrap my arms around his neck and breathe in spearmint, his cheek warm against mine.

"Guo Mama gave me your note," I say, smiling over his shoulder.

He lets me slide through his arms until my feet touch the ground, then laces his fingers with mine. "Dropped it off after youth group." His voice rumbles over, around, through me. "Guo had the guts to open it and read it right in front of me. She looked at me like she was gonna kiss me." He smiles over my head then down at me, gripping my hands and spreading our arms out like wings, pulling me into his chest. "Thankfully she only patted my butt, so I made it out unscathed. Still a little shaken, though."

I laugh into his chest, then tilt my head back to see his face. "I think you kind of like it."

He leans into me, his mouth on my ear sending vibrations through me. "Would prefer an atta boy from a certain Taiwanese girl a whole lot more, but hey—Guo's pretty hot for a 200-year-old." He smiles into the air, and I lead him down the path toward the sea of people spread across the grass in front of the giant projector screen.

"What have you planned tonight besides checking out my butt?"

I bump him with my hip. "Already done that, nothing new." I say through a smile, and he stops, turning to me.

"I've heard about you, Ms. Zhang…" He shakes his head as I pull him across the grass. "Just glad I wore these jeans 'cause they make my butt look unbelievable."

I roll my eyes at him but can't stop a smile as I wrap my hand around his bicep and squeeze.

"But really," he says, scanning the crowd, "what have you planned this fine April evening?"

"I was thinking we'd hang here for a bit. Just us. And all these people. And Audrey Hepburn." I nod toward the giant screen. "My white van is in the shop, but I brought the candy. And some Oreos, so if you don't like the movie, at least your stomach and bloodstream will be happy."

"What're we watching?"

"The original Sabrina. My favorite."

"Huh." He nods and we bump together as we walk down the grassy hill. "Never seen it."

"That's because you have no female influence to show you all the good stuff."

"Oh, I have a female influence. My aunt is extraordinarily girly, but she likes German films. Super weird. And Meemaw watches Hallmark, so no thanks. Guess you'll be my first." He stops walking and looks down at me, shaking his head. "Uh…didn't mean that the way it sounded."

I laugh but my blush goes through all my skin layers and down into my heart. "Guess we'll stick to movies for now."

We find the perfect spot by a tree behind a row of couples already snuggled under blankets, and I pull out mine.

"Kinda disappointed in my dino blankie now." Marcus spreads out the blanket. "Yours is so sophisticated."

I smile at the flowers and stripes. "It's the longest one I could find. Trying to get used to this tall person stuff." Kneeling, I open my satchel and pull out a family-sized package of Double Stuff Oreos, two small milks, two plastic bowls, and spoons.

Marcus's eyes light up. "I didn't think this night could get any better."

"I do know a few things about the infamous Marcus Miller. Even though there's one very important thing I *must* know before the movie starts."

"Okay…" He lowers himself to the blanket and I check out his bum—which looks exceptional in those jeans—before he rolls to his side, facing me. "What do you desperately wanna know about me?"

"Promise you'll be 100 percent honest?"

He frowns. "Uh, whatever you heard, I didn't do it."

I laugh and pull two bags from my satchel and set them in front of him. "Twizzlers or Red Vines?"

"Please." He rolls his eyes and snatches the Red Vines, lifting onto his elbow to rip open the bag.

"That's a huge relief," I say, dropping the Twizzlers back into my bag. "This night can proceed as planned."

He rips a piece of licorice with his teeth. "What would happen if I'd said Twizzlers?"

"I would've gotten cozy with him." I tilt my head toward a guy with his life-sized teddy bear and lay on my stomach beside Marcus, our shoulders smashed together.

"Guess it would've been me and the licorice, then." He rummages for another piece, our faces so close, I can count the freckles on the bridge of his nose. Four.

Marcus sticks a piece of licorice between his teeth and holds it toward me like a bridge between our lips. I glance at it, then meet his eyes, back to the licorice, then to his eyes again before leaning closer to him, biting the piece in half.

He sucks in the remaining piece, chews, and wiggles his eyebrows. "That was a close one," he whispers, then breaks off a tiny piece and sticks it between his lips again. If I take a bite, our lips will touch, but he laughs and shakes his head as he chews.

"Kidding. I want you to kiss me whenever you're ready.

Just like, anytime. Now's fine. Or whenever." He gives me a sidelong glance, then laughs. "Okay, seriously though. Only kidding. Really. No pressure at all—it'll happen when it happens. And it will. I'm just happy to be here, laying on a tall person blanket in Dolores Park when my dad thinks I'm playing video games at Johnny's. And Johnny thinks I'm with my aunt. And my aunt thinks I'm at soccer practice. Very delicate balance to be with you, but I'd say...304 percent worth it."

The movie starts, and I drop Oreos into our bowls, then drown them in milk. Marcus sets his phone timer for 4 ½ minutes and we wait before digging in, laying on our stomachs and watching Sabrina in all her awkwardness. By the time she gets to Paris, Marcus has had two bowls of Oreos and is lying on his back, head propped up on my bag, Red Vines in hand. I'm lying on my side, my head on his chest, arm draped over him.

His fingertips ripple up and down my spine and when he laughs at something on the screen, my head bounces, but I'm paying more attention to his heart beating beneath my ear: solid, steady, eager. I listen to it until Sabrina gets her hair cut and lift my head, resting my chin on my hand that's spread on his stomach. "What do you think about girls with short hair?"

"Ah, loaded question," he says to the sky before looking at me. "My dad's warned me about these." He smooths his hand over my hair and down the side of my face. "I think... it's just hair. Some girls, like this Asian girl watching an old-school movie right now, would look good with short hair, long hair, no hair. A bald Mei would still be a hot Mei."

I roll my eyes and pinch his stomach until he laughs.

When the credits roll, I sit up and look down at him. "Well? What did you think?"

He puts his hands under his head, his eyes glossy in the lamppost light. "That was my first black and white movie and…I liked it. Especially the part where she's in culinary school. Just glad you're not going to Paris. But if you were, I'd find a way to make it work."

I raise my eyebrows. "Make what work…?" I smile and lean closer.

"Well…I've heard rumors that there's an incredibly funny, brave…interesting…hot, talented…hot…girl with hair who's going to culinary school and will eventually be my girlfriend, so if the rumors are true, I'm gonna have to find ways to see her. A lot."

I curl my toes and flex my fingers that want to fly over my heart to keep it from flipping out of my chest. "Does this girl know how you feel?"

His eyes shoot blue light straight through me. "I think she's starting to figure it out."

I smile and pull him to his feet before we shove my blanket and the leftover food inside my bag. We toss our bowls in the garbage on the way out of the park and head toward Chinatown until Marcus tugs on my hand and stops.

"It's only 11:30. Way too early for us to go home, especially since I was hoping to stay out late and fall asleep during history tomorrow." Marcus takes my bag, throws it over his head and shoulder, then grabs my hand again and veers us out of the crowd in the opposite direction of Chinatown. "I know my dad's asleep on the couch because he hasn't responded to my text, so I've got time. Whaddya say to a midnight stroll through the Mission? Dodge a few piles of poo and some syringes? Super safe. My dad wouldn't hate this idea at all." He wraps his arm around my shoulders and pulls me into his side.

I think about the streets I walk to Nick's house and wonder what Marcus's dad would say about me walking them alone at night. Baba doesn't care when it's an errand for him. But after last time, I'm more afraid of Nick than I am of whatever or whoever is in the dark alleys.

Marcus slows in front of a shop window display, turning us to face it. He points at the mannequins. "Which outfit would you choose? Just curious. Think I know, but I wanna see if I'm right."

I smile and scan the summer dresses in all shades of blue, orange, and yellow. "Probably…that one." I point at the flowy, short blue V-neck dress with long, loose sleeves.

Marcus looks at it, then me. "I was right. And you'd look way better in it than she does. When you take your yacht to the bi-annual kitty kite festival that was scheduled for a Mediterranean island but got relocated to Nova Scotia. You might be cold, but you'll look fabulous."

I laugh so hard my face aches while I wonder how I can make nights like this last forever.

CHAPTER 14

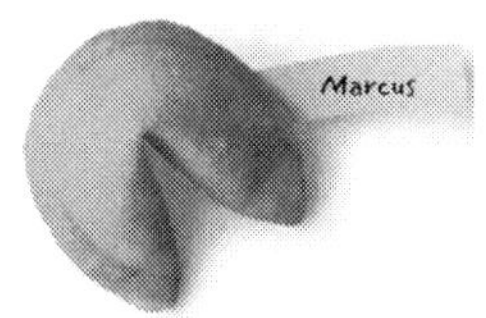

Dear Marcus,
Nova Scotia is just lovely by yacht. Yes, it's quite chilly but I look stunning in my blue dress, just as you predicted. My kitty kite won second place which was rather disappointing, but the tail did get ripped off by a rogue wind current so it's to be expected. If only my best kite mender hadn't missed the boat, but I received your telegram and will demand the captain turn this ship around at once. I'm positively dying to see you in the green and orange plaid suit I picked out for you. It's so fetching. All the elderly women onboard will positively swoon when they see you. Yes, you'll have to play a lot of Bingo but you'll get lots of birthday money for years to come and since kite menders don't make a lot, it will be very worthwhile.

All my sea-faring best,
Mei, Second place winner in the International Kitty Kite Festival

"So…" Audrey sits back in her chair, arms crossed. "How's it going? Been on a date yet?"

I mimic her, slouching with my arms crossed "Have you?"

She shoots forward in her seat. "Oh, don't worry—I've got

the baklava coming. I had a lovely lunch date this week. Just wondering if we're going to share the baklava or if I get it all to myself."

"I told you it had to be a real date. Not Stacy from accounting."

"For your information, it was Ricky from accounting. And we're going out tonight. Guess I'm eating baklava alone."

"Nope." I shake my head and tap the table with my thumb. "I earned the other half. Twice."

Her brows are super pointy when she's surprised. "Don't you dare lie for baklava. It will turn to lava in your mouth and burn off your tongue."

I smile and nod. "Oh, this is for real. I'm as surprised as you are."

Audrey squints. "Are you being serious?"

I shrug. "Yeah. A lot changed while you were in Boston."

Her shoulders drop. "That was fast." She slides a shake toward me. "I'm not even sure what to do with this information if it's true."

"Come on, Drey." I roll my eyes and shovel ice cream into my mouth, talking around it. "You knew it'd happen eventually. There just wasn't a girl I liked enough. Now there is."

Her frown turns from scrutiny to curiosity. "Have you told Ray? And have you kissed her?" Her eyes spark and I'm afraid she's gonna light the napkins on fire as she leans forward, devouring a spoonful of ice cream.

I meet her eyes, then focus on my spoon.

"What does that look mean?" she explodes, slapping both hands on the table and leaning out of her chair toward me. "Did you lose the bet?!"

Uh, thought about it. Wanted to about 325 times. But I'm keeping that information to myself. I reach across the table and poke her shoulder. "Calm down." I shake my head. "It's only been two dates." My stomach ruffles with the thought of kissing Mei. Making out with her. Doing other stuff. Later.

Audrey narrows her eyes. "I sense you're not telling me the whole truth."

I jab the spoon in my shake, sitting back in my seat. She's not gonna stop digging, so I've gotta give her something to obsess over. Plus, I'm dying to tell somebody about Mei. "Not gonna lie—the motorcycle's really hard to think about when I'm with her." I pick at the table's edge. "She's all I can think about. Her and…*that*." I need to stop. I'm saying too much. But what if she can tell me what to do so I don't mess this up? I can't have this conversation with Dad. And I've seen Johnny and Savvy make out and I'm not asking either of them for advice. They went zero to ninety in ten seconds so it's only a matter of time before they're over. Not gonna be me and Mei.

Audrey relaxes, crossing her arms on the table and leveling her gaze. "Well, it's about time."

"I'm not gonna do anything, Drey." *Even though I so, so want to.* "Don't even know what I'm doing, but…I kinda get how I could lose the motorcycle now. I won't, though. Just afraid I could. But I won't. Definitely not. But also, I'm…" I scan the hanging plants and yellow wind chimes hanging over our table, embarrassed to admit my total lack of knowledge in all things Girl. "I'm clueless," I look at her. "I mean, I know the basics, so don't give me the whole birds and bees talk—I got that much. I just didn't know…" I swallow. How strong I could feel for her. That my hormones can boss me around. That I swear I saw "I love you" in her eyes. Or maybe it was the reflection of my thoughts.

I hunch over my shake, staring into it. "Didn't know I could feel this way. Dad didn't mention it when he talked about girls messing me up. And if you tell him, I swear, Drey…"

She stares at me, a slow smile creeping across her face. "Are you kidding?! You think I'd ruin this by telling that killjoy? No way. But you should bring your lady love on our next lunch date."

"No." I shake my head.

"No?"

"Nope."

"Why? Are you embarrassed of me?" She pulls a hideous face.

"No, even though I should be."

"What's her name? What does she look like?" Audrey leans forward and twirls her spoon in her shake, her bracelets jangling.

"Her name's Mei and she looks unbelievable, that's what." I smile at the table, thinking about the way Mei's smile reflects off everything around her.

"So…I'm guessing blond? Long legs, long hair? Perfect teeth, etc., etc., etc., blah, blah, blah?"

"Perfect but in a black hair, killer smile, brown eyes, Taiwanese kinda way."

Audrey's eyebrows could climb Mount Everest on their own. "So…" Her eyes scan the café. "Not one of the screaming girls at your games."

I shake my head. "Exactly opposite."

Audrey leans forward, a weird grin on her face. "What's she like?"

My mind draws a cross-section of Mei, arrows pointing to different parts of her. An arrow labeled 'Intriguing' points to her head; her mind is an entirely new universe to discover. One arrow labeled 'Killer' points to her smile. A big clump points to all the parts of her body I like best—long, slender fingers; deep eyes; skinny bird legs. Arrows pointing to the way she dresses; how she watches me when we talk like she's absorbing every word I say. The way she floats more than moves, and how her voice calms me. The smart, funny things that come out of her mouth. The only thing I don't like about her is her taste in music, but we can work on that.

An arrow points to the tattoo on her neck and, in my

diagram, my initials are under it. It's so permanent and personal, I choke on my own air when my stomach knots.

"You okay?" Audrey tilts her head.

"Yeah. Good."

"Wow—you floated off to La-La land. You've got it bad." Her smile's too wide. "I can't wait to meet this girl who replaced my girl-avoiding nephew with a lovesick man."

"Not lovesick."

She raises her eyebrows, challenging me.

Lovesick? Is this how it starts? Oh, no way. It's been two weeks. A month if you count our notes. But why can't I sleep? I've never had a problem sleeping. I stare out the windows during class. I see her everywhere, like she's tattooed on my eyeballs, and everything I look at has a Mei on it. I repeat the word in my mind, trying to get used to it being in there. It's never been there before. This feeling can't be that. But maybe. Eventually. If things keep going. Could it?

"Take it slow, Marcus. I've dealt with enough hormonal guys to know that sometimes love gets overtaken by other feelings. There's no rush."

"Don't even know what I'm doing anyway, since, you know, not a lot of girls in my life besides you. I just…I don't wanna mess things up." Face Eater eating Mei's face in the alley flashes in my mind. "I want everything to be perfect."

I like having Mei in my world. Like having her all over my days and talking to her until way too late. Love having thoughts of her all over my head. The sound of her laugh everywhere inside it. Having her all over me would just be a bonus. My life feels bigger with her in it. Soccer and school are still cool but she's the coolest thing by far. She's the first thing I think about when I wake up, and I take her with me through my day, wondering what she'd think about the guy in history who's a total perv. Or what she looks like sitting at a desk, working out a calculus problem. And I always, always, wonder what she's doing. Thinking. How she's moving. Who's lucky enough to see her smile at that moment. Or does she save the big, sparkly, dimple smile just for me?

Mei's opened a whole new side of me. Something amazing and crazy is rumbling through my life.

It's official: I'm falling for her, big time.

My eyes snap to Audrey's. "This can't be happening—I'm eighteen. Haven't even kissed her yet," I blurt.

She smiles and tilts her head. "Your dad fell in love when he was seventeen."

"It obviously wasn't love, but he thought it was, and then everything fell apart and he's sad and alone and bored enough to want me to be there with him."

She tilts her head and gives me a mom stare. "For Ray, it was love. For your mom, maybe it wasn't, maybe it was. Love doesn't look the same for everyone. Everyone has their own experiences. This is yours."

What if I'm headed for love, but Mei's not? That would be the ultimate form of messed up. My chest tightens, air flow stops. No way. She has to be as into this as I am. Doesn't she? Or is she gonna take off like my mom? Leave me with feelings I have no clue how to handle?

"What do I do?" I ask Audrey. "I don't know the rules or how to do anything."

"You're obviously doing something right."

"I know, but like…now I wanna know everything about girls so I can do everything right and be perfect for her so she'll have no reason to leave…" I take a deep breath and let it out.

Audrey rubs one of the leaves on the plant in the center of the table, then looks at me. "When you say that, are you referring to falling in love or…other stuff?"

I shift in my chair, then press a hand to my ribs. "No! Yes? Everything. I'm just curious. For way after graduation, if this thing continues. I mean, I'm not gonna be a monk forever so I just wanna do my research for…eventually. When I make 'the big commitment,' quoting Dad."

She rolls her eyes. "You would." Twisting her hair off her neck, she pulls it into a high ponytail. "You sure you want to know *everything* about girls? It might scare you away."

I hesitate. "Yeah? I mean…yeah."

"Ah. Like you want to get straight A's in Girl."

"Yeah," I grin, "Like that."

She nods. "So very Marcus of you. And not very boy of you." She pins me with her eyes. "But that's a very, very good thing, I assure you." She sits taller in her seat and smiles. "I can tell you all about girls and answer all your questions. Shoot!"

I jab my spoon into my shake again.

"What?" Audrey leans forward. "My firsthand girl experience isn't good enough?"

I glance at her, laughing uncomfortably. "You're my aunt. You know? It's weird."

Audrey narrows her eyes, considering me. "Oh. Right. So…not a real girl. Gotcha. Well. Fair enough." She grabs her bag from the chair. "I'll direct you toward true knowledge then." She stands and scoots in her chair. "Stuff your face and let's go."

I attempt to camouflage myself in the Self Help and Relationships aisle while Audrey flips through book after book about relationships and the female brain. About communicating with women. Female anatomy.

My hoodie is suddenly too loose like it's spilling all my thoughts for everyone in the bookstore to see but it's also threatening to choke me.

"Okay, Drey—that's good. Ten books. Plenty to study."

She hoots at something she reads and slaps the book shut,

then points to the stack of books on the floor between my feet. "Pick up your pile of wisdom and walk confidently to the counter. You're on a quest for knowledge. Your girl will thank you."

Ten books are hard to shield under my arm as I dart through aisles and around brick columns toward the register. But as embarrassing as it is and as amateur as I am, my curiosity is raging. Maybe this stack will explain why Mei won't tell me about Face Eater. Or why she gets all fidgety when I ask about her family. Or how she can talk to me without saying a word. And then there's the stuff I shouldn't think about but do. All the freaking time.

Audrey pays, then hands me a gigantic canvas bag that weighs 100 pounds.

"Well, Lover Boy, you've got some reading to do. But if Ray finds these, I'll deny everything."

I shake my head. "He won't find them. Trust me. Ripping every single cover off and locking them somewhere."

She smiles and rolls her eyes. "Whatever you need to do but here's some aunt-ly advice in parting." She steps in front of me. "This is your life, not your dad's."

"Okay, yeah, I—"

"Create your own future, not your dad's or your mom's. It's an exciting time for you. Enjoy it."

I wait, knowing she's not finished, my head heavy, the bag cutting into my fingers.

She smacks her lips super loud. "Oh, and also—two hundred dollars on books entitles me to a meet and greet." She pivots in the opposite direction. "Go get her, tiger," she calls over her shoulder.

CHAPTER 15

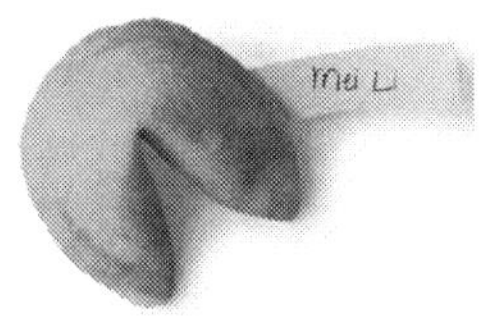

Marcus: Bummed we're not hangin' right now, but I'm dedicating my win to you tonight. And it's gonna be a big one.

"Wow." Lin shakes her head, staring at the ceiling while I lay on my stomach next to her. "You've stunned me. And that's hard to do, as you know. I mean, the only thing you could tell me that would be more life altering is that you got us on The Price is Right. But who needs *that* when you have *him*? The ultimate Door Number Two. All the prizes of all the Showcase Showdowns ever."

Dropping the Marcus bomb on Lin wasn't as weird as I thought it would be. She'd sat still for the first time in her life and didn't say a word until I told her all the details. Most of them. Maybe 50 percent.

"So..." Lin's frosty pink lips form an O, her blue-lined eyes scanning my room. "You...Marcus Freaking Miller. Before you know it, you'll be kissing and...No way you'll wait four weeks to *kiss*. I couldn't wait four seconds."

I shrug, and when her eyes go wide, I brace myself before the inevitable squeal pierces the silence.

"Wait," she blurts, cutting her squeal short. "Did you already kiss him and you're not telling?"

I swivel my head toward her and smile. "Do you really think I could keep it to myself?"

She squeals into my bedspread and squeezes my forearm with both hands. "Mei Li! This is crazy. This is Marcus Miller we're talking about. Not even going to pretend I'm not so jealous right now." She shakes her head. "I want every detail from now on—no holding back. Promise? Like, if it's a ten-minute kiss, I want you to spend ten minutes telling me every single detail. Got it?" She holds out her pinkie and I hook it with mine and press my thumb to hers, sealing the promise. She nods then asks, "Are you going to see him tonight?"

I blow my hair out of my face. "He's got a game."

"Is it an away game?"

"No. Home, I think."

Her eyes shine, and she wiggles her eyebrows. "Well…we have legs, and there are trains we could use those legs to get to. We have cards to ride those trains. We can do homework later. Catch what I'm saying?"

The stadium rumbles as the crowd stomps and chants with the cheerleaders. The bleachers are a patchwork of colorful yelling fans as Lin and I slide in next to an old man and his dog.

The cheerleaders do back handsprings across the field and my eyes move from one to another. Has Marcus ever talked to any of them? Like the blond one with the long, toned legs standing on the male cheerleader's shoulders? Or the girl with the spiky blue hair? Do any of the girls clumped along the fence like him? They're all fresh, trendy, glossy. He said he's never had a girlfriend, but that doesn't stop them from wishing they were.

The cheerleaders bounce around the field until the buzzer blares, and when the team runs onto the field, the crowd roars. My heart thumps when I spot #8 running from the far end of the field, his hair shooting from a whale spout on top of his head. A smile spreads across my face, but I casually put my hand over my mouth and lean my elbow on my knee. In a text last night, I told him he should wear his hair like that for good luck and he did it, even though he knew I wouldn't be here.

My whole body blushes as Lin grabs my arm and leans in, squealing, "Oh my gosh—those legs."

I follow his every move as he weaves and sprints, making the first goal of the game. The stadium erupts and everyone is on their feet including me and Lin. The other team kicks the ball out of bounds and my eyes are glued to Marcus as he throws it toward one of his teammates, all sweaty and serious. I want to stand and shout his name like the other girls in the stadium. He wore his hair like that for me, not them. I'm the one who was at his house until 3 AM, not them. I'm the one he texted all day.

He kicks the ball and runs toward the goal, and my legs tense. I grab Lin's arm as one side of the stadium chants *"Magic"* and the other replies *"Miller"*.

Lin nudges me with her shoulder and leans in, her eyebrows upside down Vs. "Magic Miller?! Only one of us here knows just how magic..."

Pride and giddiness swell in my chest, forceful and stretching, until doubt drops on it with a thud that sends a metallic dust cloud up my throat. Why do the girls chanting a nickname I've never heard bother me? They're clearly not here because they love soccer.

He said he likes me. Right? That happened? I take a deep breath, my attention still on the girls until the crowd erupts, and I snap my focus back to the game where Marcus just scored another goal. His teammates run past, slapping his butt and high fiving, his grin beaming across the stadium, catching all of us in it.

He bends over, catching his breath while a teammate throws in the ball, but my attention swings back to the girls, stopping on glossy brown hair. The girl's turned to her friend, her smile wide, eyes bright before turning back to the game as she yells Marcus's nickname.

I'm not flawless and I'll never be tall. I'm not beautiful like she is—confident and bright. That's the kind of girl that matches Marcus.

Swallowing the heavy sludge of comparison, I focus on the game again when a tall man in a suit and long jacket strides up the stairs to my right. I glance at him, then suck in air too fast and cough.

Lin's head snaps toward me. "You okay?"

I slouch in my seat and lean toward her. "Marcus's dad is right there."

Lin glances toward him and I put my elbow on the armrest again, hand shielding my face this time while I try my best to curl into the corner of my seat.

"Yikes!" Lin yips, turning toward me. "Okay, yes, he's a detective and everything but he doesn't even know you were in his apartment. Total stealth."

Detective Miller takes the stairs two at a time, then slips into a spot right across from us and I flatten against my seat, watching from my peripheral vision.

He and Marcus have the same straight nose, deep-set eyes, thick brown eyebrows. I wonder what Marcus's mom looks like. Did he get his sky-blue eyes from her? His dark blond hair? He has his dad's smile.

I take a deep breath, let it out slowly, and search for Marcus on the field. One of his teammates passes the ball to him and he sprints down the field, passing it to another guy who passes it back to him as Marcus runs toward the goal. The ball sails through the air and the goalie leaps for it, but the crowd's on their feet and so am I because everybody knows before it happens that Marcus will get exactly what he's after.

When the ball flies into the goal, the crowd chants his name louder and he smiles as one of the guys leans in to say something. Marcus looks up into the bleachers as girlish cheers flutter around him from the group by the fence. He runs toward the sidelines, grabs a Gatorade, and drains it in two gulps, face flushed, hair damp with sweat. Tossing the bottle aside, he smiles when he sees his dad standing and waving both arms. He waves back and runs when his coach sends him back into the game but his eyes snag on Lin and me and widen, his mouth dropping open as he slows to a stop.

I consider ducking, not sure what his reaction will be, but a smile spreads across his face. The roar in the stadium fades to static as I smile back, his eyes holding mine.

"Whoa. Hi."

"Hey." I press my lips together to keep my smile from lifting me off my feet.

"Had no idea you were coming."

I shrug and smile. *"Love a good soccer game."*

"This just became the best game of the season." A player slams into him from behind and his teammate yells, but Marcus's feet are planted, and he stares directly at me as Lin's head swivels between me and him, eyes wide.

"Oh my gosh, he's staring at you."

Her voice is too far away to bother taking my eyes off Marcus as his eyes say, *"I'll find you after the game."*

I nod and Marcus grins, sending pulses of heat down my spine before he takes off running.

"Um…what was that?" Lin asks, turning to face me.

I snap my attention from Marcus to her. "What?"

She grabs my arm, squeezing and bringing me back into the moment with her. "It's like you two just had some silent conversation while the entire stadium watched. Including his dad."

My smile plunges. "Did he look at me?"

"Yes. Everyone did. I don't know if they knew it was you, exactly, but who else would it be?" She motions toward the dog, then the old man, staring at me before shaking her head and patting my shoulder. "It's probably fine. There's no way he knows about you two. I'm sure he's got too many distractions to think anything's going on."

I shoot a quick glance at Detective Miller who's on his feet, cheering Marcus's name, and I let go of the breath hiding in my throat. But then he turns his head, and his eyes meet mine. He looks confused but smiles and steps across the aisle toward us.

"Hey, Mei Li. Lin. What are you doing here? I thought you two went to Central."

My stomach burrows deeper inside me and I swallow thick fear. "Oh…hi. Yeah, I just have a friend playing in the game."

"Ah, well…sure hope he's a Bulldog because they're gonna cream Lowell."

"You know it." The words tumble from my mouth, clumsy and heavy, but I plaster a smile on my face and Detective Miller chuckles, then steps back to his seat.

Lin slowly leans close and whispers, "Your 'friend' is definitely a Bulldog. I only wish he had four of those legs." She fans herself. "But joke's on Detective Dad, I guess. Honestly, I'd be more terrified of those girls down there finding out about you two."

When the game ends in a victory as predicted, the crowd slowly funnels out of the stadium to the sound of girl shrieks and laughter. Lin and I stay seated, watching Detective Miller meet Marcus on the field with a back-slapping bear hug. He lifts Marcus off his feet, and they laugh, Marcus shaking his head. Then Detective Miller punches Marcus's arm and turns, blending in with the leaving crowd, no glance in my direction.

The brunette and her friends stroll toward Marcus who smiles and talks to them for a few seconds before his eyes slip beyond them to me, still in the bleachers. The brunette keeps talking, and he laughs but catches my eye, raising his eyebrows, then waves at the girls when they walk away. He jogs to the bench, grabs his bags, and pulls out his phone. Two seconds later, a text pings:

> Marcus: Meet me at the south entrance in 5?
> I'll be the sweaty one.

My eyes meet Lin's which are staring intently at me, waiting, so I stand and grab her hand, pulling her to her feet. "Ready to meet Marcus Miller?"

"Oh. My. Gosh." Lin says under her breath, watching Marcus throw his bag over his shoulder and walk toward the locker room. "I've never been more ready."

We move down the steps and out of the stadium, rounding to the south parking lot, and a few minutes later, Marcus jogs toward us.

"Sorry to make you wait." His eyes move from me to Lin, back to me, streaking the air with blue. *"You totally made my day."*

I smile and glance at my feet because my eyes are reaching for him, but Lin steps between us.

"Hey…I'm Lin. Mei Li's very best friend. Also your neighbor." She does an exaggerated bow and Marcus laughs, bowing in response. She cackles as she straightens and holds up her hand. "Wow. Okay. Approval granted."

Marcus raises his eyebrows while he laughs, glancing at me, then back to Lin. "Didn't know I had to get that but I'm completely relieved to have it for…whatever." He smiles at her and her face lights up. "Think I've seen you around, so hey, neighbor. I'm Marcus."

"Oh, I know. Anyone who's female knows." She tilts her head. "But anyway, Magic Miller…" She glances at me. "Mei Li and I were just about to head home so…want to join us? Or do you have to sign autographs? Press conference?"

I want to clamp my hand over her mouth; he probably has somewhere to be with the other people—the real people in his real life. I break in. "It's okay. You probably have plans. We just came to say hi so…"

He smiles down at me, shifts the bags on his shoulder. "Nothing important going on so…I'll head home with you." His eyes grab mine and hold on. *"Let's take the long way."*

"Well, I'm headed this way." Lin hugs me. "Call me later with every detail," she says in my ear, then turns to Marcus. "Nice to meet you, kind sir." She tips an imaginary hat and skips down the street toward her apartment building.

Marcus watches her, smiling and shaking his head. "Wow. That's a lot of energy in one small person." He glances down at his phone in his hand and texts someone before shoving it in his bag and wiggling his fingers. "Empty hands. Just in case they want to wander toward yours. Or yours toward mine. Just…whatever…"

I smile as his pinkie catches mine, then his other fingers weave into place.

"So." He looks down at me, his eyes roaming my face as we walk toward the crosswalk. "Nothing better to do than watch soccer tonight, I guess?"

"It's what girls whose favorite number is eight do. Turns out there are a lot of us." We turn the corner, and he smiles into the purple haze.

"Good thing there's only one girl #8 secretly/not-so-secretly wanted there."

My cheeks ache from smiling as we cross the street, ecstatic except for the sliver of my brain that wonders how safe PDA is right now. "Should we go to our separate sides of the street?"

Marcus stops, looks down at me, then up the street and shakes his head. "I mean, yeah…we probably should but…I don't want to." His face is outlined by the lights, his cheeks splotched orange and pink from neon signs. "I'm kinda tired of doing things I don't wanna do, so I'm not letting go of your hand."

"Are you sure? What if your dad sees…?" Or Nick…

He glances around, then pulls me back down the street and around the corner. "Know how I said we'd take the long way home? I meant the really, really long way via back-streets." He squeezes my hand and veers me in the opposite direction of our neighborhood. I laugh and talk so much I'm hoarse when we finally walk down my alley and stop under my fire escape.

I press my lips together and look at his chest, his school's bulldog mascot glowing in the dark. I want to kiss him. I want him to kiss me. He said it would happen; I just hope that doesn't mean in four weeks. I want to know what a real kiss is like and then experience it a hundred more times before I go to L.A. and my life dumps Marcus out of it.

He watches his fingers play with mine. "Thanks for coming to my game. Although you almost made me lose it. And other things."

I hold a shrug and tilt my head, playing with the string on his hoodie. "Had to see what all the hype's about."

"And?" His eyes gather my erratic mind and heart into our dark, warm circle.

"I very much understand it now."

He meets my eyes, his gaze falling on my lips, staying there for two heartbeats before he groans and steps back. "Nope." He shakes his head, holding his hands up. "Not gonna kiss you in the same alley Face Eater earned his nickname. No way." He runs his fingers through his hair, takes a deep breath, lets it out in a sigh that ends in a smile. "Still… you have no idea what you do to me."

My heart jumps up and down, flops around, drops into my stomach, and has a seizure before tangling in the realization that he really was going to kiss me. It was going to happen, right here, right now. But now, he's gripping his backpack straps, his knuckles white, my thrashing heart jostling breathless words out of me.

"Call you as soon as I can." I give him a quick hug and race up my fire escape ladder even though my mind stays in that hug. Against his chest, inside his arms, wrapped in heat. I glance over my shoulder. "And see you tomorrow?"

He puts his hand over his heart, his fingertips digging in. "Definitely."

I scramble up onto the landing, my body tingling as I push up my window, then look down to where The Moment almost happened. The Almost Kiss, My Heart's Best Memory, The Explosion of My World, The Guaranteed Best Moment of My Existence—right as Marcus steps out from under the fire escape and looks up, his smile shooting light into the dark alley.

He takes a few steps backward, smiling up at me when our eyes collide. *"Can it be tomorrow yet?"*

I smile so big, the corners of my mouth threaten to tear,

then I wave, my hand going to my chest as he turns and walks down the alley toward the street, disappearing around the corner.

Squeezing my eyes shut, I hold my breath before letting it out in a whispered squeal as I crawl through my window. My phone buzzes from my jacket pocket as I drop to the floor.

I slip it out to see "Mmm" scroll across the screen, but someone knocks on my bedroom door and Mama's voice drifts under it. "Mei Li?"

"Yeah?" I send the call to voicemail and crack open my door.

"Can we talk?" Her words hang in the air, waiting for me to notice them, but Mama steps through my door and lowers her voice. "I came up earlier, but you weren't here."

"I went to a school soccer game with Lin," I rush as my phone buzzes with a new text. "Sorry I didn't tell you." I glance down, tilting the phone to read the screen.

> Marcus: Why wait until tomorrow? My dad's not home for a few more hours. Meet me behind my building in 10?

My heart shoves its way up my throat and my eyes snap to Mama who's studying my face as I think of excuses to get her out of my room so I can sneak out and meet Marcus.

Mama glances at the phone pressed into my thigh, then nods, looks at the floor, then me again. She reaches out but I stiffen, and she drops her hand, talking to her silk slippers. "I know what's happening, Mei Li."

I press the phone tighter against my thigh while my mind flips through possible meanings, like I'm in a crowded clothing store, flipping through racks to find something that could fit. This rack of me sneaking around with Marcus? Me obsessing over Marcus? Me finding ways to be with him? What does she know and how did she find out? Guo Mama said she'd never tell. Did Mama see us together? We weren't careful walking home tonight. My thoughts turn to the conversation I almost heard between mama and Guo. Was this what they were discussing?

I swallow and grip the phone tighter like my fingers will relay the message to Marcus that I'll meet him as soon as I get Mama out of my room. "Happening with what?"

She hesitates, scans my room, then levels her gaze with mine for the first time in a long time. "With Nick."

My knees lock, blood flow freezes. "What do you mean?" My voice is dry and crackly, thin and wary, like his name sucked the life out of me.

"I mean…" She sits on the edge of my mattress and grips her hands in her lap. "What he's doing to you. What he's done."

I stare at her, and when she looks away, I clench my jaw. I don't want to pretend. She does that enough for all of us. I don't want sunken, sad eyes or to be invisible like her. She's faded and wispy, her sharp cheekbones the only part of her that isn't two-dimensional. She used to be vibrant and fun. We laughed. I idolized her back then but stopped when Baba hit her and she did nothing to stop him.

My stomach tenses against the realization bubbling up from deep, deep cracks. If I keep letting Nick do this, I will become her.

I square my shoulders and meet her eyes as resentment erupts from me. "Then why don't you stop it?" I want her to see it all in my eyes, but she won't look at me. "Oh…I remember why: because you're as powerless and trapped as you've made me." I shake my head, the words filling my mouth dripping with the acid they've been swimming in for years. "But I won't stay trapped. I want something different."

Her folded hands grip each other like my words hurt when they hit, and my insides curl away from the cruelty I hurled at her. I close my eyes and formulate an apology, but she stands.

"I want something different for you, too." Her words huddle behind her as she walks out of my room and closes the door, leaving me alone to wonder what she meant. But her words don't matter. Maybe she's stuck, but I don't have to be. I still get a choice, and I choose Marcus.

CHAPTER 16

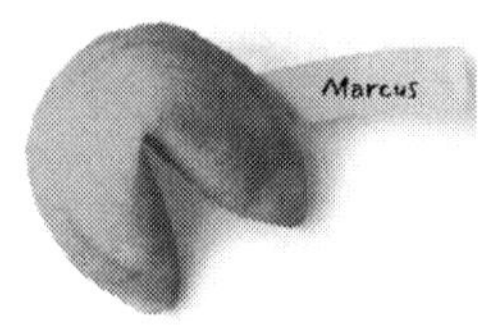

Now I've done it. Crossed some line in my head and somewhere near my heart. Slammed the door on what I used to think and know and barged through the forbidden portal into Mei Land. All new territory and I'm *all* in. So, so far in.

The yellow light glowing from building windows looks like evil Halloween pumpkins, scowling at me. *"You're such a liar, just like your mom."* I look away 'cause I don't want guilt smothering all this goodness happening inside me right now. Big win at the game. Big win with Mei. Big win with my self-control, though I wouldn't mind losing that. I've got it bad for Mei but there's nothing bad about it.

When I saw her in the stadium, my heart did this thing it's never done before. Like it was on a half-pipe doing 360s. And winning my game wasn't even close to as exciting as seeing her. Not sure what Dad's talking about, because nothing in my life so far has felt as good as Mei does. He just forgot. Or my mom wasn't as cool as Mei. Something inside me swears I've always known Mei was out there and was just waiting for me to find her.

I grip my backpack straps and smile as I turn out of her

alley, but I don't wanna wait at the crosswalk; gotta burn this extra energy Mei pumped into me. Gotta control this smile before Dad notices the Mei all over it. He won't be home until at least 2 AM, but…it could take that long to tame it, especially if she meets me tonight. I glance at my phone. She hasn't responded, but she will, and then…two more hours in Meiland.

I call her again, and it goes straight to voicemail, but a text beeps:

Mei: I'll be there.

I practically skim the asphalt, my smile taking up all the space on my face and crowding the empty sidewalks and streets.

I head behind my building to wait for Mei and figure out where we can go be invisible together when two guys cut across the intersection toward me. When I make eye contact, they walk faster and my heart thuds, pounding out a warning.

One of them calls to me to stop but my brain yells for me to run. I toss my bags aside for later and take off, even though I have no clue why I'm running from a huge dude and one half my size.

Footsteps slap behind me, closer, I pick up speed, glance over my shoulder just as Small Guy grabs the back of my neck.

I swear and twist, throwing elbows, but Small Guy slows me down and Extra Large pins my arms behind my back, shoving me against a wall.

"Stay away from her," he growls into my ear, and I freak, wrenching my arms free. He goes down and I rush Small Guy, fear shoving hot energy through me. I plow into him, knocking him to the ground and throwing punches that hit air because Extra Large yanks my hoodie from behind. He hauls me to my feet, then shoves me against a metal service door, his face in mine.

"You have no idea what you're dealing with," Extra Large growls and I shove him, but his chest is double mine, his giant gut like an anchor. He grabs my collar and twists until I'm choking. Over his shoulder, I see Small Guy scramble to his feet and sprint toward us as I thrash, but Extra Large flings me sideways, and my ribs connect with a metal railing.

Rage erupts inside me, flowing into my legs. I hurl myself at him, shove him against a garage door, white knuckles gripping his collar as I slam his head back against the metal, my face so close to his I can smell the weed coming out his pores. "Who are you?" My spit lands on his face and he flinches, but Small Guy grabs me from behind and throws me to the ground. Extra Large barrels toward me, so I scramble up and swing, slamming my fist into his face.

A growl erupts from his bloody mouth before he rushes me, throwing me against a garbage can that launches into the middle of the alley with a boom.

I skid across the sidewalk, anger sloshing in my chest and through my veins, exploding from my mouth. Spitting blood on the sidewalk, I push to my feet, hurl myself into his stomach, propel him backward into a lamp post. He drops and yanks me down with him but Small Guy's standing over me, his face in mine.

"If you ignore this friendly warning," he pants, "you won't walk away next time."

I grab his leg and twist, but he grips my arms as he goes down, and we roll, kicking a row of garbage cans at the curb, grunts and swear words echoing off metal until Extra Large kicks me. Sharp, shooting pain bursts in my ribs and I curl into the gutter when someone yells my name.

"Marcus!"

Frantic.

Fuzzy along the edge.

Wakes up my stunned senses.

Mei.

Rolling to my side, I curse to the sidewalk where I rest my forehead before slapping my palms against the cold cement and getting to my feet.

Mei shoves Small Guy in the chest while he holds her phone above his head.

"What are you doing?" she screams in his face, slapping him over and over until Extra Large grabs her.

Anger rockets out of my buzzing pain, sound roars back into my ears, and holding my ribs, I launch myself toward them.

"You're not keeping your end of the deal," he growls at Mei as I stumble toward them, but when metal clicks, my head snaps up. Extra Large stands behind Mei, pointing a gun at me over her head, and my eyes flick between the glint of metal and Mei's horrified eyes.

"Don't take another step," he booms, "or I'll end this."

Small Guy curses and drops Mei's phone before slowly approaching Extra Large. "Put it away, man. Now."

Extra Large's eyes never leave my face as he leans closer to Mei, the gun still pointed at me. "If you think this is some kind of game, go ahead and keep playing, but remember we know how to hurt you." He shoves the gun in his waistband and takes off running, Small Guy limping behind him.

CHAPTER 17

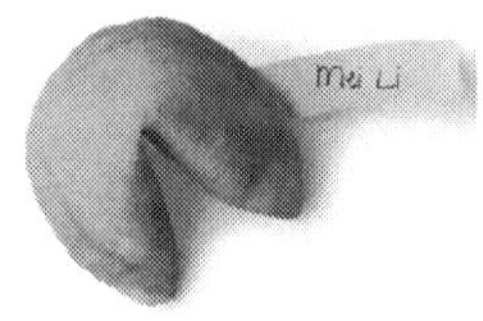

Marcus leans against a brick wall, catching his breath. "Who were they, Mei?" His left eye is swelling, blood trickling from his eyebrow.

How am I supposed to answer that? If I do everything ends here. If I don't, everything ends anyway. How's he supposed to trust me after this? I glance up the street, down, across. Nick may be out of town, but he has his guys watching me. I clench my jaw and swallow the metal taste coming from anger and my bleeding heart. He's ruined everything.

"I'm so sorry, Marcus. I didn't mean for any of this to happen."

He growls in frustration and pushes away from the wall, hunched over, limping toward his building. I follow him, not sure I should. Maybe I should just go home and lock myself in my room. Or run in the opposite direction. When I turn the corner, I see his bags. At least I can use them as an excuse to follow him into his building. But when I pick them up, he stops.

"Why are you protecting them?"

"I'm not, I'm..." Protecting myself? My family? Not

Marcus.

"Are they your friends?"

"No." My voice rises, desperation pushing it out of me.

He turns to me, clutching his ribs. "Then tell me who they are, because I'm sorta confused. Maybe I have a concussion from being slammed against concrete." His eyes are clouded with anger, pain, exhaustion. "I just got jumped by someone you know. Think we're past the point of secrets, don't you?" Blood drips into his eye and he swipes at it, swearing.

When I don't answer, he swears at the cement before grabbing his bags from me and limping around the corner. I close my eyes, the darkness in the dingy alley settles inside me, but I don't want any of it. I want to tell Marcus everything. He deserves to know.

I turn the corner and he's punching in the code to his building. When it beeps, I pull the door open for him. He said his dad's gone, but if he happens to be home, this night will get much, much worse.

Marcus grips the railing and hauls himself slowly up the two flights of stairs. I wish I'd never brought him into my world. That I'd never gone to his game. That this building had an elevator. That dealing with Nick was as easy as calling the police. But nothing's easy about this. Ending it is the hardest by far. But this has to be the end of us.

When we finally reach his apartment, Marcus's hands tremble on the doorknob, and he throws the door open, his anger like a heat wave as he drops his bags on the floor.

I follow him inside, pulling out a bar stool for him. He eases onto it, then talks to his hands pressed against the countertop. "Who were they?" His voice is raspy, his eye swollen, cheekbone purple and splotchy.

I pull a bag of peas from the neat stack in the freezer, and he closes his eyes, takes a deep breath, and lets it out with a string of swear words.

"What can I do? How can I help you?"

"There's a first aid kit in the hallway closet."

I drop the peas on the counter and dash to the hallway, bracing myself for the questions that will build a barrier between us now that the world is still and the truth is all over his bruised face.

Opening the closet door, I snatch the red box before hurrying back to him, flipping it open on the counter. He pulls it toward him and rummages until he finds a roll of medical tape. When he lifts the hem of his shirt to chest level, he hisses through gritted teeth and I step to him, fingers trembling as I help him pull his shirt over his head. He catches my eye as it comes off but drops them to his swollen torso and fumbles with the end of the tape.

He rips off a piece with his teeth, then sets down the roll and spreads the tape over a spot below his chest while I watch and feel helpless. He rips off a few more pieces and sticks them on the same spot before I take the tape from him, my fingers stiff and shaky.

Goosebumps rise along his skin as he watches my fingers smooth the tape, then closes his eyes and exhales, long and heavy. When he looks at me again, I drop my focus to the final piece of tape before handing him the bag of peas.

He hesitates, then takes it from me and holds it over his eye while I grab a dish cloth, soak it, then step in front of him and dab blood off his eyebrow and lip. He inhales sharply and tenses.

"I'm so sorry," I whisper. "For everything." My voice is uneven, and I should have stayed quiet. Any word I say is one more piece of myself I have to leave with Marcus.

"All I gotta do is call in an anonymous tip. Those guys'll leave us alone."

I step to the sink, rinsing the cloth. He's right. If the cops know, Xander and Holden will leave us alone because the Zhangs will be on the other side of the ocean. Twenty minutes ago, I wasn't going to end up like Mama. I chose Marcus and was going to tell him everything tonight. But now…I'd rather become Mama than do this to him. There can't be anymore us. If there is, this will keep happening. I'm being watched. I never thought Nick would go this far, but I don't know him anymore.

"They would have never done this to you, if it weren't for me." Clenching the cloth in my fist, I close my eyes. I let myself believe and hope and wish that Marcus and I could be real. That Nick would find something better to do than manipulate me and my family. I thought I was smart enough to keep my dream life from my real life.

I turn back to him but can't meet his eyes as I dab at his eyebrow that was perfectly fine before we met. I wish I could wash away my bleeding heart so easily. "We can't see each other anymore, Marcus." The words are raw, soaked in the tears and blood they've been drowning in.

His eyes fly open and he grabs my hand. "What did you say?"

Tears blur my vision. "We're too different. I never meant for you to see my world."

He shakes his head, body rigid. "This isn't about where we come from, Mei. This is about everything you're not telling me."

"I won't let you get hurt again."

"No more excuses, no more lies, no more secrets. Who is Face Eater and why are his guys after me?"

I press my lips together, dab at his eyebrow.

"The least you could do is tell me why you're protecting him. I thought it was you and me, and that you—"

"It is—was," I say to my hands, "but we can't."

"That doesn't even make sense." He shoves his fingers through his hair, grimacing and swearing.

"I'm not safe, Marcus."

He swears at the floor, then looks at me. "I don't want safe—"

"Everyone wants to feel safe. Not everyone gets the luxury, but you do. You can have it all—everything you want."

He stands, tipping the stool backwards, and grabs the counter with one hand, his ribs with the other. "Stop treating me like I'm some golden kid who gets everything he wants. I don't. Look at my life—my mom left because she didn't want me. My dad's never gotten over it, and drilled the fear of women into me. I'm terrified of doing the same thing to my dad, so I'll be here indefinitely. I turned down my full-ride to Stanford because my dad needs me here. But the worst part is, there's a girl I want but can't have and I don't know why, so no, Mei, I don't get everything I want." He grips the counter, his eyes pulling back from me, like he's emptied himself, his heavy, secret pain hanging between us.

My vision of his shiny, perfect world dims, the shadows in its corners coming out in the shadows under his eyes I thought were from all our late nights, but now…

We've both been running from our real lives, but they've detoured, cut us off, and are coming right at us. But his world would still be here, in this country. His dad would understand if he just talked to him about Stanford. I heard him celebrating the night Marcus got the offer. And there's no way his mom left because she didn't want him. There had to be another reason. And if she were here, she wouldn't hold him hostage with secrets that could ruin them all. He could figure it all out. He's Marcus, and no matter what he says, he'll get everything he wants.

"You do have it all. And you could have anything you want." My words are hot and sharp. "I'd take even a fraction of your life."

He looks at me, then shakes his head, his eyes holding me in place. "You obviously have no clue what I want because, right now, I want you to be honest and I can't even get that much." He swallows like the words are burning his throat as much as they're burning my chest. "And I want you and this thing between us," he blurts, "but I can't stop you from protecting Face Eater. So maybe he's what you want."

I shake my head, swallowing tears, blinking. "He's not."

"Then tell me you never wanted me. That I imagined it all. That it was all some kinda sick game and didn't really mean anything to you. Tell me. Go."

I talk to my hands. "I chose what I wanted, and look what happened."

When I meet his eyes, he holds my gaze before staring into the dark living room. I reach for his face again, but he jerks back, yanking the cloth from my hands and flinging it at the sink. "Why are you letting him do this to us?"

I shake my head and want to tell him I have no choice, but he goes on.

"Because I honestly thought we had something, Mei. I let myself think I was your boyfriend, crazy enough." He takes a shallow breath, then grimaces, frustrated.

My thoughts grind to a stop as the word breezes through my overheated, aching head.

Boyfriend.

"Maybe it's my fault, though." He throws his hand out. "I assumed things and haven't been honest enough about how I feel about you."

I swipe at a tear, and he grabs my hand, his eyes reaching so far inside me they scatter my resolve. Turning, I step around the counter to the sink, yank on the faucet, and watch water flow down the drain, wishing my reality could flow with it. But as much as it hurts Marcus, and as much as it will kill me, this has to end. "I have to let you go," I say to the draining water.

I wring out the cloth, cursing myself until Marcus's chest warms my back. I hold my breath as his hands smooth up my arms, his fingers playing inside my sleeves before moving to the nape of my neck.

"I don't believe you," he breathes, starting a fire on my skin that flares over me, and when he presses closer, I exhale, gripping the edge of the counter with both hands. "You're saying one thing, but your eyes are telling me something completely different."

I tremble as he sweeps my hair over my shoulder, all thoughts of goodbye burning to ash in the heat between us. "You do have a choice. We could figure this all out together. I'm not running, and you don't have to either."

His finger traces my tattoo, his other hand eases down my arm, and I close my eyes as his fingers slip between mine.

"Say what your eyes are telling me," he whispers, his voice rumbling through me. "That we're not over." His words reach around me, turn me toward him.

His gaze moves from my eyes to my lips then back again, carrying a silent question.

I nod, not taking my eyes off him as one trembling hand moves to the back of my head. He leans in, hovering over me, and when his lips find mine, heat sizzles down my body like I'm being filled with warm water. Marcus grips the back of my shirt, his lips coaxing me closer until I'm on tiptoe.

His hands move to my waist, my hips, his fingertips urging me closer until I wrap my arms around his neck and press my chest to his. He grimaces and I pull back, but he tugs me to him again. I grip the counter and lift myself onto it so he doesn't have to bend over so far, and he steps into me, his teeth grazing my bottom lip. I gasp, knotting my fingers in his hair before sliding them down his neck.

"I'm so sorry," I say with my eyes, and we hold each other's gaze, his palm cupping the back of my head as his other hand grips my shirt along my waist. "For everything."

"Does this mean we're not over?" he asks, his breath warm and ragged as he lowers his mouth to mine. "That's kinda the message I'm getting, but I need to hear it," he whispers against my lips, pulling back to look into my eyes while his hands circle my neck, tilt my head back, his thumbs running over my jaw.

"We're not over," I murmur, circling his wrists with my hands. If Marcus is right and I have a choice, this is it. He's it. We can figure the rest out together.

He lowers his forehead to mine, his lips so close I can feel their pulse. He curses through a groan before his lips crash into mine again, unlocking three words I've kept sacred and nurtured since the night I met him. I close my eyes to keep them hidden, but this close, he'll feel them in my heartbeat:

Wǒ ài nǐ.

I love you.

CHAPTER 18

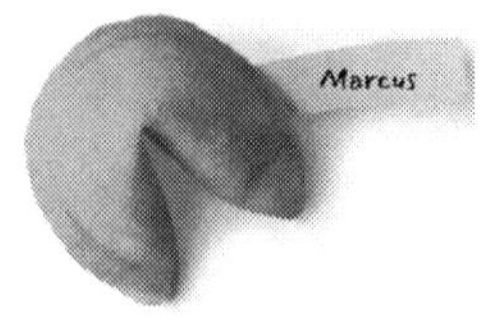

Mei: In the fortuitous words in the song Unsent by Alanis Morissette, "Dear Marcus, you rocked my world."

Marcus: That's all great what I did to your world, but you blasted me to a whole new one.

When my alarm goes off, I slap it quiet and roll over. My ribs don't appreciate it, so I unwind the warm ice pack around my torso and ease back onto my pillow. No way am I going to school today. Forget my ribs—don't want anyone to see my black eye. There's only one person I plan on seeing today. And every day from now on.

I close my eyes, replaying how the hair on the back of my neck stood up when Mei touched me last night. How my blood pumped so hard, my veins feel stretched out and floppy. I have so many questions. And so many feelings. I plan on asking her all the questions and showing her exactly how I feel. Show and Tell with Marcus and Mei. And that'll definitely involve kissing her again. A lot. Like…maybe all day. While keeping my hands to myself. Which just became a whole lot harder.

I snatch my phone from my nightstand and grimace at the painful reminder of the pounding I took last night. I'd expected brass knuckles. Nun chucks. Sabers. It wasn't Ugly Chao who'd trashed me, but felt like a message directly from him.

My thoughts circle over each other, trying to figure out what his deal is with Mei. Why does he care so much? Mei seems to be freaked out over the guy, should I be just as freaked?

When I check my phone, there's a Mei text, sent at 2:48 AM.

Mei: How are you feeling?

You don't fight off thugs or kiss someone like I kissed her if she's not your girl. My senses rocketed, and I hadn't thought, just done. I smile at my phone and dial her number. Probability of Mei and Marcus togetherness=99.98 percent. It's the 0.02 percent I'm after today.

She answers on the first ring. "Hey."

Ah…that voice.

"Hey, so…" I put my arm behind my head, pausing when my ribs scream at me. "That whole kitchen scene?" I let the words and the scene float through the phone. "That was hot, Mei." My legs go numb, and I wiggle my toes to make sure these thoughts haven't paralyzed me.

"I know." She's still smiling, probably touching her lower lip like she does when she's holding back emotion.

"I can't stop thinking about it."

"Me neither." Smile. Lip touch.

"And that's why I'd like to say thanks in advance for skipping school and spending this magical Friday here with me."

Smiling. Biting her lip. Closing her eyes.

"I can't." She's quiet for a minute. "But I can meet you after—"

I cut her off with a dramatic sigh. "It's just that Buddha's raging. He's throwing stuff and yelling. Think I heard swear words. And a threat to hurl himself off the windowsill if you don't come. And then he raged when I told him you tried to break up with me last night. I can't handle his rage in my delicate condition."

"It must be tough..."

"Especially after last night."

The pause is filled with her smile's electricity. "How are your ribs?"

"It's not my ribs I'm worried about."

"What are you worried about, then?"

"My lips. They need like..." I squint at the ceiling. "A lip gloss transfusion or something. From a willing donor."

Beams of smile light are shooting through the phone. "That sounds life-threatening."

"It's a slow, painful way to die."

"I should come pay my last respects."

"You definitely should." My abs tense just thinking about kissing her again, and it hurts. In a good way.

"Maybe I will."

"Then maybe I'll see you in an hour? I'll try to stay alive until then," I whisper. Our smiles meet somewhere between our phones before I sign off, then grit my teeth and slide off my bed, swearing at the rug while holding my ribs as I shuffle to the kitchen. I hate those guys so much. Hate that I can't tell Dad. Hate that, if I wanna keep Mei, we have to sneak around.

Dad's at the table, reading something on his phone. "Hey." I ease toward the cupboard as fluidly as I can.

He shoves his phone in his pocket. "What's up, M.C.?"

"Not a lot." Yet.

"Whoa." Dad stands and steps closer. "Where'd you get the shiner?" He tilts my head back and inspects it.

"Header gone wrong. Practicing last night at Johnny's." I swallow the sour lie. "Guess I should've gone to youth ministry instead." The lie combusts in my chest and burns up my throat into my eyeballs.

Dad nods. "Yep. Jesus saves." He smiles and pretends to slug me in the chin before patting the side of my head. He pulls out his phone and finishes texting while I pour a heaping bowl of cereal and ease onto a bar stool like today's any other school day, and I'll head off to fill my mind with knowledge. Definitely gonna learn—all about Mei. Her secrets. Her lips. But nothing else. Motorcycle.

"Marcus?"

I look up from my Froot Loops. "Yeah?"

He raises his eyebrows. "Did you hear me?"

"Oh. No—sorry."

"I just said I'm sorry I was so late last night. Things have been heating up at the precinct. I hate being gone so much."

"Any leads?" I shove cereal in my mouth.

"If it's who I think it is, the guy's a thug to the bone. Can't wait to lock him up." He glances at his phone. "Sad thing is, I think there are a lot of people involved. Undocumented immigrants." He shakes his head. "People come here to make a better life and get caught up in stuff they never dreamed of doing just to stay." He grabs his plate, puts it in the dishwasher, and glances at me. "Text when your homework's done, and Lex and I'll meet you for dinner somewhere. Take Lex's bike for a ride, maybe?" He rubs his hands together. "You need some practice. Graduation's coming right up."

"Yeah." The word squeezes through my tight throat. "Could definitely use some practice."

When Dad leaves, I ease into the shower, brush my teeth, and text Mei. Ten minutes later, I lean against the open door of The Clubhouse and almost don't recognize her skimming the stairs in a baseball cap and giant sunglasses. But the way her hips move when she walks…it's all her. Her skinny jeans ride low, the V-neck underneath her jacket clinging to her, and I swallow my pounding heart, grabbing her hand and pulling her inside before shutting and locking the door.

"Hey." My hands circle her waist, my body heat sufficiently burning through the cold, morning air swirling around her. She grins up at me and my lips hover above hers. "Just gonna make sure you brought the lime kind." I smile as I kiss her slowly.

She stretches against me, and my fingers press into her back, holding her against me until my ribs protest. "Sorry," I whisper against her lips and my fingers reluctantly ease up. I take off her baseball cap and sunglasses before resting my forehead against hers. "Little sore."

She closes her eyes. "I'm so sorry, Marcus. I don't know what I was thinking last night," she murmurs, her lips brushing mine, her arms draped around my neck. "But there's no way I could ever stay away from you. Thus, the disguise."

I curl my toes into the carpet to avoid floating into Mei Land. "Speaking of last night…I think we're official. Am I wrong?"

"You're not."

I lace my fingers through hers and walk backward, pulling her to the couch. Holding my breath, I ease onto it, then tug her down beside me, ignoring my screaming torso as she snuggles closer. "So…maybe we should do some actual talking since our mouths got a little distracted last night. Maybe talk about how we're gonna make this work without getting jumped every day. I mean, here we are, not at school. Our lips aren't busy. Yet. And before they get that way, we should talk about what happened."

She's silent for a few seconds, my question hanging in the air. "Okay…"

"Why do those guys care we're together? And were they watching you this morning? Like, are they gonna burst through the door and kill us?" Uncertainty from last night crushes my preoccupation with her lips.

She takes a deep breath and lets it out as a long sigh of surrender. "I made sure no one was around." She picks at the hem of her jeans. "Nick's…protective."

"Ah. Yeah. Kinda." A lump grows in my chest. "But why? What is he to you? And don't say nothing because…this," I lightly pat my taped torso, "isn't nothing."

She shakes her head, her eyes grabbing mine, holding on. "He wants there to be something between us, but I don't. He must have found out about you somehow."

"So…he's the jealous type." Marcus slides a hand lightly over his ribcage. "Checks out. Your parents know?"

She nods.

I raise my eyebrows and wait for words to form. "And they're cool with the way he treats you?"

She glances around the room. "Not exactly, but…"

"But what?"

"Like I said last night, you and I come from the same neighborhood, but completely different worlds. Our parents worry about different things." Her jaw is set like she's not gonna let anything slip out of her mouth.

I lean my head back against the couch. "That is so messed up. No offense, but seriously."

"Maybe in your world."

"No. In every world. That's not okay." The edge of her words rips open the place I'm storing my anger, leaving the silence jagged. "So, just to clarify: Face Eater's not your boyfriend. Swear on Buddha."

"I swear, Marcus. There's just…a lot of family history, that's all. If I could tell you everything, I would. But I can't, and that's how it has to be. I promise I'll tell you everything I can." Her voice is a whisper and I grab her hand, bringing it to my chest. "And..." she continues, "if we're going to be together, you can never tell your dad any of this. Or you'll never see me again."

Whoa. My head snaps back like she threw a punch. "Seriously? It comes down to that?"

"Yes."

I let the information sink in, kinda like a blow to the head, then scan the living room before looking at her again. "You part of the mafia or something?"

She throws daggers with her eyes, and I hold up my hands. "Pretty sure Face Eater is, so..." She turns away, looking out the window, and my thoughts stumble over themselves to push out words. "Okay. Whatever. Fine—I'll let it go for now, but I'd prefer not to fight those guys again, and I just...I don't want this to sound demanding or anything but if we're together, I can't stand the thought of Face Eater kissing you in that family-friendly way anymore. Or punching you. Or touching you in any kind of way. Unless you want him to, and then...whatever. Your choice, but...I just can't." I sit forward on the couch, gritting my teeth against the pain as I run my fingers through my hair and talk to the carpet. "I promise not to tell my dad and you promise to stay away from Face Eater."

She rolls her eyes and looks away, but I turn her face toward mine. "And...promise you're not playing me. That what happened last night meant something to you..."

Her eyes search my face. "Marcus, I..."

"Because if it didn't, please—"

"I swear."

I grab her hand and pull her down the hallway into my room. I shuffle to the windowsill and snatch Buddha. "Swear on him and I won't ask any more questions for now. You can tell me when you're ready. If you swear on Buddha, I'm in this thing for good." I hold Buddha between us, looking down at her. "Like...for good, good. Like...we'll lie low until we figure out how to be together in a safe, normal way." She seems so much smaller than when she got here. I tip her chin up and our eyes lock. *"You in this thing with me?"*

She closes her eyes and nods before looking at me again and whispering, "I'm in" before grabbing Buddha and wrapping her arms around my neck. "100 percent. But we have to be completely secret."

When I grunt and reach for the wall, she lets go and steps back, hand over her mouth, but I smile through a grimace and slide onto my bed, stretching out on my back to breathe through the pain. "I swear you and Face Eater are both trying to kill me."

I stand in Lex's garage that smells like his neighbor's weed farm growing on their balcony. I keep my sunglasses on despite the setting sun so Dad won't see everything I'm hiding from him. As far as I know, Mei's the only one who can read my thoughts, but just in case.

My temperature's still significantly elevated from today's make out which went on a whole lot longer than last night's. *Way* longer. Making out with Mei is straight up magic, but I had to remind myself about the motorcycle a few hundred times. Luckily, my crying ribs helped keep things under control.

"Let's see what you got, M.C.," Dad says, lifting the garage door. He throws me a helmet and I pull it on before sliding onto the motorcycle, steadying it as Dad climbs on behind me.

I clench my jaw and swing my leg over the seat like moving's not grinding my ribs to dust, and grip the handlebars, peeling out of the garage. Dad slugs my shoulder to slow it down but I haven't slowed down anything since I met

Mei, and definitely haven't honored his wishes. I let up on the gas.

A few minutes later, we pull up to Golden Gate State Park and I kill the engine and take off my helmet. Dad slides off the bike and I put down the kickstand and step off. We sit on the railing, overlooking the bay, our heels kicking against the metal, helmets in our laps. I focus on the water instead of letting my eyes wander to the bridge where Mei and I were last weekend. Gotta stay here with Dad.

"Big month, my man." He wraps his arm around my shoulders, slipping me in a headlock and knuckles my head, then lets go, his Adam's apple bobbing.

I look across the bay and blink away the sting in my eyes. This is it. Last few weeks of life as I've known it. Just me and Dad, doing our thing. After graduation, things will change. Especially if Mei sticks around for culinary school. We'll keep dating and, eventually I'll tell Dad about her. Once he gets to know her, he'll approve, and everything will be cool.

I swallow nausea and anxiety. Sadness. Disappointment in myself. The combo tastes like rusty metal and puke. Curling my toes in my Adidas, I fight to keep my mouth shut when I wanna tell Dad everything like I always have. Wanna tell him about Mei and how I'm starting to feel about her and hear him tell me he gets it, and I don't have to sneak around. That he'll lock up Face Eater and fix everything that's messed up with Mei's family. That everything's gonna be okay. I want Mei and Dad. Why do I have to choose?

"How you feelin' about graduation?" He keeps his eyes straight ahead, but his jaw clenches and pulses like he's pushing back emotion.

I take a deep breath, hoping fresh air will yank all the sadness out of this freaking moment. "Excited. Nervous. Ready. All of it."

He glances at me. "Yeah?"

I keep my head turned from him so I can blink away tears

of loss from signing with USF instead of Stanford. From lying to him. From growing up and considering leaving him. "Just getting kinda real."

He shifts on the railing and clears his throat. "Yeah. Came way too fast but I'm so proud of you, son." He blinks and tightens his grip on the railing.

"Dad." My voice breaks. "You're kinda killin' me."

His eyes are glossy as he smiles. "Should we have a sob fest and get it over with? It's a happy time, right? My son's going places I never went, doing big things I never did." A tear slides down his cheek and I lean my elbows on my knees like someone just punched me in the gut, and my insides hurt way worse than my ribs. I let out a long, shaky breath, and he laughs.

"Raising you's been the best eighteen years of my life." He nods and swipes at another tear. "I've spent a lot of time burnt over your mom leaving but…it was her loss and my luck."

I wipe both palms down my face to clear the tears and groan. "You gotta stop, Dad. Seriously."

"No way. It's how I feel. And I don't let myself do that too often. So deal with the love coming out of my eyes." He bumps my shoulder with his. "Love you, M.C."

I open my mouth to tell him I love him, too when a group of women next to us asks him to take their picture, one of them smiling at Dad a little bigger than politely. When he comes back, I nod to the group, grateful for a conversation detour.

"Think that lady wants you to ask for her number."

He glances at her, then back at me. "Not happening."

"She not your type?"

He watches a boat creep under the bridge and shrugs. "Not sure what my type is. Thought it was your mom. Thought she wanted the same things I did. I had big plans for us. I was gonna get recruited to the FBI and eventually marry her, but then she wound up pregnant and took off after you were born." He studies his feet. "I hate the way things ended with her but glad I got what I got. She's the one lacking." He squints as he looks out over the water, his feet kicking the railing. If there's a crack anywhere in Dad's campaign against women, I need it to spread wide open. Maybe I could tell him that I'm merely interested in Mei. Make the lie a little less sharp.

"Not every woman's like my mom." Now it's my turn to watch the boats, the setting sun glinting off their windows.

He raises his eyebrows. "You speaking from experience?"

Okay. Nope. Not ready to tell him. "No." I shake my head probably a little too fast. "Nah…just thinking. Probability's low."

"Why risk an amazing future by betting on probability?" He shakes his head, staring out at the ocean.

The lump in my stomach sprouts legs and crawls into my throat, digging in like a tick that sucks out all my Mei confidence. I wanna ask him if he ever felt about someone the way I feel about Mei.

"I know there are good women out there, but you're young. And you never really know what'll happen until you take the dive and then it's just…messy."

Since when does he think there are good women in the world? His newfound attitude lands in my head with a thud and springs a leak in my confessions holding tank. The leak picks up all the words I've been hiding from him, and they slide down to my mouth. Don't know what to do with this conversation. Where was this crack in his hatred toward women a month ago? But before I can confess anything, I slide off the railing, my torso screaming as I nod toward the motorcycle.

"Welp…better get home. If I don't get my homework done, I won't graduate." I pull on my helmet and we slide back onto the bike, my white knuckles on the handlebars having nothing to do with driving or my ribs.

"How 'bout we grab dinner with Lex first?" Dad asks as he pulls on his helmet. "I've got a hankering for Zhangs since we didn't go on Tuesday."

CHAPTER 19

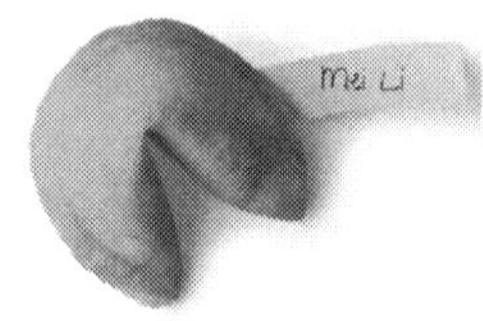

WANTED: An everyday kinda thing with a fine-lookin' Taiwanese girl. Call Buddha if interested.

My face hurts from smiling as I turn the corner into my alley and scan the street for Nick's guys, but Guo Mama steps out of her shop and I veer toward her.

"Ah! That's the look," She smiles so big I can see all her dentures

"What look?" I shift the grocery bags in my hand.

"Girl in *love*," she says through a grin. "You can't deny it—I read it in here." She holds out a folded note and heat rushes my face when I set down bags and snatch it from her, shaking my head.

"Seriously, Guo Mama?"

She holds up her hands. "Can't help it. I am so happy."

My eyes trace Marcus's handwriting, and I smile at the lopsided letters of my name. "I need to get to work. Thank you!" I call over my shoulder as I hurry out the door and slip around the corner, glancing at Marcus's apartment as I slide the envelope in my pocket and go through the back entrance.

Guo Mama's right: I am a girl in love and want to tell him. The words bubble to the surface every time I'm around him. He's going to see them or feel them, but I want to say them.

Dropping the grocery bags on the counter, I sneak upstairs and throw my bag on my bed before closing and locking my door. I roll my sore neck where Holden grabbed me. Another reminder that things will get much worse if anyone catches me and Marcus.

I stare at the envelope until my phone buzzes, and I yank it from my pocket, but it's only Lin, saying she'll be here after my shift. At least it's not another text from Nick. Every time I get one, I fight to type one-word responses with happy, friendly exclamation points so he'll never suspect anything. The responses in my head are anything but happy or friendly.

Stepping to my desk, I shove Marcus's letter inside my 'CALC' folder with the others and head downstairs for work, smiling to myself as I picture us curled together on his bed earlier, on a blanket under his window. That room was on a completely different planet, far from this one. I could easily give up everything here for everything there. Permanently relocate to his world that might not include culinary school but has unlimited Marcus. If I disappeared from my world, Nick would have to move on. My parents would stay in the States. Everything could be okay.

The kitchen is busy, and I stand on tiptoe to look out the blurry swinging door window to check the crowds. My eyes skip over the sea of red tables, customers' heads thrown back in laughter or leaned over their dinners.

Wishing it was Tuesday, my eyes skim Marcus's usual table and skid to a stop on Detective Miller, Detective Robinson...Marcus. Detective Miller's son who made out with me all afternoon. Not long enough.

My eyes dart to Nick's usual table, which is empty again tonight, and I let out a shaky breath and close my eyes, remembering his text from earlier: You are going to love L.A. I can't wait to show you around in a few weeks. I'd texted back that I couldn't wait, but Nick's absence tonight is a gust of relief trailed by a hot, fast memory of me and Marcus from earlier, his lips on my neck, hands struggling to stay in the safe zone. Me hoping they wouldn't.

I press the Sharpie heart he drew on the inside of my wrist against my hip as heat flares in my stomach and into my face.

I turn from the window, my lungs burning as I haul in a deep, shaky breath and walk to the back of the kitchen, behind the shelves, my fingers fumbling with my apron strings, arms and legs numb. Detectives can smell lies, and I'm splattered with them: my Nick lie, my family lie, my skipping school in Detective Miller's house lie. Making out with his son in his very own house last night *and* today. Marcus's fingerprints are practically all over me. His heat is still trapped in my permanent blush. Like a love sunburn I hope never fades.

Baba walks into the kitchen, barking at one of the chefs, and I grab a tablet, gripping it until my fingertips go white. I push through the swinging door, my eyes above customers' heads as I weave around tables toward Marcus, my heart pumping too much blood to my head. I think I'm going to explode.

I smile at Detective Robinson first, my eyes straining so hard to stay on him, I'm sure I'm glaring. "Hello," I say with a shaky smile, then tense when I feel Marcus's eyes rest on my face like a warm hand.

I curl my toes and concentrate on Detective Robinson, hoping I'm not squinting. "Can I get you anything to drink or are you ready to order?"

"Hey, Mei Li!" Detective Miller booms, spinning a spoon on the tabletop, grinning at me like a spotlight on all my guilt. "Looks like we're getting special Zhang treatment tonight!"

Marcus smirks at the table and rests his forearms along the edge, drumming his fingers, The same fingers that touched me all day. A new number blares from his arm in red Sharpie: 3/1000. I need to look at Detective Miller, but Marcus is leaning on his elbow, chin in his hand as he watches me. Detective Miller drops the spoon he's spinning, and it clatters to the ground. When he bends to pick it up, Marcus's eyes meet mine.

"Speaking of special Zhang treatment. Meet me in the pantry?"

My legs go tingly, and I wiggle them as I bite my lip to control my smile, then yank my eyes back to Detective Miller when he sits up.

"I'll get you a new spoon," I say to him, standing on one foot and wiggling the other.

Detective Miller leans back in his chair and smiles. "I was thinking of ordering something different tonight, but…"

"Or…" The word jumps out of me, my whole body jittery. "I could do an order of extra lo mein…" I say, then laugh like a hyper butterfly. When my eyes skim Marcus's, he raises one eyebrow, his eyes sparking.

"Whoa." Detective Miller whistles. "Impressive. Guess I really am that predictable if everyone here knows my usual."

"Not everyone. That's my own detective work."

Both detectives laugh and nod while I smile at Detective Robinson's badge, grateful the lighting is dim for my hot cheeks' sake.

"And what can I get you?" I ask Detective Robinson, my finger hovering over broccoli and beef.

"Well…if you know his usual, you probably know mine." He points to my tablet. "Let's see if I get a surprise, or if we really are Zhang's VIPs." He grins, showing the gap between his front teeth.

"Challenge accepted," I say to my tablet, but my eyes slip to Marcus who picks up his glass and drains the water in two gulps.

Detective Miller laughs and slaps the table. "Big, fat tip

from Lex for dealing with this crew." He reaches across the table and slaps Detective Robinson's shoulder.

My neck is kindling a bonfire that will flare out the top of my head any minute, but I smile, feeling like I'm breathing in hot air. I bend one knee so I don't pass out. "Anything to drink?" I hit the buttons before they tell me. Dr. Pepper, Mountain Dew. Dr. Pepper.

I breathe through my nose to keep a straight face and ignore Marcus, but he leans into the table and drops his hands under it. A second later, his fingers trail behind my knee and down my calf. My heart jumps and I inhale sharply, shaking my leg like I'm flinging off a bug.

"You okay?" Detective Miller's eyebrows furl but Marcus's fingers drift to the side of my knee while he pretends to study the menu on the table in front of him.

I lock my knee and snap my eyes to Detective Miller and smile, nodding spastically while my stomach squirms. "Yes. Fine." My thoughts travel at the speed of light down my leg to Marcus's fingers. "Sorry. You said large Dr. Pepper, right?"

He nods and hands me his menu as I bite my lip, hauling my focus back up my body to Marcus. "What can I get for you?"

He leans back and crosses his arms on his chest, rocking on the chair's back legs. I glance at his fingers that just secretly left lava trails down my legs, then the fraction on his arm.

"What's 3/1000?" I ask with my eyes.

"Show you in the pantry. But that heart on your wrist looks serious. You got a boyfriend?"

I look at my tablet, then back to Marcus, talking with my eyes. *"Look at your menu before your dad notices."*

Luckily, Detective Miller is discussing something with Detective Robinson, and Marcus sighs, long and loud.

"Well…if you know what these jokers like, I bet you know what I like." His eyes widen. *"And it has nothing to do with food*." I grip my tablet tighter while he scans the menu, then sighs and looks at me. "I had Zhang's earlier today but can never get enough. I love everything about it. So good." His eyes spark and set tiny fires in places that make me want to crawl into his lap or run and jump in the ocean. He grins up at me and I kick his ankle. Hard.

He flinches, then straightens, and smiles at me. "Sweet and sour pork for me, please."

I'm combing my wet hair after a shower when Lin trots up the stairs, blowing a bubble as she sails into my room.

"Hey, hot stuff." She flops on her stomach across my bed. "Will you promise we can talk about something more exciting than calculus? Does anyone actually like it? Or use it?" She swings her head toward me where I've dropped into my desk chair. "The answer is decidedly no. So, let's talk about something useful as a warm-up. Like…the real reason you weren't at school today. Hmmm? Could it have something to do with a soccer player?" She stares at me and taps her chin. "Which would positively dash Harvey in pieces since he thinks you two are going to end this year with your lips locked while you're on some super-scary rollercoaster on Senior Day."

"How do you know that?" I prop my feet on my desk, remembering my lips locked on Marcus's while I was supposed to be at school with Harvey. Marcus's lips affect my stomach way more than any rollercoaster could. That stomach-drop feeling happened repeatedly in the last twenty-four hours. I put my hand over it, then pretend to straighten my shirt when Lin looks at me weird.

She digs a pen out of her bag. "Heard he's going to ask you to prom."

Oh. That. I haven't thought about prom since Marcus took over all sections of my brain.

When my phone buzzes on my desk, I pick it up to see Mmm on my screen and control my voice to keep from shrieking. "Be right back." I jump up and bolt into my bathroom, swinging the door closed behind me. Climbing into the shower, I huddle in the corner and answer. "Hi," I whisper through a spreading smile.

"Hey," he sighs into the phone.

"Was it your idea to come in tonight? That was the best kind of surprise."

"It was actually my dad's, so that worked out nicely. Maybe he senses how much I crave Zhang's these days..."

There's a honk on his end of the phone. "Where are you?"

"Staring at your window."

I straighten and put my hand over my mouth as ice crawls through my veins. "Xander and Holden could be anywhere."

"And?"

I burst out of my bathroom and yank my curtains aside while Lin watches from my bed. Marcus is standing across the alley, one hand holding his phone to his ear, the other over his heart. His hair waves at me in the breeze, his smile lighting the alley.

"Come up here. Hurry."

"Is that who I think it is?" Lin asks over my shoulder as I shove open the window.

"Hurry," I rush into the phone, then hang up and shove it in my back pocket, watching Marcus. There aren't many places for a human to hide down there, and there are enough neon signs to outline shadows. Unless my stalkers are hiding in the dumpster, the coast seems clear. But we can never be too careful.

Lin grabs my arm and murmurs, "You've been keeping secrets, and you promised you'd tell me every detail."

I swivel toward her. "Okay, don't kill me, but...Marcus and I are..."

"Are *what*?!" Her eyes spark and she sticks her head out

the window beside me, then jerks back inside the room. "What are you?!" she gasps, then says, "You two have kissed haven't you?" When I don't respond, she gasps louder. "I could murder you with my bare hands for not telling."

I duck back inside and turn to her. "I swear I'll leave nothing out. But you have to swear you'll *never* tell a soul what you're about to witness. I mean it, Lin. Promise." I glance out the window when Marcus pulls himself onto the fire escape, gripping his ribs and swearing, then I turn back to Lin and hold out my pinky.

She holds up hers, then grabs my wrist, and inspects the Sharpie heart before tilting her head and squinting at me. "Where did this come from?"

"Promise you won't tell any of this."

She holds her breath, then lets it out while squeezing her eyes shut and nodding. "Fine. But…" She wraps her pinky around mine and presses her thumb to mine, sealing the promise. "You have so much to spill."

"Oh. Hey," Marcus says when he ducks and leans through my window. "Nice to see you again, Lin."

Her mouth is open and smiling and Marcus glances at me when she doesn't say anything.

I push her shoulder. "Will you make sure my door's locked?"

She blinks, then nods and turns toward the door, squealing at it before glancing over her shoulder at Marcus who's easing through my window. He drops into my room, swearing at the ceiling as he holds his ribs. I slide the window shut and close the curtains.

I hold my finger to my lips, and he nods, then reaches for my waist but pulls back when Lin slides beside me.

"You two…" She shakes her head slowly, her eyes stuck on Marcus. "This is…"

"Secret," I say, turning to her. "You promised." I widen my eyes at her, sending the message loud and clear.

"Oh, it won't come out of my mouth, but my head is nothing but raving about this entire situation." She waves her hand between us. "A lot has happened since I left you two after the game, hasn't it? Including that." She points at Marcus's eye. "Which I'm sure Mei Li kissed better."

Marcus raises his eyebrows and laughs once as she takes a few steps backward, grabs her bag off my bed, and mouths, "Oh my gosh" to me while Marcus watches. She opens the door and I mimic zipping my lips. She holds an invisible phone to her ear and mouths, "Call me" as I close the door and lock it, then turn to Marcus.

"Are you crazy coming here?" I whisper.

He shrugs and grins. "Couldn't help it. Told Dad I was taking a run, but he's waiting for me to get back so we can do movie night. If I'm not there, he'll send out an all-call."

I stand on tiptoe and hover my lips close to his, smiling. "So, what do the numbers on your arm mean?"

He grips the hem of my shirt, pulling me against him "Let's just say it changed from a 2 to a 3 this afternoon and kinda wanna change it to four right now…"

I laugh to the ceiling, then press closer until his shirt crinkles and I frown.

He pats his chest and whispers, "Massive amounts of tape. Like, two rolls."

I tug on his hoodie zipper until he bends toward me, our mouths crashing into each other.

"I knew," he says between kisses, "if I came here…I'd get all sweaty…" He pauses and gets too involved with my mouth to talk, gripping my hips. "Gotta get sweaty enough my dad'll believe I went for a run." He guides me backward and presses me against the wall, our mouths telling everything we can't put into words until footsteps come up the stairs.

I push him toward the window, and reach around him,

yank aside the curtains, shove it open. "You have to go," I whisper.

He ducks through the window, turning back to me and grinning. *"Sufficiently sweaty."*

When someone knocks on my door, I whirl around. "Yeah?"

"I need your help downstairs, please." Mama's voice is barely loud enough to make it through the closed door.

"Okay," I call. "Give me a minute. Finishing some math." I cringe, then whirl back around to Marcus, leaning out the window, our faces close. "I'm sorry," I whisper.

"I'm definitely not," he whispers back, the lamplight from my window and his smile combining to spotlight him.

"Wait," I whisper.

"Yeah?" He sticks his head through the window, and I take it between my hands and lean toward him, my lips on his ear, my heart pounding the words out of me.

"I love you," I say then pull away, but Marcus grabs my wrists.

"Whoa. Wait. What did you say?"

I hold my finger to my lips and glance over my shoulder, then back to him. There's no way he hasn't seen it in my eyes. But just in case, I say it again, my throat throbbing. "I love you."

He stares at me, frozen, then shakes his head. "No…no, no, no." His palm goes over my ear, his fingers tangling in my hair. "That's not how this goes." His forehead meets mine and I close my eyes, breathing in his heat. "It's supposed to be like, a…moment." His voice ripples around me. "I'm supposed to say it first and then you say it back and—"

I cup my hand over his mouth. "Shh! You're going to get me in so much trouble."

He pulls away. "Then tell me again so I can see what it looks like when you say it." He runs a finger over my bottom lip, watching it before meeting my eyes again.

I grab his hand. "You should've been listening."

"I was," he murmurs, searching my face. "But…whoa." His throat bobs as he swallows, his eyes roaming my face. "I was waiting for the perfect time to say it and—"

"You worry about perfection, and I'll say what I think when I think it."

"Is that the first time you've thought it?" He arches one brow and grins.

"Not telling."

"That's okay. I've seen it. You want me."

Blood surges through my veins and I'm lightheaded. *"You're right."*

"Prove it."

The adrenaline surge leaves me coiled and ready to spring through my window, but I lock my knees. *"Not until you say it back."*

"This isn't how I wanted to say it. Or where or how or any of it," he whispers.

"So you've thought about it…" I tilt my head, smiling.

He nods slowly. "Yeah, like…every time I look at you or talk to you or text you or read your texts or write you notes or read yours. When we're video chatting and I'm wishing you were in bed beside me instead of all the way over here."

My stomach flips and I squeeze the windowsill. He glances to his right, his face smooth in the castoff light before he meets my eyes again, glossy and soft.

"I think about it when I daydream about you in biology and English and math and history and during practice and church and riding the train and walking home. And breathing. So yeah…" He nods slowly. "I've thought about it a couple times." He shrugs. "Seems crazy but doesn't feel crazy." His eyes hold mine, and I beam at him.

"Mei Li?" Mama's voice calls from the stairs. "Downstairs, please."

"Coming!" I whip back around to face him. *"You have to go,"* I say with my eyes, reaching to shut the window.

"But I haven't said it yet."

"Guess you'll have to find the perfect time."

He smiles as he backs down the ladder, patting his hand over his heart before he disappears.

I pull the window down, take a deep breath, and release it in a silent squeal so no one will sense that I was just telling Marcus Miller I love him.

CHAPTER 20

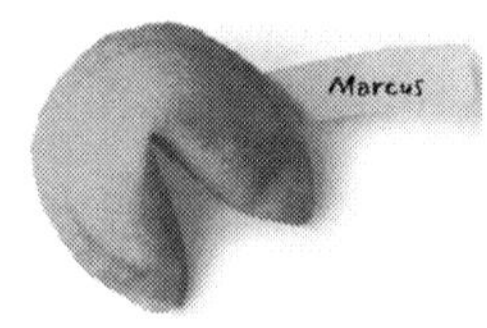

Marcus,

Like how I folded this note? I YouTubed it. Guo Mama shouldn't be able to open it which means this is my chance to say something really juicy like…continue our game of 3 Random Objects from last night. Actually, from 2 AM. (Shouldn't I be more tired than I am?) First 3 random objects: Marcus Miller's smile, Marcus Miller's laugh, Marcus Miller's lips when they're on mine. Your turn.

I toss my AP chem book beside my lawn chair and scrunch down, my hoodie shielding my face from the crisp April breeze sauntering down the street. Every chemical equation I try to solve comes to the same conclusion: Mei Li Zhang, the element MLZ. And that's it—there's not much else in my head. Just her and a whole lot of the last three words she said to me: *I love you*. Then the three words she texted at 3 AM after our two-hour video chat: See you tomorrow.

It's tomorrow. Almost 7 PM tomorrow, and I still haven't seen her. But man, I need to. She texted at 4:45 to say she'd sneak over as soon as she could, and I gave her the green light. Sat on this fire escape. Tried doing chemistry, and it really needs me to pull my head out of last night—Mei's face on my phone screen, the questions we asked each other but would never ask anyone else before we signed off way too late as usual—very, very reluctantly, stretching over twenty minutes. Her good night text is lodged in my brain. My reaction to it still burns through me.

My foot taps against the metal, clanging all the way down the building. We need to figure this out. How, where, when… she's gotta be an everyday thing. We have to figure out more undercover meeting spots, more ways to see each other. I gotta figure out how to keep my hands off her enough that I earn my motorcycle, but the motorcycle kinda feels flimsy now. If I had to choose between the two…

The thought stumbles over itself when Mei finally rounds the corner of her building, I'm out of my chair and gripping the railing, watching her cross the street. Her hands are shoved in the pockets of an oversized coat, her hair tucked inside a beanie to disguise herself as she jogs toward my building.

I sweep the street for any lurkers, then back to Mei who's watching her feet until old man Huang stops sweeping the sidewalk in front of his apothecary shop. He bows and smiles, adjusting his glasses as he speaks to her.

No, no, no—keep moving. Her disguise obviously didn't work for him, and it won't work for Face Eater's guys either, especially when she smiles at Mr. Huang, exploding the whole world.

Gripping the railing, I watch her cross the street toward my building then scramble back into my living room and dart to the front door before my heart beats twice. I've waited almost twenty-four agonizing hours to see her. Couldn't concentrate in class, thanks to the buzzing in my head, and every time I blink, I see her smile, feel her lips.

I snatch a piece of gum from the cupboard, straighten my jacket, and run my fingers through my hair. Stare at the door and wonder if she got the note I left with Guo this morning.

One of my best by far. Had me squirming when I wrote it. It's like the thought of her split me open and a bunch of feelings hiding inside spilled onto the paper. Big ones. I told her all about them but left out the three words that have been sprinting through my mind. Saving them for face to face, perfect time, perfect place. Not here and not tonight since now, I only have two hours until Dad comes home from his meeting. Hope he doesn't sense the words I wanna say or the female voodoo. If he just knew Mei, he'd change his mind about all women. I mean, five weeks ago, I was pro-motorcycle, anti-girl, anti-love. Then I met Mei. Now it's pro-motorcycle, totally pro-girl, completely pro-love. And I like it.

Love it.

Love her.

Love? Really, though.

I smile at the door. Yeah. Really. Definitely.

The intercom beeps and I buzz her in, count to seventeen, then swing the door open before she can knock. "Hey." I pull her inside and close and lock the door before wrapping my arms around her "It's been twenty-two hours too long since I've seen you," I say, leaning my forehead against hers.

She wraps her arms around my neck and laughs into my ear before whispering, "Did you mean all those things you wrote in your note?"

My pulse bounces in my neck as I pull her beanie off and smooth the static from her hair. This is the moment. It's not where or how I pictured telling her, but the words are coming out and—

"It sounded kind of like you might have a crush on me, but I don't want to assume anything." She stands on tiptoe and presses against me, pushing me into hyperdrive.

I turn her and pin her against the wall, my mouth finally —FINALLY—all over hers like it's dreamed of being all day. Mmm…strawberry bubblegum…She tastes like strawberry freakin' bubblegum. Her mouth's so warm and it's telling me things she'll never have to say out loud. It's speaking its own language and I understand every word. Mm-hmm…aw, yeah…Comprende, baby…I want you that much too… gotcha…loud and clear…

"You're the best kind of torture," I groan against her lips, catching my breath. If she knew what she was doing to me, she'd be scared, because my thoughts are not the purest. I haven't even told her I love her, but I do, and it makes keeping my hands off her like resisting gravity.

She unzips her jacket without breaking lip contact, and when my eyes snap open and meet hers, I grab her zipper and yank, shoving the jacket off her shoulders until it drops to the floor. Only her jacket. Still safe.

But her hands are in my hair and a hormone tornado rips up my insides, uncovering all my Mei feelings, flinging them through my body. My fingers flex over her hips, urging her closer until she breathes my name and something powerful—like superhuman powerful on a natural disaster scale—has to stop me because my hands are on her thighs, lifting her so she can wrap her legs around my waist, crush my ribs, squeeze the life out of me, kill me in this most heavenly way.

Blood and adrenaline drag race through my veins, flames trailing them, no brakes. Like my hands, lifting off her shirt. My eyes slip and my control follows. Mei. Black, lacy bra. Hints at everything it's hiding.

Motorcycle, Mei, motorcycle, Mei, motorcycle.

Mei.

Now.

The silky skin under her ear melts beneath my mouth, and I rip off my jacket, my shirt following with her help. Her hands are on my bare chest, and I close my eyes, wishing there wasn't a huge tape barrier between the rest of my skin and her fingers.

Her hands make their way to my back, and she pulls me

closer, her fingernails digging in. Everything goes into overdrive and I'm frantic—need her so much, I'm shaking.

When her hands go to the button of my jeans, I almost choke, pull back. "Stupid proverb," I pant. "Bad joke—anything." But her mouth is on my neck and she's pulling me closer. If something stupid doesn't come out of her mouth right now, I'll do something stupid. But Dad's gotta know how amazing this feels. Why has he kept me from this? Why did I ever decide to wait? The world could detonate around me, and I wouldn't notice because it would match the white-hot fire in my body.

I'll buy my own motorcycle.

I lower her to the couch, my hands gripping her thighs, a siren blaring in my head. It mingles with the crackling in my brain, and I force myself to diagram the moment at lightning speed:

Mei—red hot. Me—in flames. No space between us, just a tangle of arms and legs and enough oxygen being heavily breathed to keep multiple cardiac arrest patients alive. Flaming arrows point out all the hot spots and the percentages of me messing everything up blinks in red: **99.99999%**

A picture of Mei from the night I watched Nick eating the bottom half of her face flashes in my mind. Another of her bruised face, Nick's signature all over it.

No.

I don't wanna be like him. Don't wanna take and don't want this to end the way these things always end. Guys on the soccer team brag all the time about who they got with the night before, laughing when they tell the guys what they said to the girl to get what they wanted. Jeff and Ty both lost their girls after they did it. Same story for every guy on the soccer team. Dad. My mom. Too many endings.

But how is that even possible? My hands know exactly what to do. And she's telling me without saying a word how much she's feelin' it and I'm feelin' it and it feels better than any motorcycle and—

I lose it, crawl over her, lacy bra and everything under it pressed against my chest. Heart against heart, mine pounding a warning.

I drop my forehead to hers, squeezing my eyes shut and thinking of the ugliest thing I can. A landfill…steaming, filthy landfill. And rats. All over. Flea-infested, rabid rats. Or a report card riddled with Bs, Cs…Ds…Tiny baby Marcuses everywhere. The end of us.

I pull away, dropping my head to her collarbone. "Just… give me a minute." I rub her arms, willing myself to cool down.

Cool. Cold. That's it—glaciers. Glaciers everywhere. Ice cold water lapping at my feet. And I'm shivering. In my underwear. No—not my underwear. Fully clothed. Layers and layers of clothes. Shivering fully clothed. In Antarctica.

"I'm sorry." I breathe, raising my head to meet her eyes as I shift her knee off my ribs. "I almost wrecked everything."

"You could never wreck anything," she whispers, her words trailing down my neck. "Everything with you is perfect."

Her hands grip my hair and somehow, her body's even closer. I grit my teeth as I try to shut down my senses. My hands grip her waist.

"Mei." My voice is gone, my resolve shattered in tiny, heroic pieces around us. "This isn't me just saying no for the fun of it. If we do this now—and trust me, I want to—I just… don't want us to end like my mom and dad did. I don't wanna rush any part of anything with you. I do, but I don't."

She catches her breath and sits up, then presses her lips together before talking to her hands. "Or this isn't the way you pictured it happening. Not perfect enough." She looks up, holds my eyes.

I swear. "This has nothing to do with perfect, obviously. I

just…why does it have to be here? On my couch, when my dad could walk in any minute?"

She swallows and looks at me, then slides off the couch, her back to me.

"Can we talk about this?"

She shakes her head. "I shouldn't have come over tonight."

"Mei…" I swallow the heat scorching my throat. "I wanna take things slow so we don't mess everything up. I don't wanna keep lying to my dad and really earn my motorcycle."

"I can't compete with a motorcycle. Or be perfect for you." She looks away, shaking her head. "This was never going to work."

Her words roll over me, circle like a hurricane. My mind slams on the brakes, skids, tries to understand what she's really saying. "Wait. So you're out?" The words are so heavy, they drop between us like boulders I have to scramble over. "Is this all you wanted from me? And you didn't get it so you're done?" I swear and shake my head. "I happened because my mom took what she wanted from my dad and left. And yeah, he's not blameless, but I don't wanna make their mistakes." Frustration, anger, and confusion tangle in a frayed ball in my chest and press against my aching ribs until I'm on my feet.

"And you think I'm like her?" She turns, shaking her head and swiping at a tear, but when I can't find a response, she scoffs, "You do. You think I'm her even though you don't even know her. And obviously you don't know me, either."

"You're right—I don't know you because you won't let me in. For all I know, you've been having a good laugh with your friends and doing whatever you do with Face Eater when I'm not around."

Her mouth opens, and I wish I hadn't said it like that but I'm ready to catch whatever explanation comes out because at least it will finally be something. But she closes her mouth, shakes her head, and all the words back into their hiding place. "I have to go."

I swear, hands on my head as I turn away from her. I should stop her, but I need to puke. Throw up regret. Fear. Panic. Dad's right: girls just mess with you. I forgot Mei's one of them. But she so, so is, and she's officially messed me up.

I whirl back around when she crosses the room toward her shirt, then her jacket. "Why won't you tell me what's really going on?"

She shakes her head, her shirt and jacket pressed to her chest like a shield as she crosses the room, bending to grab her beanie, her hand trembling.

"You can't just leave. We—"

My head snaps toward the door when someone punches in the code on the other side of it. My eyes skid back to Mei who's frozen in the middle of the living room, no shirt.

I dive toward her, but I'm too late and light from the hallway spills into the dark apartment and all over us as Meemaw breezes into the living room in a flutter of scarves. I whirl around as her hand finds the light switch, one million watts spotlighting me, frozen, choking on hysteria, an almost-topless Mei behind me.

Meemaw jumps when her eyes land on me, and she drops her bag. "Oh!" One hand flies to her chest, the other braced against the wall. "Marcus!" Her face falls while her eyebrows leap, taking my heart and temperature with them.

Mei's a blur as she sprints past me and out the door, disappearing into the hallway. My eyes flick to Meemaw who watches Mei go then stares at me, and I plaster a tight, wobbly smile on my face. "Hey…" I'm breathing like I just scaled the wall and dropped in through the window.

She pushes the door shut behind her. "Oh my." Her eyes run up and down me. "Oh my, oooh my." She clears her throat, blinks a few times, then bends and picks up her bag.

My eyes follow every movement as she sets it on the table and pats it a few times before looking back at me and sighing.

"Why don't you put on your shirt." She waves her hand toward my bare chest. "Then come give me some sugar." She opens her arms, waving her hands for me to come closer. "Seems you have plenty to spread around tonight. Come 'ere, baby."

I blink and swallow scorching, metallic panic and grab my shirt from the floor. I pull it on before jerking toward Meemaw and wrapping my stiff, paralyzed arms around her. My whole body has seized. I've gone from overheated to hypothermic.

She squeezes me tight while I try to ignore that she just saw Mei shirtless and knows I'm the one who got her that way. She'll tell Dad. He'll take back the motorcycle. If Mei's not already done, she will be now.

"Sorry to interrupt the festivities," Meemaw says as she rubs my back, then pulls away and holds my shoulders, plastering a smile on her face. "Thought I'd surprise everybody but turns out, I'm the one who got a surprise!"

I run my hands down my face, shaking my head, my eyes on everything but her face when I drop my hands.

"Didn't realize you were throwing a topless party tonight but looks like I kind of ruined it for you two." She gestures toward the door.

I close my eyes, swear under my breath, and nod. "Meemaw…I…" I what? Just wanted to see Mei's underwear? Was getting ready to check her for breast cancer? I shake my head, my face burning, legs numb. Testosterone slumps in a cold, hard lump in my toes and I drop to the couch.

When her hand rests on my face, I open my eyes. "Ah, Marcus, hon. This isn't the first time I've walked in on an eighteen-year-old male Miller in a compromising situation. Just didn't expect to find my grandbaby fixin' to make a great-grandbaby for me." She pulls a Dr. Pepper from her purse and drops beside me, taking a long swig.

I open my mouth, but she goes on. "You best be glad it was me and not your daddy. You might've found yourself in a closet until you die." She turns her head toward me, blinking. "Does Raymond know about this young lady? Because he's never mentioned her and I'm pretty sure he would…"

"No—he doesn't. And we…she and I…haven't…" The words squeeze out of my raw throat. "We've never done anything like that before. Just…got carried away."

"So, I *really* interrupted, then."

I lean forward on my knees and clasp my hands between them, hanging my head. "I totally lost control."

"Mmm. Yes, well…happens to the best of 'em."

"I promised I wouldn't," I say to my feet.

She rubs my back, her nails trickling over my t-shirt. "Seems you need to find a reason that will help you keep control. Especially if you really love that gorgeous girl." Her voice smiles. "Do you love her?"

I close my eyes and dig my toes into the carpet, nodding. "Yeah. And I know it's stupid—we're eighteen. Trust me—given myself that talk a couple hundred times. But I just…fell hard for her the night we met. Couldn't shake it. Tried to control it. Massive failure, as you saw." I rub my hands down my face.

"You've always felt things deeply. Girls like that about boys. Probably the reason Raymond made that silly bet with you. Not that I disagree with him insisting you keep things tucked away." She takes a sip of her soda. "But what boys your age don't understand because your hormones are like fireworks, is that sex is not love and love is not sex. No sense confusing your brain with all the emotions that come with playin' tangle toes too early."

I glance at her, my face blazing. "Where do you come up with this stuff?"

She cackles and pats my arm. "The motorcycle bet was just a way to keep you from makin' the same mistakes your daddy did. But…" She sighs. "Raymond really needs to stop makin' you a prisoner of his past choices. He's carried that around for way too long. He could have been married and happy all these years instead of beatin' himself up and hating womenkind." She plays with the tab on her soda can. "But I'm only his mama so what do I know?" She rolls her eyes, her earrings swinging against my shoulder. "Your daddy has done an incredible thing, raisin' you into a spectacular young man but it hasn't been easy on him or you." She rubs my back and goes on. "I'm happy you've decided to give girls a chance. Maybe consider your speed, though. Find that reason to keep control and think about what's best for both of you long term. Saves you a load of heartache and regret down the road."

We sit shoulder to shoulder in silence like we did every summer on her porch swing during storms, talking about things that should've been embarrassing but weren't with her. My body relaxes and I wish I could curl up against her like I did when I was a kid so she can tell me everything with Mei's gonna be okay.

"Your mama decided not to be a mama and even though she's moved on, I know in my mama heart that she regrets it every day. Even models have regrets. Especially when she saw your graduation announcement, I bet."

I turn my head toward her. "How'd she see my announcement?"

Meemaw sets her empty can on the coffee table and sits straighter on the couch, then turns toward me, her hands folded in her lap. "Your mama's in L.A. I saw Iris—her mama, your other meemaw—at the Piggly Wiggly a few weeks back and got Olivia's address. Sent her an announcement." She shrugs. "Thought she'd want to see her baby who's not a baby anymore and looks an awful lot like her."

I stare at Meemaw, thinking about the only two pictures I've seen of my mom. What her face might've looked like when she got my announcement—a stranger she never wanted to know. Half of her somewhere in the world—up the coast—she didn't care to meet.

"Why'd you do that? I don't need her in my life."

"I know, hon, but your mama has a right to know the fabulous person she brought into this world. I'm just proud of you, that's all. Wanted to show you off a little, I guess. Show her what she missed."

A wall of emotions made of my feelings toward my mom, disappointing Meemaw, lying to dad, and my argument with Mei barrels toward me, slams against me. I need to call Mei and explain—talk it out with her—but the way she looked at me right before Meemaw walked in said things I don't wanna hear. It can't be over. She didn't mean it just like I didn't mean some of the stuff I said. But what if she did?

I grunt like I've been gut-punched, then lean forward, elbows on my knees as I stare at the carpet. I squeeze my eyes shut, but too late. Tears burn down my face and I swipe at them. "Please don't tell Dad," I say into my hands. "I promise I'll tell him, I just…please."

Meemaw sighs. "I won't say anything to him, baby. This is your deal. But in the meantime, why don't you tell me everything that's causing those tears."

CHAPTER 21

Wrapping my coat tighter around me, I walk faster to outrun the last hour, sweating despite the crisp night. Burning with shame and embarrassment after Marcus's grandmother walked in on us half naked. Fighting. Frustrated. Messy.

I walk faster, like I can get away from myself. Things were just fine until my hormones took control. I shouldn't have thrown myself at him even if I'm completely in love with him. I thought he felt the same way. I thought I saw it in his eyes. But he wasn't so ready to throw away his future and his relationship with his dad, and I wasn't ready to tell him the truth about my mess of a life.

I haven't seen him that frustrated, even after Holden and Xander. When it poured out of him tonight, I emotionally retreated. Like I've done my whole life with Mama and Baba and, more recently, Nick. But never with Marcus.

When he asked me to tell him the truth about my life, everything inside me shut down, reminding me to stop pretending. Telling him won't change my life, and Marcus deserves the truth. Until tonight, he's allowed me to keep my secrets, even gotten hurt over them. He didn't do anything to deserve that. So we're over before we even really started.

Tears prick my eyes as I round the corner, but my Marcus thoughts screech to a halt because Nick's standing at the front entrance of the restaurant talking to Baba. I take a step back, but Nick's gaze flicks to me and pins me in place while a thin smile stretches his lips.

"Just the person I came to see." He holds out his arms and walks toward me, dark memories running ahead of him and slamming into me. Blood on a flower rug. Chandelier. King size bed. Pain. Shame. Realization.

I swallow all of it in a bitter lump. I'm trapped between him and all the secrets I'd have to dodge to run back to Marcus's. My voice cowers deep inside me when Nick wraps his arms around me in a full body strangle.

"I've missed you. But I have good news. Great news, actually." He pulls away, his hand sliding to my lower back as he turns us toward Baba. "My table ready?"

I straighten to minimize contact between his hand and my back where Marcus's fingers were ten minutes ago.

"It is." Baba gestures to the door.

"Wonderful." Nick reaches for my hand, pulling me behind him, my legs stiff, ready to run in another direction—anywhere that's not here. But I have to stay and pretend Nick matters to me, just like I've been pretending in my texts to him.

I follow him through the dining room to his table where he pulls out my chair. I slide into it, the wood hard and unyielding, and I swallow fear as he sits across from me. The flame of the flickering candle on the table bends in his breeze, throwing sharp shadows on his face.

Ya Ting glances at me and my eyes never leave hers as she gives a weak smile and sets down water glasses before taking our orders. I will her to see my desperation to get away, but Nick's attention is fixed on my face like a set of claws piercing sensitive skin. He's going to peel me open, put slashes in me that leak all I've hidden from him. But maybe he'll see how empty I am and realize I'm not worth his time.

Ya Ting leaves, and I try to think of any excuse to call her back, but Nick's attention digs in deeper, clawing at nerves, and I almost dare him to rip me open. He throws a beaming smile at me like a blade, severing my thoughts.

"Tell me everything I missed while I was gone."

I stare into the dark holes that are his eyes. Does he not remember what he did to me? Is he going to say nothing about his guys following me? Hurting Marcus?

I dig my nails into my thigh under the table. "Umm…Just homework and restaurant." My restless hands go to my fork, and I rub the handle until my fingertip burns.

"And that's exactly why I will get you out of San Francisco. You'll experience something new and exciting. In fact," He pulls his phone from his pocket and clicks it on, swiping the screen. "I showed Chef Torres a few pictures of your creations and she was impressed." He flashes me a picture of a French Asian fusion recipe I made up a few months ago. When I thought my future was straightforward. Back when I wasn't afraid of Nick. Or aware that Marcus and happiness could be part of my life.

"She said she'd love to see more from you."

I press my lips together and force them into a wobbly smile. "Wow. That's great." If only my heartache and fear would let some excitement through.

"It takes a lot to impress her, but I think I managed to." He leans back, folding his arms over his chest. "And it's only going to get better. I found us an apartment in L.A. with unbelievable views, brand new, best of the best. All it's missing is you."

I swallow and glance at the table, hoping to find a response written on it, but he squeezes my hand and I look up at him. My emotions are no longer rooted, and words fly past them. "It sounds amazing, but I'm not sure I'm ready for all that and…I don't know, I just—"

"You're just confused." Nick tilts his head. "That's the natural consequence of playing house with the detective's son."

My eyes snap to his, my pulse rapid gunfire, and I open my mouth to fire back an equally rapid denial, but Nick shakes his head.

"While I've been busy coordinating a beautiful future for us, you've been betraying me and your family." He shakes his head slowly. "I don't know this side of you—the total disregard for our plan and for what I'm doing for you." He reaches for my hand, but I pull it back. He hesitates, then goes on. "I know I've made mistakes, but we've gotten through them. Would you turn your back on everything you could have for some little boy whose father could snatch your dreams and send you all back to Taiwan?"

"That's not—"

"Don't interrupt me." His voice lunges at me and I ball my fists in my lap to resist throwing my hands over my face like a shield. "I've given you everything you could possibly want, but it's not enough, I guess. And what's so baffling is how much you're willing to throw away for a boy. I understand being curious, but you and I both know this can't last. It's impossible. You know that right?"

"Let me just tell you what—"

"No. Let me tell you." He sits forward, his voice a low clap of thunder. "You're a brilliant chef but not brilliant enough on your own, so next Thursday, you're going with me to L.A. to meet Chef Torres. You will intern with her over the summer because I will not let you embarrass me by backing out. You've been telling me about your dreams for years and I'm making them happen. We'll live a life of complete luxury —culinary school in Napa in the fall, open a restaurant when you finish. Become the next big thing on the L.A. food scene. What more could I possibly give you?"

My eyes strain to hold in confused, misdirected tears I should have cried for Marcus but will waste on my own stupidity. I bite my quivering lip. What I used to see as my chance at freedom is coming out of Nick's mouth like chains. I don't want to work with him, but I don't want to be stuck here forever, around the corner from what could have been. Even though what could have been ended when my shirt hit the floor.

My face burns and my voice is thin like it might snap. "I could have done it myself and saved you the trouble." I picture Chef Marco in his white coat, elbowing his way through a crowd to tell me I'm going places. On my own, not because of Nick.

Nick smiles at the table, then looks back up at me. "You'd have to start at the bottom like everyone else. It would take you years to get a chance like the one I'm handing you."

I curl my toes and search his face, my neck tight with anger and hatred. "Why?" He knows about Marcus. And that I've been avoiding him—lying to him with every text. He has to know I don't feel the way he wants me to feel about him. I dig my nails into my thighs. "Why are you doing this?"

He tilts his head. "Because. You didn't get to this country without my father's help and I'm the one keeping you in it. You want out of your house but can't do it without me. I'm making that possible for you because I've always loved you, despite how you choose to repay my generosity." He folds his hands on the table and talks to them. "All I want is the best for you. So, tell me how that makes me the bad guy."

When he looks up at me, my thoughts slump, deflated, because he's right. I can't get out of my house without him. I can't get into culinary school—or into any college—on my own because I'm not even supposed to be in America. Nick and his connections are the only way for me to stay and do anything. Not even Marcus could have changed that.

Nick reaches across the table and grabs my hand, his thumb moving along my knuckles. "I know you're scared, and I know you have your plans, but they won't work without me. People will get hurt. Your family…me." He rubs my hand. "The detective's son." His voice scrapes against my ears as he tightens his grip on my hand.

I tense, fighting the urge to rip my hand away.

"You can have everything. Or nothing. Your choice."

The meaning behind his words oozes into my empty spaces.

"Don't you see how beautiful your life could be? How easy and different from all this?" His dark eyes scan the dining room before landing on mine again, pouring black into me and just before I drown in realization, I nod once. An hour ago, I was ready to give myself and all my secrets to Marcus. Now, I'm reminded I have nothing that's mine to give.

Nick's smile broadens but doesn't add any light to his tone. "There's the girl I love. I knew she would come to her senses. You've forgiven me and I forgive you." He picks up his water glass and takes a long, demanding drink, then sets it down and leans toward me. "So let's talk about L.A."

He shifts the conversation to Chef Torres's restaurant. A black-tie event. A dress. Jewelry. Something about showing me off. How I should act and what I should and should not say. I can't hear any of the details over the sound of my mind frantically beating on Marcus's door. But I can't run to him. I can never see him again. His voice will never rumble through me, saying nerdy things that make me laugh. Asking questions that dig around my soul. I'll never feel his hands running through my hair. His body wrapped around mine like a shield.

I'll never get to tell him the truth.

If I let Nick's darkness flow into me, it will suffocate all my secrets, all my guilt, all my Marcus memories and happiness and hope. But empty has to feel better than fragments of myself tearing me open from the inside. Letting Nick in is the quickest way to kill it all and put me back in reality.

I stare right into the darkness behind his eyes through the rest of dinner, only closing mine when Nick's lips force mine open in his version of making me understand before he leaves the restaurant.

When he's gone, his darkness hangs from me, trails me up to my room. It pulls me to the floor and floods me as I sob out whatever's left inside me until my phone buzzes, throwing light into the black silence.

I uncurl from my ball on the floor and pull it out, clutching my throat as I read:

> Marcus: I'm sorry Mei. Everything was moving so fast and then Meemaw walked in and holy freak. I'm sorry about all of it. All the things I said before she came. How frustrated I got. Meemaw wanted to chat me up so I couldn't text until now. Can you talk?

I blink through the haze in my head made of hope mixing with reality. End it. Now. If Marcus and I weren't already hanging by a thread, Nick cut it, and what we had dropped to the ground and shattered along with my hope. Marcus would have eventually seen my world and ended things, anyway. He would never have understood. I don't understand it either.

I hold my breath, stare at the screen that's alive with Marcus's words. But my stiff, cold fingers type, then slide over the send button:

> Mei: I think we should take a break.

Another buzz:

Marcus: WHAT...? No. We just need to talk it out. I'm sorry I got mad and said things I didn't mean. I talked to Meemaw and everything's cool with her. We can work through this. Just please answer your phone.

My phone vibrates with an incoming call, and I put my hand over my heart so it can't hear Marcus's call, then quickly text before I lose my nerve:

Mei: I need some space.

My video chat beeps and Marcus's picture grins at me so brightly I squint, then close my eyes and trap the picture, dropping my phone face down on the carpet to suffocate the beeps. Two seconds later, another text vibrates my phone, and I take a deep breath, flipping it over to see the screen.

Marcus: Literal space or figurative?

My chest tightens, but this is the only way to keep my hope dead:

Mei: Both.

I hurl my phone at the wall, hoping it shatters, then curl back into a ball.

A few minutes later, someone knocks on my window and I press my palms to my eyes, swipe at tears. Three taps—three times, pause, two more taps. Not any someone. Marcus.

Sitting up, I stare at the drawn curtains like I can sweep them aside with my eyes. My feet flex. All I have to do is open the window, tell him the truth. Run from here, go wherever he goes. But Nick's darkness is all over me; I don't want Marcus to see it, so I curl back into a ball on the floor, digging my nails into my arm until the knocking stops.

The bell rings and everyone in my calculus class pours from the room to start their three-day weekend. The seniors are going to Santa Cruz tomorrow for our final class trip. Most of them, anyway. I can't step out of my apartment without worrying Nick's guys are following me. They're constant reminders of my consequences. Xander followed my bus to school today and I just hope Marcus made it home last night after he came to my fire escape. He's been hurt enough by my mistakes.

I slip across the hall to the bathroom and lock myself in a stall. Taking a shaky breath, I pull my phone from my satchel, turn it on, and wait for the buzz that is Marcus on the other end. Not reading his texts for the last four hours is me putting space between us. Even though what I want is exactly the opposite and my eyes are starved for his words:

> Marcus: Trying to respect your "SPACE" but withdrawals are killing me. Will you please call me? Text, note, whatever. Just talk to me.

I hold my phone to my heart like I can shove his words inside me, and close my eyes, swallowing a sob when it buzzes again, my heart beating toward it.

> Marcus: MEIIIIIIII!!!! *#@%, *#@$, *#@%!

> We are not over. We're not supposed to have an end remember?

I stare at my phone until the words go blurry. Marcus will eventually find the end, but right now, his texts are all I have, and I read them over and over until my phone buzzes again. I take a deep breath, letting it out before reading:

Marcus: I miss you so bad. Please talk to me.

A tear escapes and I swipe it away. If I could respond, I'd tell him 'miss' isn't a strong enough word for what I'm feeling. Sorry isn't a strong enough apology. I'd tell him I meant it when I said I loved him. That it hasn't changed and never will. I'd tell him the reason for the secrets. If I was in charge, I'd never give Marcus a reason to run from me like I ran from him.

My phone rings and I silence it when Mmm blares from the screen. I stare at the beautiful letters, picturing the beautiful boy they belong to until the call goes to voicemail, joining eight other messages I've forced myself to ignore.

I burst out of the stall, clutching my phone, not caring which of Nick's guys will be waiting outside the school to make sure I go straight home without any detours. I don't care if I never make it home. All that's there is fear and dread over going to L.A. with Nick next week and what my life will look like after that.

What I want is Marcus's arms wrapped all the way around me until I am hidden in his safe, happy world. I want the tenderness of his lips on my neck that tell me exactly how he feels without saying a word. His laugh and the funny stories he tells me and the way he points out weird things I never would have noticed. Our hours of talking because we always have more to say but never enough time. His confidence. How he always wants to know my opinion and asks me a million questions. The way his brain works, and his smile when I walk into the room. How much he loves his dad. That he keeps the promises he makes. How, for one brief, shiny moment, he pulled me into his perfect world, not knowing anything about me, not caring when he found out I'm not safe or perfect. In that small moment, I felt what it was like to be perfectly happy.

I hurry down the hallway, past my classroom, past the

offices. Running from everything and toward nothing. My phone buzzes again and I veer toward a corner, look at the screen, the words squeezing oxygen from my lungs. I lean against a locker as what's left of my heart crumbles:

> Marcus: I love you Mei.

CHAPTER 22

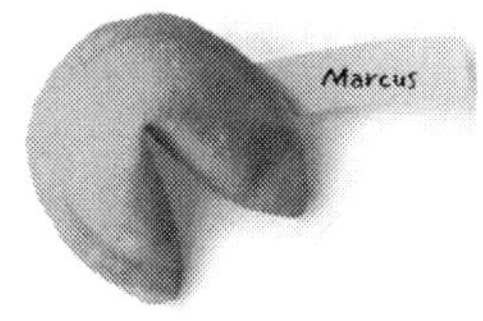

Mei,

Three days. No response. Seems kinda permanent. If you were here, like you were three days ago, I'd tell you I love you at least once a minute. Maybe open my window, yell it to all of SF so maybe you'll hear me and come back.

I stare down at the street from my lawn chair on the fire escape. Maybe if I concentrate hard enough, Mei will appear, and everything will go back to before we fought. Before Meemaw walked in.

I shift in my chair, away from the embarrassment that's stalked me since that night. I usually hate when Meemaw leaves, but this time, I'm glad she's staying at Aunt Audrey's so I don't have to put so much effort into avoiding eye contact.

Now if Mei would just call me, I could apologize. Again. She could explain everything she's left unexplained and prove she meant what she said when she told me she loved me. I'd know she wasn't playing me. We'd keep making plans that have nothing to do with her family or Face Eater or Dad or a motorcycle. I'd show her she means way more to me than any of it.

But it's 5:30 AM. She's probably not awake. Unless she can't sleep, either.

Pulling my beanie down lower, I tighten the blanket around my bare legs. Haven't been warm since Mei ran out. Been out here for hours and my eyes still refuse to shut. My hands won't let go of my phone. Just in case Mei decides she's done with space.

"Hey."

I look over my shoulder as Dad climbs out the window to join me on the fire escape. He's shirtless, and for 36, still rockin' it. I feel like the old man here.

"Hey." I turn back around in my chair.

"Kinda early to be out here. Everything all right?"

No. I'm so messed up. I went to her apartment after she left, but her curtains were closed. I climbed her fire escape, knocked on her window, but the curtains never moved. Her ladder's been pulled up every day since, shutting me out. I've sent 43 texts. Left twelve voicemails. No response. Nothing.

"Yeah. Fine."

Dad nods as he leans against the railing, looking out into the foggy morning. "You've been kind of quiet the last couple days. You feeling okay?" He gestures toward my beanie and blanket.

Kinda like I've been ripped apart.

"Just cold."

He frowns and turns to face me, crossing his arms over his chest. "Well…you were a rock star at your game yesterday. Perfect one for your meemaw to see. She screamed like a madwoman, and you kicked the hell out of that ball. Not sure where you got your skills, but hey—I'm proud of you, even if I can't take credit for it."

He wouldn't be proud of me if he knew what Meemaw knows about me and Mei. If he knew how many times she's been in The Clubhouse, and what I almost did with her in our living room...

My stomach flips. "Thanks."

Dad studies me. "Something's up M.C. What's on your mind?"

She's not on my mind—she's in it, through it. All over it. So much for space.

I shrug. "Why do you think you and my mom didn't work out? I mean, I know she left, but, like...why...?"

His eyebrows jump and he goes still, then clears his throat. "Uh...well...that's actually a question I don't have an answer to. I only have guesses."

"What do you think happened? Besides her not wanting a kid." Did he ever have this feeling in the pit of his stomach that makes me wanna turn myself inside out to get rid of it?

"I think...uh..." He looks around like someone somewhere in San Francisco will answer the question for him. "I think we were too young." He meets my eyes. "And she had a different idea about where we were headed."

"Where did you think you were going?"

There's a question in his eyes, but he goes on. "I thought we'd always be together." He's far away now—eighteen years ago away. "Honestly didn't know what we were doing most of the time. Figured we'd just make it work no matter what." He shakes his head and laughs once. "We were on and off a lot. One night, we were at a party and things got a little intense and she ended up pregnant."

I shift in my chair. "So you wish you'd had a motorcycle bet with your dad?" I look down onto the street, my eyes wandering to Mei's building, mentally standing on her fire escape, waiting for her to open her window and her life to me again.

Dad laughs again, and it ricochets off the buildings as he shakes his head. "Nah. I mean, I wish I'd made different choices, yeah. But a motorcycle bet would mean you wouldn't be sitting here, so…wouldn't change it for the world. Things with your mom were just…one of those complicated things, you know?"

Yeah…complicated I do know.

"Listen, if you want to meet her or something, I can find out where she's at. Last I knew she was in New York, but I can ask around."

"Nah. No. Just wondering. Like you always say—girls just mess you up." So he doesn't know Meemaw sent her a graduation announcement, or that she lives six hours south of here. I wonder how bad it will mess Dad up if my mom shows up to graduation. Or me?

"Most do, yep." He stretches and I grab onto his words.

Most? What happened to "all women are awful"?

"That's why it's just you and me. Girl-free apartment without a trace of the feminine touch. But who needs it, right?"

It had a whole lot of feminine touching in it three nights ago, and I think I need it. My chest still tingles where Mei's body pressed against it. Pretty much all over it. I shift in my chair.

"Especially when you have a gorgeous, shiny new girl waiting for you in Lex's garage."

My eyes snap to his. "She came?"

"Couple days ago. I'm surprised you haven't seen the key hanging in the kitchen, teasing you." He rubs his hands together and smiles. "It's definitely teasing me, but gotta get you graduated and slip a big, red bow on her. Then? She's all yours."

I stare down at the street. The moment I've been anticipating for the last four years and I feel…nothing about it.

"Still planning on Stanford campus tour this afternoon?"

"Oh." I jerk my eyes to his, clear my throat. "Yeah." Totally forgot we signed up for that months ago. Pretty much forgotten everything in the past few weeks. My loyalty to

Dad. Promises. That I still need to tell him I'm not actually going to Stanford.

"Because I was thinking...Since your meemaw and Audrey have plans, maybe we could check out the new branch of The Clubhouse together. I'll get a couple hotel rooms, you can invite the guys, and we'll be back before church tomorrow. Sound good?"

I look up, surprised. I've been pretending this long, why not keep it up? Plus, it will get me out of here and might be the only time I step on Stanford's campus. "Sounds great."

Mei's everywhere. In the song playing in the restaurant at dinner. On the crumpled Chinese restaurant takeout flyer that tumbled across the sidewalk during the campus tour. In the package of vending machine Sour Skittles I couldn't stop myself from buying. She's in the lime air freshener in the elevator and the girl who was laughing hysterically at something her boyfriend said while we were supposed to be listening to the admissions counselor. She's in my head, on my skin, in my heart...her absence from my life stabbing it violently. It drops me to my knees on the abandoned soccer field and I clutch my stomach. Somehow, Mei's even affecting my digestion.

I have to talk to her. Tired of talking to myself, imagining what happened. I have to talk to her in the only way I can right now. I didn't wanna leave a note with Guo because I don't want her reading what I need to say to Mei, but I'm desperate.

I pull the Sharpie from my pocket and color another letter in "THE END" I drew on my arm in block letters. Once they're all filled in, it's safe to say Mei's gone for good. I take out the local real estate flyer handed to me on my way across campus and flip it over, using my leg as a desk:

Mei,

I'm sitting on an empty soccer field at Stanford. It's 8:21 PM. A bug is crawling up my leg. I'm overwhelmed with the details of my future. Wish I was coming here in the fall. Dad bought me a Stanford shirt and I'm wearing it, but still not sure how to tell him I'm going to USF. I have a headache, but nothing close to my heartache. Everything feels all wrong. Like that I had Greek fast food for dinner but wanted Chinese. That I haven't talked to you in three days. I can't stop freaking thinking about you but can't leave you another voicemail. I've already left 12. The worst (best?) thing is that I can't stop thinking about the way I felt when you told me you loved me. I can't stop thinking about how incredibly cool I am with being messed up as long as you're the one messing me up. It's been 76 hours, 12 minutes, and according to my very reliable watch, 34 seconds since I last saw you. 3 DAYS. I can't do this, Mei. I want you to mess me up every day because at least—

"Marcus?"

My head snaps up. Tavah Riggs walks cautiously toward me, and I shove the letter in my back pocket.

"Hey. Johnny invited some of us to meet you guys at some party, but you weren't there, and after bugging him while he and Sav were making out, he told me you were here. Mind if I join you?"

I stare up at her. Don't know what to say.

Tavah stops walking. "You do mind. Sorry."

"Hey, no—you're fine." Ah, seriously? "I don't mind. I'm just…sitting."

"You sure?" She tilts her head. She has incredibly shiny hair and lips. The combination is…bright.

"Yeah—definitely."

She sits on the grass beside me, leaving plenty of space between us. Just pretend I'm in chemistry and she's sitting next to me at our table. Easy.

"So, umm, Marcus…can I ask you something?"

I glance at her. She's pretty. I forgot. She's also the least complicated person on this soccer field right now and it's calming.

"Is it true, what everyone says about you?"

"Depends on what everyone's saying."

She tucks her hair behind her ear and stretches her long legs in front of her—tan, smooth, stretching for miles. "That you don't like girls. That you think you're too good for anyone at our school."

I laugh into the night, a burst of amusement and annoyance. "I like girls."

"I don't believe you," she grins.

If you'd been at The Clubhouse Wednesday night and seen what I was doing with a girl, you'd have no doubt. "Why not?"

"Because. It's like everyone's invisible to you."

Not everyone. There's one girl I see every time I blink. I choose my words carefully, scanning the field. "I just have this bet with my dad. I get a motorcycle if I stay away from girls." I shrug. "That's it."

Tavah's eyebrows rise. "Oh. Does he hate girls?"

"Kinda. He doesn't want them messing me up." Too late.

Tavah's laugh sounds like some kinda Middle Eastern musical instrument. "How would a girl 'mess you up'?" she asks, her eyes intent on mine.

Uh, she could walk into my life with her perfect skin and perfect hair, perfect body and her skinny jeans and let my hormones out of their cage. Everything that comes out of her mouth could be the most fascinating thing I've ever heard. She could smile at me for no reason and make me laugh until my stomach hurts. She could mess with my mind until I think I'm in love with her. Rearrange my priorities with one look. Thoughts of her could keep me up at night, hijack my homework or soccer or future. She could be carbonation in my veins. She could become everything to me. For starters.

"You okay?"

"Yeah." My voice is lower than usual, like it's taken the deep dive into my thoughts with me. I clear my throat. "Totally fine."

Except I'm totally not. I miss the way Mei checks out my legs. How she squealed when we rolled down that grassy hill on our walk around San Fran. How grass stuck in her damp hair. The way she watches my face when I touch her. How she bites her lip when she's trying not to smile. The smirk on her face when we talk with our eyes. Her eyes. Really miss those. And the way she fits inside my arms. How she lays her head against my chest and interlocks her fingers around my waist like she'll never let go. The way she said she loved me like it came from a secret place deep inside her only we'd ever been. And I believed her.

"Ah. A girl's already messed you up, hasn't she?"

I'm momentarily tempted to spill my emotions all over Tavah like some clumsy accident. But they're so close to the surface, I swear she can see them swimming. Like I'm an emotional aquarium.

I laugh. Not like Mei makes me laugh, but like if I don't laugh, I'll cry, but I need to keep my mouth shut because if I start talking about Mei, I won't stop. Then my head will catch up with my heart and I'll realize I'm not actually talking to Mei.

"What's so funny?"

I shake my head to my lap. "Was just thinking I'm like an emotional aquarium right now. You're looking right through me." Tavah looks through me, but Mei sees everything inside.

She throws her head back. Another musical moment. When Mei laughs like that, she puts her hand over her mouth, like she's trying to hold back her crazy girl. Tavah lets it fly.

"I'm curious to know what exactly an emotional aquarium looks like..."

"I don't know—you tell me."

She laughs again and shakes her head, glancing at me, then to the grass. "Okay, so…" She pushes hair out of her face and looks to the sky. "Really attractive." She picks a handful of grass. "I've had my eye on your emotional fish for a while."

Crickets chirp. A plane drones overhead. What do I say? WHAT DO I SAY? THAT SOUNDED LIKE A CONFESSION.

"They're more like attractive sharks, though." She throws the grass and watches it fall.

Oh. "Sharks?"

"Yeah—intimidating. Scary." She shrugs and looks at me.

"I'm not scary," I lock eyes with her, wondering if they've learned Eye Language yet. Nope. I miss Mei.

"Yes, you are—girls never know what you're thinking."

There's one girl who can see exactly what I'm thinking. I wish she could see what I'm thinking now. She'd call me back. She'd—

"I wish I knew what you were thinking right now." Tavah won't look at me. But I'm glad. She's new territory—all honest and ready to confess her deepest feelings and drag mine from me. "Sorry." She shakes her head and takes a deep breath.

"Why?" My voice is rushed, outrunning thoughts of Mei.

Tavah swallows. "I think I just needed to tell you how I feel so I can get over you."

Whoa. Hold up. Over me? "Over me?"

She smiles and nods. "Yeah. Over you."

"What exactly are you trying to—?"

"Please, Marcus." She rolls her eyes. "I'm not subtle. Surely you saw the neon signs saying I like you. A lot. Too much and for way too long."

Whoa. Okay. Aquarium closed. Come back…never.

"Give a crush six years and it feels bigger than a crush. And that's just the part of you I see. I mean, I definitely like what I see." She glances at me, suddenly shy. "I just wish I knew more about what I see." She pauses, takes a deep breath, and lets it out slowly. "Wow. This is harder than I thought it would be, although, to be honest, I knew it would be really hard."

I smile at her. "What do you mean?"

She tilts her head back and smiles at the sky. "Just…Okay, here goes." Straightening, she swivels to face me, crossing her legs and gripping her knees. "I've been asked to prom. Skylar Sanchez texted me tonight. He's great. I was super excited and was about to respond and say yes. But…what I really want is to go to prom with you." She swallows and nods, and her words float to me like dust that hasn't settled. "Johnny said you aren't going, but it's our senior year, and I just…" Looking at the grass, she closes her eyes and rushes, "Want to go with me? Maybe? Even a little bit?" She scrunches her nose and smiles, then glances at me before picking more grass. "Holy cow, this is hard. Sharks all over the place."

I open my mouth, close it. Stare at the dark field. I wasn't gonna go to prom. But I also wasn't gonna fall for a girl and then get messed up by that girl who won't talk to me.

Tavah's fingers play with a strand of her hair. This girl tells me exactly what she's thinking. So easy—no guessing. The guys are going to prom. I have nothing better to do but sit home and think about how not with Mei I am. "Yeah." I nod. "Sure. Let's go to prom."

CHAPTER 23

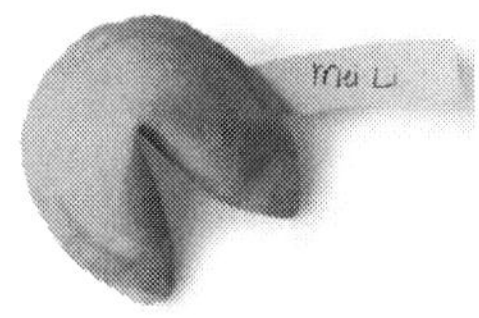

> Mei: My Nai Nai once told me that only 3 things matter: how much you loved, how gently you lived, and how gracefully you let go of things not meant for you. I experienced the first two with you. I'm not ready for the last. I don't know how to do that part. I'll never want to.

I lie on my bed and stare at my unsent text until my eyes well, then delete it. I've typed and deleted hundreds of texts this week, but I can't send any, ever again. Funny how "ever again" feels so long and so short at the same time. I've worked more in the past seven days than I have the last month and done homework in the time between to catch up before "ever again" starts today.

When I told Baba I didn't want to go to L.A., he said there are worse things that could happen to me. He said I'm going with Nick because he's done so much for our family, and "we" can help him with this new venture. It's the least we could do. "We", but not really *we* since it's my future that depends on Nick, not Baba's. Also, I'm going to L.A. because he said so.

As an added restriction and command, I'm not walking with my class during graduation next Wednesday because "we don't need to showcase ourselves."

So, in three hours, a car will pick me up. It will take me to the airport. When we land in L.A., I'll be escorted to Nick's penthouse suite in some hotel. Then, I'll wait for whatever happens next. Today, "ever again" can't last long enough.

All I can do is wish I wasn't going. That I wasn't part of this family. That I was with Marcus instead of moving farther from him. Or with Lin instead of hiding from her worried texts. I don't know what I would even say, though. I've written Marcus notes I'll never deliver, typed texts I'll never send. Told Harvey I can't go to Prom with him tonight. Avoided Guo Mama. Buried my face in my pillows to muffle the sounds my heart makes as it sinks in my tears. Stopped hoping. Marcus's texts stopped coming two days ago and my heart stopped beating and drowned.

But according to Baba, I'm so lucky. If this is luck, then Marcus did me a favor by taking Buddha even though he's no longer on his windowsill. He must have figured out Buddha brought him bad luck, too.

I lift my head off my bed and reach for Magic 8. I've asked it over and over if there's a way out of this. It hasn't given me a straight answer. But when I ask if Marcus is thinking about me, it says "Yes" every time, including this one.

I toss it to the end of my bed and grab my phone. My chest tightens and my body leans into hope but there's nothing from Marcus.

I roll to my back, scrolling through pictures for the 500th time. Us in front of Hippie Thai, me rolling my eyes and Marcus jutting out his chin. Marcus laughing and reaching for my phone as I snapped shot after shot of him. Marcus laying on his bed in a white tank top and loose-fitting sweatpants, one hand behind his head, blue eyes looking straight into the camera. A video he sent me of him shaving. The secret code he drew on his arm that translated to Marli, our couple name. A selfie with the chemistry equation he created to prove his chemical reaction to me. Selfie after selfie he took with weird things he saw on his walks home, funny captions for each one. Marcus lying on his back with a licorice rope jutting from his mouth while he winked at me. A shot of his wall chalkboard and the pie chart he drew about me. Him, wearing his lucky soccer socks, my name drawn in Chinese characters on the bottom. A shirtless selfie, a red Sharpie heart drawn on his chest with my name inside it. Another screen shot of a video chat when he showed me his new Adidas. An overhead shot of us lying beside each other under his window, Marcus kissing my temple while I smiled at the camera.

I shut off my phone on picture 134 of 368 and my heart retreats into its dark corner, but the phone lights up with a text from Lin: Coming your way babe. You can't avoid me forever.

I set it face down onto the nightstand, mad at myself for indulging in Marcus and making my chest tighter, my body achier. I drop my head back onto the bed until the door flings open and Lin's energy rushes in, pressing me further into my bed.

"Okay. What's wrong?" She drops onto my bed, snuggling me from behind and laying her head on mine. "You've been too quiet. Spill."

Her concern is permission for my tears and my silent sobs shake the bed while she rubs my back until words scratch up my throat. "Marcus and I broke up." I haven't said his name out loud for so long, it's grown too big inside my head and hurts coming out when I tell her everything about the fight and Marcus's grandmother and Nick and the threats. I can't stop the words once the verbal flood starts. "And now, I have to go to L.A. with Nick. Tonight, and there's nothing I can do about it. I tried."

She bolts up, looking like she's trying to chew and

swallow metal. "Are you serious? No. No way." She shakes her head as she slides off the bed and paces the room. "You can't go. I won't let you."

I watch her, my cheek smashed against my wet pillow. "He found out about Marcus. He'll retaliate—hurt him. Shut down the restaurant, get us kicked out."

"Tell Marcus. His dad—"

"Can never know," I break in, lifting my head. "You know why."

She drops to her knees in front of me, squeezing my hand. "You know I love you. But part of being your best friend is telling you when you're being stupid. And you are. In two major ways." She holds up her finger. "Number first: he's about six foot two, I think, but you've been all over those measurements, so you tell me. His legs are objects of greatness, his face was sculpted by the gods, and his body is—"

"Stop, Lin." I close my eyes, then snap them open when a too-clear picture of a shirtless Marcus rises in my head.

"That's what you had, and you can still have it. Unless you go to L.A. You had your first fight, not a breakup. One word from you and he'll be here, not me. And while I love hanging out with you, I won't make out with you. You're beautiful and everything, just not my type."

"In this easy solution, does Nick magically disappear?" I sit up and slump against my headboard, my body heavy. "If I don't do what he asks, people get hurt."

"What do you think is going to happen to you if you go with him? *You'll* get hurt, and not in the emotional, heartbreak kind of way. Don't even try to deny it. You know I'm right. And I'm so done talking about him. It's like pouring slime into my ears."

"Let him finish me off."

She rolls her eyes and pretends to vomit on my carpet. "You're being super dramatic. Ever thought there might be other options? Like running away?"

"And go where?"

Lin throws out her hands. "Anywhere. Somewhere Nick's not." She taps her chin and looks at the ceiling. "You can leave—start a new life. Avoid getting raped. Or worse." She grabs my hands. "You'll be safe. I mean, you won't get the boy, but you won't be with Nick. And I'll know where you are. We can talk every day. And when the coast is clear, and the dust is settled, I'll tell The Boy where you are, and he'll come for you."

The thought sinks in and spreads through me, taking root. This could work. I won't have to be with Nick. Not here, not in L.A. Except. I have about $350, a fake passport, and no driver's license.

I look at her hand, then her, and we sit in the idea until Baba's voice calls for me. We look at each other before I hesitantly push myself off the bed and step to the door, opening it just a crack. "Yes?"

"Hurry up, Mei Li—Chaz is here to take you to the airport."

I grip the doorknob as reality pours through the crack like liquid steel, hardening my insides. I turn to Lin. "What time is it?"

She checks her phone. "Almost four..."

Nick said six.

Baba's voice booms up the stairs. "Mei Li! Now!"

I close my eyes, mentally say goodbye to Marcus, then grab my duffle. Avoiding Lin's eyes, I open the bag and nestle Magic 8 inside before zipping it and hauling it onto my shoulder. It's 500 pounds of fear and regret, just like my feet, my head, my heart.

Lin stands between me and the door. "I'll go downstairs, create an emergency. We need to figure out a plan."

Baba's footsteps pound up the stairs and I jerk into motion, grabbing Lin's hand. "Walk me out. I'll text you on the way to the airport."

I stiffen in my seat as the plane dips into a right turn and descends toward L.A. I don't want any part of me to touch Chaz on my left or Xander on my right during this flight that can't possibly last long enough. The last time I was on a plane was from Taiwan to America. I hadn't known what was ahead of me then and wish I didn't now. This plane couldn't crash hard enough to satisfy me. Couldn't find a hole black enough to slip through and disappear.

When the fasten seatbelt sign went off earlier, I'd locked myself in the bathroom, connected to wi-fi, and texted Lin. We'd hurried through possible escape plans until Chaz had knocked and called my name. I'd stashed my phone in my bra and zipped my jacket. It's stayed zipped, heavy with unread texts full of ideas that could get me out of here.

I wish Mama had stopped this, but I guess whatever had been so important that night in Guo Mama's backroom wasn't important enough to actually do anything about it.

There's a car waiting for us when we land, and I expect it to take us to the hotel, but it pulls in front of a warehouse surrounded by a chain-link fence. My heart pounds in protest until Chaz talks to me over his shoulder from the passenger seat.

"Nick has something for you to wear to the gala. He's being generous, so take advantage of this rare moment."

"There are benefits to playing nice," Xander adds, and I throw open my door and get out of the car, slamming it to trap Xander's words inside. No amount of money or fancy clothes could make being with Nick worth it.

Xander and Chaz jump out of the car and walk on either side of me toward a warehouse door. I wait for them to slip a collar over my head and attach a leash. Nick must have told them I'm a flight risk. He's not wrong. But it's not just a risk

—I'm going to disappear as soon as I have a private moment to call Lin.

An elderly woman bows and tells Chaz and Xander in Mandarin that they can wait on the sofa before leading me through a towering maze of boxes and garment bags. Her enthusiasm bounces off the metal walls as she slides open a large door and scurries into a room made almost completely of mirrors. There are dozens of me, each a small, expressionless puppet on invisible strings.

"Mr. Nick picked a dress just for you. He says it would fit your curves perfectly." Without looking at me, she ushers me into a drafty, flimsy dressing room, then looks at me expectantly, motioning for me to undress.

I wait for her to leave so I can text Lin, but she motions again, so I turn my back and slip my phone out of my bra, zip it into my jacket pocket, and stiffen when she helps me out of my shirt. She unzips a garment bag hanging from the door and pulls out a black gown, motioning me closer. She helps me into it before leading me to a platform in front of the mirrors.

My eyes roam the black satin hugging my hips, gathering in the back before flowing to the floor. The V-neck dips to the middle of my sternum and the open back drops to just above my backside.

"You like it?" the ancient seamstress asks as she pulls the dress tighter, pinning it.

All I want is for the woman to leave the room so I can text Lin and continue our conversation about escape plans, but she's staring at me, waiting, and I swallow and shake my head. No. It's my funeral gown.

She stops and her eyes widen. "No?"

This dress shows more of me than I ever want Nick to see. It won't stop him from getting too close. I need a suit of armor. So no, I don't like it. The one thing I like—love—and that fit me perfectly is off limits thanks to "Mr. Nick."

"Mr. Nick came in and made sure all is taken care of. I do as he says."

She's frantic and there's a familiar fear in her eyes so I place my hand on her delicate shoulder and force a smile, responding to her in Mandarin. "Mr. Nick will be very happy." But Mei Li will never be.

"Good, good. I will have it delivered to his hotel room by 9 AM tomorrow." The old lady grins and nods, pinning the dress so tightly my breasts practically burst out, and when she shuffles out of the room, I stare into the mirror. This costume tells me everything I need to know about what this life will be.

The seamstress hurries back in and finishes pinning the dress, and I peel it off like I wish I could peel off this moment and all the moments waiting to pounce on me. She waits while I throw on my clothes, then walks me to the front. I need to find a bathroom and hopefully the lady won't follow me inside.

"All done?" a girl asks as she comes out of an office. She flips through a notebook, then looks up at me. "Mr. Chao's fiancé, yes?"

My eyes widen and I shake my head. "No—not his fiancé."

"Mei Li Zhang, yes?" She smiles through tight lips and when I nod, she says, "Come with me," then motions for me to follow her into the office. "Mr. Chao requested you choose something in here." She opens a door behind a curtain and when I step through it, the room shimmers. Jade pendants, cuffs, and earrings wink at me from shelves and hooks. Diamonds catch the light and throw it across the floor as I follow the girl to a glass case filled with jewels.

The girl smiles and raises her eyebrows. "Choose whatever you'd like, and we'll put it on Mr. Chao's account, per his instruction."

Account? In a warehouse full of dresses and jewelry? How

many fiancés does he have? But my pulse quickens when a thought shimmers off the diamonds and settles deep inside my mind. A future-changing thought that echoes Lin's words from earlier.

Diamonds could be the "how" part of my escape plan.

Show me more," I say to the girl, walking into the room.

Chaz pulls a keycard from his pocket and swipes it over the door which beeps then clicks. He pushes it open to let me in, but my legs lock, so he grabs my elbow and pulls me inside.

I step into the foyer, scan the sunken living area. The lights of L.A. blink beyond the floor to ceiling windows, a sectional sofa facing them like a throne for royalty to look over their kingdom of small, insignificant lives below. Chaz motions over his shoulder and I follow him toward an open door across the living area.

"This is your room," he says. "Be ready to leave for Chef Torres's restaurant in thirty. Nick will meet us there."

I close the door and lock it, then toss my bag on the bed and pull the velvet box from the gift bag nestled among my clothes. I swallow and peer inside at the diamond choker with matching bracelet and earrings that have to be worth more than a car. Definitely more than a plane ticket to wherever I decide to go. According to the sales lady, they were the most expensive items in the room. I don't think this is what Nick had in mind when he said to pick whatever I wanted, but this is my ticket out of here. My courage to survive this moment until the moment I need arises. This will pay for my new life.

I pull my phone from my jacket and send a picture of the jewelry to Lin: I have an idea. I set the box in the nightstand drawer and double check the bedroom door is locked, but Chaz's voice drifts from the other side of it and I lean closer.

"What's the ETA?"

"10:30," Xander answers and I hold my breath and lean closer to the door.

"Anything else I should know?"

"Nick wants them here thirty minutes after they land."

"That's not enough time," Chaz growls. "The ride from the airport takes that long."

"Wish I could give you more time, but—"

"No…you've done more than enough, Xan…"

I frown at Chaz's soft tone. Xan?

"What about Nick?" Chaz asks and Xander laughs once.

"You think he'll get his hands dirty? He'll make sure their dinner goes long so the job's done when they get back."

Chaz swears. "Yeah, okay. We'll make sure it gets done. It just might not be in the way Mr. Chao prefers."

"Don't take any chances, C." Fear and longing weigh down Xander's voice and I press my lips together and think about the women usually draped around Chaz. Maybe they're his suit of armor…?

"I'll be careful. I'm just tired of this. Nick crossed a line with Su Ling."

I straighten.

"She has kids. Nick played too close to home this time. He's being reckless and we're all gonna pay."

"I agree, but we can't turn him in. He'll retaliate."

"If we can't turn him in, maybe it's time to turn myself in. I can hand over what's left of the fentanyl, give the cops any info they need. I'd get ten years max, but it would get me out of this."

"Whoa, whoa, whoa. What?" Chaz's voice gets rough. "No, Xan. Don't leave me in this."

Everything on the other side of the door goes quiet, and I put my hand over my mouth, knowing I've heard way too much. But maybe it's exactly what I needed to hear.

CHAPTER 24

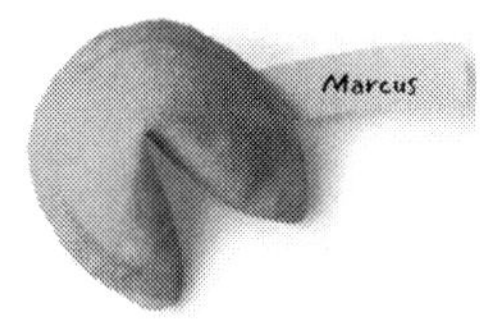

Mei,

It's Saturday. Ten days since we've talked. Tavah's gonna be here in a few minutes and I feel like I'm cheating on you. Is it possible to cheat on silence? On last week? On a ghost? If so…here goes.

Blue and orange strobe lights flash over our group as we mosh to the music thumping through the speakers. Heat and humidity stick to my neck and I unbutton my collar, then rip off my tux jacket and fling it onto a nearby table. Sweat slides down my temple and my face hurts from smiling, my throat hoarse from laughing and yelling over the music. No one in our group had a drop of alcohol at dinner but we're wired.

Ty and Raj take turns chest bumping me to the beat and rebel yelling while Tavah and her girls wind around and through us, breathless and laughing with their hands in the air, hips swaying. And, no surprise, Johnny and Sav are tangled together, moving in a slow circle as they make-out. As stupid as it looks and is, I turn my back to them because it hurts like Mei.

The crowd swells and Tavah jostles into me, ripping me out of the Mei moment, and I start jumping again, right in the middle of our group, Tavah in front of me. When the song ends, we stay facing each other, laughing and wiping our foreheads. I laugh down at her, plumping her puffy sleeves like pillows. "Oh no!" I yell over the thumping bass of the next song. "You're deflated! The 80s are dying!"

She throws her head back and laughs, her hair flying around her face since she danced it out of its clips earlier. I don't bother backing away as the crowd presses us together. I wanna know what it feels like to be close to this girl who's a popped bottle of champagne, bubbling and fizzing all over the place.

Her friends wiggle into our space, their neon dresses streaking in the dark, and we all sing along with the song at the top of our lungs, Tavah by far the loudest.

"No way!" I yell down at her, eyebrows raised. "You like this song?"

"Are you kidding?" Her smile explodes in the dark, reflecting pink light. "I LOVE this song. Can't get tired of it. I've tried." Her face shines with sweat and glitter from the sparkly stuff on her eyelids.

We jump to the beat, bumping against each other and everyone else, and when the song ends and slides into a slow one, I slip my hands around her waist, pull her to me, and lean in. "Slow dance?"

She smiles and nods, pressing her chest to mine as she wraps her arms around my neck. My fingers flex on her waist, sliding a little lower to her hips. Our knees and thighs brush against each other as we sway, her body moving with mine. She rests her chin on my shoulder, and I close my eyes. Mei would have to wear ten-inch heels for her chin to reach my shoulder. I clench my jaw. She'd also have to be here with me so her chin could be on my shoulder. Ten days. No calls, no texts. No late-night video chats. Just nothing but guilt, shame, regret, pain. Unanswered questions.

I lean my head against Tavah's, and her arms tighten around my neck, her body melting into mine. Her heart pounds against my chest, making me all warm and tingly, but I shift when my ribs complain. Everything about Mei hurts. Everywhere Mei used to be. If Tavah had bodyguards, she'd at least tell me ahead of time and explain exactly why they wanted to whoop me. She'd tell me when so I could prepare. And if Tavah and I had once been together but were over, she'd tell me exactly why. I'd never have to guess. Haven't had to guess once tonight. She even called me on Monday and asked for my measurements so she could get the perfect baby blue tux and shoes to go with the 80s theme. Told me all the plans. Warned me about the shirt ruffles.

When Audrey came over tonight before Tavah picked me up, she'd stroked with joy when she'd seen my ruffled shirt, then practically chained me to the toilet seat so she could do my hair in a big 80s way. She'd tried to get the details about what was happening with Mei. When I told her we broke up, she asked if I was okay. Told me she was concerned like any loving aunt would be but congratulated me for moving on and not holing up in my room. I avoided her eyes, just in case Meemaw had told her what she walked in on. I'd changed the subject and when Tavah had shown up at The Clubhouse wearing puffy sleeves and equally big hair and earrings, they'd cackled about it all. I'd watched the second girl to ever be inside The Clubhouse and wondered how Audrey and Mei would have gotten along. Doesn't matter anymore.

Dad had been surprisingly chill about the whole Tavah and prom thing. On the train ride home from Stanford, he'd been distracted by a text that made him oddly hyper, so I'd taken advantage of the moment and told him Tavah had asked me to prom. Maybe should've done that when Mei was a thing. No need now. Motorcycle's mine. Especially since

Dad gave me a 2 AM curfew and warned me for the zillionth time that only pregnancy happens after midnight, not motorcycles. In order for that to happen, I'd have to get these pants off and they're so tight, it would take serious effort from multiple people.

Now that the bass is mellow, I can feel my heart and wanna rip it out and put it in all of Mei's newfound space instead of having it trapped inside me. Wonder what Mei would think of the lack of space between Tavah and me right now.

If I never hear from her again, will I start something with Tavah? Will I feel the same way I did about Mei? Tavah's feeling pretty great right now, all silky and tight. She doesn't fit in the same places Mei does—did—but she fits in others I could definitely get used to. But would I hop a train to go see her at Berkeley? Would she do the same to spend the weekend with me?

Our heads rest against each other, our stomachs moving as we breathe, and when the song fades into another fast one, I pull back. "Gotta pee. Sorry—went a little crazy on the virgin daiquiris at dinner."

Her hands slide from around my neck and down my shoulders. "'Kay. Probably a good idea for me, too. Lots of jumping." She smooths her hair and smiles.

We ease apart and Johnny knocks his elbow against mine, whispering, "Gentleman's room. Now."

We weave through the crowd toward the door and when a couple of guys from the team yell my name, I stop to talk then catch up with Johnny. A cold rush of dry air washes over us as we step into the hallway and veer into the bathroom.

"Dude." Johnny unzips his pants and stands at the urinal.

"What?" I step to the one beside his and unzip.

"You and Tavah?" He gives me a sidelong glance, his popped tux collar jabbing his chin.

"What do you mean?"

"Pff." He shakes his head. "Kinda cozy, aren't you? For a guy who pretends he doesn't know about these mysterious creatures called women but somehow has all the right moves?"

"Got any pointers on how to slow dance without touching?"

"It's not just the dancing part." He zips his pants and steps away from the urinal and I meet him at the sink.

"Then what?" I focus on scrubbing my hands.

"You haven't laughed like this for a while. It's like you went emo and got all depressed and dark last week, but tonight, you're all laughing and off in your own little beautiful people world. And dinner?" He turns toward me, his hands soapy. "Talking the whole time, no pauses, sharing food. You took a sip of her drink, dude. I saw. I'm not even at that level with Sav yet." He rinses his hands, then shakes them dry.

"That's because you just share spit through direct contact *all* night. Why bother with straws?"

Johnny snatches a paper towel and checks himself out in the mirror while I stick my hands under the dryer. "You're into her," he calls over the roar. "Glad you're finally gonna make your move, Miller. Atta boy, that's all I gotta say. Atta *boy*." He flicks my ruffles as he passes toward the door, slapping the wall as we head into the hallway.

We turn toward the soda bar near the gym entrance. "Gonna get the lady a drink. See you back on the floor. Make your move, Miller. Make. Your. Move." He holds up a finger and tilts his head. "Motorcycle approved, of course."

I stand, straddling the lit hallway and the flashing, pulsing gym, and swallow guilt. I've had a great time with Tavah. I was all worried about the conversation, but we have too much to talk about and haven't really talked to anyone else. At dinner, we ordered things to share because we couldn't decide and were starving. And when she scooted closer, I'd checked out her lips and wondered what it would be like to kiss her now that there's permanent space between mine and Mei's.

But I shouldn't be thinking that about Tavah when last week, I was making out with Mei in my living room, only focused on her mouth and her body rippling beneath mine. Because if Mei called me right now, I'd drop everything to be with her again. But she hasn't and I can't keep pretending or hoping. I filled in the D in THE END on my arm just before Tavah came and Mei never showed up to stop me.

My throat burns with tears I've shoved down all week, and I close my eyes when my heart curls in on itself to smother the ache. I swear to myself. It's not possible to go from loving Mei to getting down with Tavah tonight. Unless I never really loved Mei.

No. I know what I feel. It's boiling me from the inside out. So, what am I feeling for Tavah, then? Felt pretty great before I talked to Johnny. Having her that close suffocated Mei thoughts. Now that I'm not next to her, Mei's moving through me again.

I push through a group of girls dancing up on their guys. Wave and nod to a few people as I slip around couples curled around each other, girls draped against their guys. Lights flash and I squint into the crowd, looking for Tavah.

I wave away a cloud of weed someone snuck in and edge along the flailing crowd. The rock in my stomach rolls around, and I spot her, dancing with her friends, all shimmery and silky. She's safe. Comfortable. I could easily slip into something with her. Couple more nights like tonight and I'd be all in. But no way would my feelings for her scare me like my feelings for Mei do. Which means there's no possibility of them being as big.

Tavah's completely beautiful and bright and hilarious and smart. She's everything a guy could want: sexy, confident, honest, even blunt, which I never thought I liked but do.

She's going to Berkeley on scholarship. She has goals. I'm definitely attracted to her. Everyone likes her, and she's an open book. My body reacts to her. I felt the hormonal flow a few times tonight, like when she fixed my collar or when she pressed herself against me as we danced. She's all those things plus probably a hundred more.

I keep my eyes on her as she blurs in the dark. She laughs at something another guy says, then does a frantic dance to match the beat, throwing her head back and flipping her hair around.

My heart clenches and I drag in a breath. Tavah is definitely a lot of things but…she's just not Mei.

CHAPTER 25

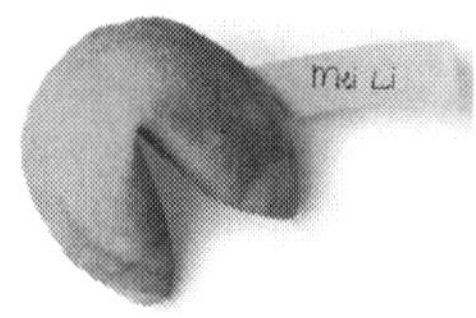

I don't dare touch anything in the hotel bathroom, afraid I'll smudge the gold fixtures. If I'd come up with an escape plan sooner, I'd be so far away from here. Even if that far away was also far from Marcus.

Squeezing my eyes shut, I grip the edge of the counter to pull my thoughts back down to the cold, marble floor under my bare feet. The overhead vent blows stale, icy air on my exposed shoulders and my gaping, tattered heart slumps inside me. It beat slower and slower last night in Chef Torres's kitchen where the ghost of my old dream trailed me, confused and misplaced. Three months ago, my heart would have leaped at all the exciting possibilities. Now without Marcus, it barely beats.

Chef Torres is as detached as the steam billowing above the grills in her sleek kitchen where I'm supposed to spend my summer. No amount of hiding in her kitchen will change the fact that every night during my summer, I'll have to return to the apartment Nick secured after Chef Torres offered me the internship.

When we got back to the hotel after a late dinner, Nick staggered to the couch and passed out and I'd hurried to my room, locking the door behind me. All night, I watched time move across the ceiling, afraid I'd hear the doorknob wiggle, wishing I had the guts to take my things and run. But Nick was between me and the door.

This morning, he'd told me through my closed bedroom door that he had meetings most of the day but would be back for the gala. I'd thought for that spark of a moment the gods had answered my prayers. I'd stared at the box of jewelry and pictured myself disappearing with it, but my hope vanished when Nick added that Chaz and Xander would be here all day if I needed anything.

I turn back to the vanity mirror, my eyes tripping over the selection of makeup Nick bought for me. I don't want to cover up anything; I want him to see exactly how I feel about him. No more pretending.

The heaviness in my chest tugs me down to the padded bench, and I slide my phone off the counter and clutch it to my chest, the metal frigid against my bare sternum. All I have to do is call Marcus. He's begged. I've dialed, but never called. I open the messages he's sent for the past ten days and scroll to the final one, blinking through tears.

It's been a long day. Don't know what day it is. When you left, everything just kind of stopped. I was late for school today because I couldn't get out of bed. Just laid there and stared at the fan. It was too dark. My dad assaulted me with questions yesterday after I said I didn't want Chinese. Said he doesn't like the dark circles under my eyes. Asked if I was on something. I was last week. Not sure how long withdrawals last. The way everything in my chest feels right now tells me they're not leaving anytime soon. Johnny texted an hour ago and said he doesn't like how many times I've avoided hanging this week. Audrey hates that I canceled our lunch date but eating makes me wanna puke. My AP history teacher didn't like my final paper. Know what I don't like? That I used to like my life but don't anymore. Know what else? That you're gone and I have no idea why. I also don't like feeling this mad at you. I don't like how much you've messed me up. Don't like myself for letting you. I hate that I have memories. That I make up conversations with you in my head so I won't forget your voice. Hate that I'm not strong enough to delete your texts or voicemails from when things were good. Know how many texts we averaged every day? 410. Averaged. One day, we sent over 1,000. Someday maybe I'll delete all 20,960 but I hate thinking about that, too. Just can't hate you, no matter how hard I try. Too much love I don't know what to do with now. I'll start working on that so in 50 years, maybe I'll finally love something besides you.

His words slam against my heart like someone pounding fists against a locked door. I read one text after the other, tears sliding down my face, then I click on my voicemail. Twelve messages stare back at me; they've almost killed me every time I've listened. Hopefully they'll finish me this time. The last thing I'll hear is Marcus's voice. I scroll to the second to last and close my eyes. Leaning back against the wall, I grip the phone with one hand, the other pushing my heart back into place.

"If anyone ever tells me I'm too young to fall in love, I'll freaking lose it." I pause the message, let his voice melt over all the painful, aching places inside me.

"I didn't even recognize myself this morning. Don't look like myself, don't feel like myself, and honestly…I don't wanna be myself right now. I know it sounds dramatic, but I'd rather be anything than without you. You're the one thing I want. I got up and left class today because someone said May—like the month—and I broke. Don't even know how to do this. Maybe you don't wanna work it out, but…" His voice drifts away and when he speaks again, it quivers. *"I need you."* He pauses again, letting out a long, weary breath, and I picture him sitting on the edge of his bed, staring into his dark room. *"We can't just leave things this way. I can't, anyway."*

I can't either. But I have to. So I'll go downstairs and pretend with Nick with Marcus's words in my ears.

I scroll to the last voicemail, push play, close my eyes. Silence, rustling. I picture Marcus running his hand through his hair, elbows on his knees, head hung. Then his voice crackles: *"I love you, Mei."* A click. The end of that world.

Nick's invisible leash tugs me through the sprawling ballroom dripping with chandeliers and wrapped tightly in gold wallpaper. I'm nothing but a pet dressed in satin and diamonds. Fancy pets on fancy leashes want the same thing ordinary pets want: freedom.

My dress clings to me, and I want to rip it off so I can breathe. The diamonds hanging from my neck and ears are so heavy, the only comfortable position is looking down at my crystal hors d'oeuvres plate. They'll have to come off when I run.

I scan the room for exits, sip the bubbling champagne. It mixes with the acid in my throat and almost erupts out of me and all over the starched tuxes and flowy gowns draped on women who laugh through their noses, their eyelashes reaching out to scratch me if I get too close. But I won't. I'll slip out one of the four exit doors. My only hope of that is to make Nick as drunk as he was last night.

"So you're the lucky plus one for Mr. Chao." A woman twice my age wearing a dress that looks like a vampire cape gives me a toothy smile that fades as she inspects the diamond necklace glittering on my exposed sternum. "We were wondering who he'd bring tonight." She tilts her head, waiting for my answer.

I smile and shrug once, wondering what I'm supposed to say to this woman who sees Nick as some kind of prize, but he kisses both her cheeks and beams at her.

"Yes, this is my fiancé, Mei Li. Mei Li, Rosa."

The bubbles from the small sip of champagne in my stomach multiply and I want to throw them up along with fear and disgust but instead, I pretend to take a sip of champagne and the conversation flows between her and Nick. I nod in all the right places as servers in short, shimmery dresses circle our group, taking empty glasses, replacing them with full ones. One of the girls reaches for mine but I hold it up so she can see it's still full. I need something to hold onto. But then our eyes meet, and I freeze, my throat dry. Su Ling. She hesitates, then turns away, and my fingers choke the glass stem.

My eyes follow her from where I'm frozen in the crowded ballroom, people drifting around me like water around a glacier. She has the same, faint birth mark on her lower jaw and even with bleached blonde hair, I know her face.

My eyes follow Su Ling from table to table, her short skirt climbing her legs as she bends and twists. She says something to a group of men whose eyes are focused everywhere but her face until one of them stands and takes her hand.

They walk toward me, and my heart trips over itself like I should meet her halfway or run the other direction. But as they pass, I open my mouth, stiffening when her hand catches mine and slips something hard against my palm. I look down at a keycard and a note scrawled on the back of a cocktail menu: *Meet me in 2803 before the toast.*

I look up in time to see her slip out of the room with the man. People are looking for her. Detective Miller. She didn't run away to work here. She'd never leave her kids. Why would she choose this? Maybe she's running from something. Or someone.

I hurry toward the door she walked through but someone grabs the back of my arm and whirls me around. I almost lose balance on my stilettos, but Nick's firm grip keeps me upright, his face in mine.

"Where'd you sneak off to?" Waves of sharp, tangy liquor jab at me and I hold my breath.

"I got lost in the crowd. This place is so big."

His eyes shift and he pulls me closer. "Perhaps we should get lost together, right after the toast."

"I'm not feeling great. My stomach is upset," I lie, praying he'll believe me. "Would it be okay if I go lie down for a bit?" I pause, pulling all the strength I can find to say the rest through a weak smile. "Maybe I'll feel better after the toast..."

Nick squeezes my arm tighter, sucks in a deep breath, and lets it out slowly. My stomach churns until panic is swept away by hope and relief when he hands me the keycard.

The thought of running and not meeting Su Ling pounds through my head as I slip inside the dark hotel room, counting the silent, frantic seconds. I shouldn't waste time; I should be running. But why is Su Ling here and what if she needs help and I'm all she has?

On second 683, she pushes through the door, frantically locking it behind her and turning to me. "What are you doing here, Mei Li?" Her eyes are all over my face in the gray light.

Mine go from her platinum hair to her sunken eyes. She looks like she's aged forty years in the past three weeks. "I'm…here to meet a chef. For an internship. Nick set it up."

She swallows, her fists clenching at her side. "I was afraid—"

"Why are you here?" I rush, my whisper harsh against the stillness of the hotel room. "The police are looking for you."

"I know," she nods, her neck tense.

"Then why haven't you told them where you are?"

"Nick threatened my boys." Her words come out in a strained puff of air, her eyes piercing mine. "I overheard information I shouldn't have. At the restaurant. He said he would hurt my boys if I didn't do as he said. But we don't have time to talk about this. Just know I'm not the only missing woman here, and if you don't leave, you'll be one of us. You can't tell anyone you saw me. Get your things and meet me on parking level 2. A car will be waiting. Stay away from Nick."

I search her eyes. "Why does he want you here?"

She grabs my arm. "Whatever you're thinking, you're probably right. Get as far away from him as you can." She lets go of me and rushes to the door, pulling it open. "Five minutes."

I stare at her, then slip out of the room and take off my shoes, running down the hallway to the elevator. I jab the button until the door finally opens, but a hand grabs me from behind and whips me around. Hot, sharp fear flares up my throat when my eyes collide with Chaz's.

"What are you doing?" His fingers bite into my arm and my heart claws up my throat, choking any words as I search his eyes for a hint of what he plans to do with me. "Answer me," he hisses, tightening his grip.

I go on tiptoe to relieve the pressure on my arm. "I was headed to my room…I'm not feeling well."

"You're on the wrong floor."

"I…got lost."

"With Su Ling? Nick won't be kind when he finds out."

My pulse jumps under Chaz's fingers and I struggle against his grip. "Let go!"

But he pushes me back against the hard wooden wall. "I should let him deal with both of you."

His words strike at me, igniting my anger. "Do it," I spit. "But I'll tell him about you and Xander."

"What about us?" Chaz narrows his eyes but not enough to disguise the flicker of fear.

"I heard your conversation in the room."

Chaz gets in my face. "Hard to talk with a slit throat."

I tilt my head to expose more of my neck. "Go ahead. You'd be doing me a favor."

He shoves away from me, turning his back, hands on his head before whirling back to me. "If you breathe a word of anything you heard, you're dead."

I clench my jaw, drag in a breath through my nose. "I won't say anything." My voice is thin and strained, like the risk I'm taking with him. "But you have to promise the same."

Chaz's breathing quickens and I tense, but he punches the wall beside me, and I flinch, the overhead light fixtures rattling. "You're on your own," he growls, "and you better not get caught."

He takes off down the hall and I let out the breath

cowering in my throat before pressing the button with a shaky hand. When the doors open, I dash inside and punch the 46, flinching as the beeps grow louder and shriller with each passing floor. 43. 44. 45.

When the elevator stops, I hurl myself out of it and down the hall toward the room, the carpet coarse and unforgiving under my feet. I swipe the keycard and rush inside, pressing my forehead against the closed door. My breathing matches the frantic speed of my mind and I try to slow it until a voice slices the silence.

"There you are."

I whirl around, my palms pressed against the door behind me for support as blood plunges to my feet.

Nick sits on the sofa, one leg crossed over the other, arms stretched along the back of it. Black on black on black. I lock my shaky knees.

"I was getting worried." His voice is smooth, his eyes sludgy as they sweep my body.

I press my toes into the cold marble.

"I promised you some fun after the toast. But maybe a little trivia first. Like where, oh where, has my little Mei Li been?" His words tumble over each other, but the sharp point of his voice impales me. "Or did I interrupt an important phone call with the boy?"

I shake my head so fast I lose balance and grab the door handle. "No—I…threw up. In a planter. I had to clean myself up. Too much champagne. First time."

He laughs dryly, but it drifts away like dust. "Why must you always be so defiant?"

I should plead for mercy. Beg, cry, do whatever he asks so I can stay whole, but his twisted face and words wind something inside me that uncoils in rage, shoving words out of my mouth. "I'm not your pet. You can't cage me."

He laughs more black into the darkness as he stands and stumbles up the two steps from the sunken living area, swaying across the marble toward me. "That's unfortunate. I prefer my women caged." He reaches for the wall, and I throw frantic words at him.

"I know what you do." I crank the door handle but he's a dark smear as he rushes me, slamming his hand against the door before his body crashes against mine.

"You have no idea what I can do."

I tense as he fists my hair with one hand, the other slithering to my backside, yanking me against him. "You could have had the most glamorous cage, but now, I'll strip it bare. No internship. No school. Nothing but you playing whatever role I give you. Doing whatever I want you to do."

I squirm in his grasp, but his hand tightens. "Why are you doing this?"

"Because I always get what I want." He presses his mouth against my ear, hot and sticky, and I squeeze my eyes shut as he pins me against the door with his hips. "Every last bit," he snarls, tugging my dress down.

I shove him, but he pins me tighter, his mouth forcing mine open so hard I thrash and dig my fingernails into his face. His hands fly over mine, but he loses balance and grabs at me as he falls, catching my earring and ripping it out.

I scream and grab my ear, warm blood pooling in my palm as I'm dragged to the floor. Tears flood my vision when I yank my leg from under him and crawl away, leaving bloody handprints on the floor. My dress peels off me as I scramble toward my room, but he catches me around the waist and jerks me backward, his rough hands gripping my stomach.

Rage and terror explode in a scream, and I kick as he drags me to his room and throws me on the bed. Rolling me to my back, he pins my hands above my head.

"I was going to ask your little boy how you taste but I'll just find out for myself."

When his mouth slams against mine again, I shove my

knee into his groin. He curses and jerks away enough that I heave myself against him, knocking him onto his side before crawling off the bed.

I'm halfway out of the room when he grabs my waist and jerks me backward, the air lurching from my lungs with a grunt.

He spins me around, hurls me back on the bed, straddles me. His hand clamps over my mouth, the other tightening around my neck until he chokes my scream, and my eyes burn. I claw at his hands as blackness edges my sight and a static buzz drones through my head until his hand connects with my face.

The world slows, and acidic fear drips down my throat. My chest tightens with a trapped scream, my head vibrating with its echo. I use my waning energy to focus on the one thing that makes me feel everything but fear.

I'm at Marcus's. His leg bounces to some awful hip hop song. He's drawing a diagram on my arm. I laugh, then laugh harder when he protests. I've messed up his masterpiece. But he doesn't care. He looks up at me. One glance sweeps away all thought and leaves only feelings.

My chest aches, and I struggle for air, but it's too thick with dread. I can't breathe...Fear pounds at me. There's nothing between me and Nick. No—I'm not here. Not here.

When I was a child, mama told me about reincarnation. When we die, our bodies turn to ash, but our souls live on and, how good we are in one life determines the consequences for our next. But I always wondered what happens if your soul dies first.

My soul is dying. I hear it. I thought it would sound like Marcus's voice since he keeps it alive, but...it's...shattering glass. Crushing weight. Silence.

My eyes fly open, and I gasp for air but choke in darkness and cologne. Nick's body slumps to my side, pinning my legs, and my eyes dart to Su Ling standing above me with a broken vase in her shaking hands, her eyes panicked.

She steps back, drops the shard of glass, and I wrestle my legs from under Nick and scramble off the bed. But my eyes land on his pants around his knees, blood pooling under his head on the white comforter.

Su Ling tears me away from the room. "Put on your dress, I'll grab your things. Your ride's here."

She runs to my room, and I stumble to the living room, grab my dress off the floor, quaking as I struggle into it.

When Su Ling returns, she's holding my duffle bag. "Follow me."

She leads me down the hallway until we reach a set of maintenance elevators. She swipes a keycard, and when the door opens, pulls me inside. We stop on P2 and rush out the elevator and through a double metal door.

A car is waiting for us in the parking garage, and she opens the door for me while she gives the driver hurried instructions. Her eyes skitter across mine before she closes my door and disappears inside the building.

The driver pulls out of the garage and looks at me through the rearview mirror, his long, wavy hair ruffling in the breeze coming through his open window. "You okay, love?" His British accent smooths the jagged edges of my fear, his eyes intent before he focuses on turning the corner when the light turns green. He puts down his visor against the setting sun and asks again. "Do you need me to take you to hospital? There's one a few blocks away."

I dab at dried blood crusting my nostrils but shake my head too fast and metal shards fly around inside my skull. I hold my head. "No. I just need to get home, please." I touch my neck to hold myself together but the diamonds still dangling from it get in the way, cold under my palm. I reach for the earrings, hissing against the pain. There's only one earring; the other is somewhere on the hotel room floor.

He glances at me through the mirror again, then nods and talks to the windshield. "You can borrow my jacket if you'd like." He grabs it from the passenger seat and holds it over his shoulder.

I ease forward, holding my ripped dress up, and slide my arms into his jacket, wrapping it tightly around me like it will erase the marks and bruises rising on my skin. "Thank you."

He nods. "Take a load off, yeah? Looks like you could use some rest. If you need to stop, just say so and I'll pop off the motorway."

I whisper another thank you past the lumps, knots, and raw spots in my throat. What would it feel like to "take a load off"? If only I could take off everything that happened tonight and hurl it out the window, watch it bounce down the freeway, get crushed under semi-truck tires. Smash against concrete barriers.

Panic and fear tangle in my chest, writhing as they grow bigger, overtaking me like sticky, black syrup inside me. What did Nick do to me?

I squeeze my eyes shut and focus on all the sore spots. My cheek…neck…angry carpet burns on my stomach…rising bruises on my back from falling on the marble floor. I swallow, not daring to let my focus move lower. But my knees are stiff, bruised. Nothing between my stomach and knees… between my legs.

I snap my eyes open, tense, focus again. But nothing. I shift in my seat. Still nothing. He didn't get that far. I send a silent prayer of thanks to Su Ling and unzip my bag, pulling out a pair of underwear and shimmy them on. The worst didn't happen. But it still could. Nick could find me. I can't go home or to Lin's. I can't go to Marcus's. I should have left when I had the chance—skipped meeting Su Ling and run. Now I'll be followed, stalked. Caged. Su Ling, too.

Unless…Nick gets caged first.

I fumble in my bag for my phone, grateful Su Ling threw

my clutch in my duffel. Clicking it on, I open a browser and find the right number, then hit send with stiff, cold fingers, holding my breath.

Two rings later, a tired woman answers. "San Francisco Police Department."

"I know where you can find Su Ling Wang," I blurt before I can think about what I'm doing. "And other missing women from San Francisco."

CHAPTER 26

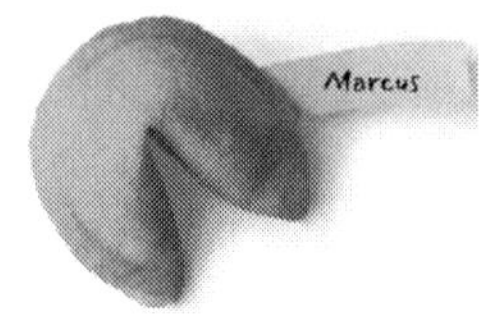

Tavah slips off her sparkly, neon heels and holds them as we stand on the corner under a streetlamp. "You don't have to walk me all the way home. This hill is a killer."

"I love killer hills."

She smiles and shakes her head as we turn onto her street. She swings her heels between us, her strides getting wider as we make the climb.

"This has been the best prom ever." She talks to the air ahead of us. "Last year, I did Sav a favor and went with her cousin who we now refer to as Gropey, and…the year before *that*, I went with Brandon Sotheby who's way more in love with himself than he'll ever be with anyone else. Also, he lit the restaurant's cloth napkins on fire during dinner. So…."

"Sotheby's a tool." I smile at her, then the sidewalk, wishing I had my Adidas right now. "I'm really glad you asked me."

"Well, thank you for humoring me. You're a fabulous date. Ten out of ten. Five stars. And now…I can check Go to Prom with Marcus Miller off my bucket list and move on with a smile on my face. I know there's someone you would have rather been with tonight, so I'll take what I can get."

I shake my head. "Tavah, it's not like that, it's just…"

"You're not over her. It's obvious, and I get it. I wasn't going to propose to you or anything." She punches my shoulder and I smile at the ground. "I'm also not going to lie and say I'm not jealous of her in a big way because I am. Like so, so jealous. Especially after tonight. But! Like all good crushes that start in seventh grade, I'll get over you." She bumps my shoulder with hers and I smile. "Tonight made it a lot harder so…we have a ten-minute walk. Help me get over you faster by telling me all about The Girl. I'll go into a jealous rage, throw a tantrum on this sidewalk, deflate my beautiful sleeves, and be over you by the time we reach my house. Ready, set, go."

I glance at her, then shove my hands in my too-tight pockets and watch the sidewalk cracks slide under my too-tight high tops. It took me five minutes tonight to decide I like Tavah. She's so easy to talk to. Honest, straightforward. I never wonder what she's thinking. Feel twenty pounds lighter around her. But…I don't just like Mei and it's not going away.

My hand goes to my chest, and I hurry and move it, acting like I'm straightening my ruffles. "This is kinda weird," I admit, taking a sledgehammer to the surprisingly little amount of awkwardness. "It's not as weird as it should be, I guess, but still. I feel bad. Guess I just…didn't know or didn't—"

"Stop, Marcus." She smiles, light from the line of street-lamps beaming off her teeth. "There's nothing to feel bad about. I like you; you like someone else. That's how it goes. I learned that in third grade. Ricky Archuleta." She pats her heart and gazes at the sky as she walks, then laughs and talks to the sidewalk. "My goal was to tell you how I felt before graduation. I've wanted to so many times but lost my nerve, so in a way, this is perfect."

No. This isn't perfect. I shouldn't be listening to another girl spill her guts to me. I should be with Mei, spilling mine to her.

"So, thanks," Tavah says, smiling before looking away. "Mission accomplished. It's done. Right? You know how I feel?"

I nod.

She nods. "Cool. Now we can all go about our business."

No. It isn't cool. I'm not cool at all. I haven't told Mei that I love her to her face. Tavah makes it look so easy, and all I've managed is to tell Mei in one stupid voicemail and a text. I need to tell her in person. I can do whatever she wants me to do, be whatever she wants me to be. Whatever she needs. We have to talk—honest and open, like Tavah is with me.

There's no way I wanna move forward without her. I'll think about everything else I thought I wanted later. I just need to tell her I want it all with her.

Mei and I aren't over yet.

I look at my watch. 12:53. Train ride home=20 minutes. Change clothes=2 minutes. Sprint to Mei's=1 minute.

Tavah slows in front of a giant three-story hidden behind an ivy-covered gate. Wide, brick steps lead to her front door where kissing is supposed to happen after a date, or so I hear.

I stop at the gate. "Thanks again for asking me. That was surprisingly fun for prom and the ideal way to spend a Saturday night." I rub the back of my neck and flex my toes in my high-tops, minutes ticking in my head.

Tavah smiles up at me. "Thank you, Marcus. For showing me what a perfect prom looks like, and being a sport. And… letting me say stuff I probably should've kept to myself." She laughs and rolls her eyes. "But…good luck with The Girl and I'll see you in chemistry." She touches my arm, then turns and rustles her dress through the gate, smiling over her shoulder as it clicks shut.

My legs flex, ready to run, but I stand on the dark sidewalk by a bush humming with crickets and watch Tavah walk up the steps and through the white door. And then I take off down the hill. Tonight's not over yet. In an hour, Mei will know I love her. She'll hear it, see it, and I hope—more than anything—she'll feel it. Because I'm feeling it. More now than ever.

Thanks, Tavah.

When the train door opens, I hit the pavement running because I almost went crazy on the ride back to Chinatown—ripped off my jacket, unbuttoned my collar when it choked me. Counted billboards. Prepared my Mei speech. Shoved my earbuds in and tried drowning my thoughts in music.

My high-tops grind into my ankles, but when I round the corner into Chinatown, I push harder. If I was on the soccer field and Mei was at the far end of it, I'd break land speed records. But running isn't responsible for my racing heart and mind right now.

What if she doesn't wanna see me? Never really loved me? What if she's with Face Eater? What if she has been the whole time? What if…what if…?

Easing open The Clubhouse's front door, I step into the inky living room. The smell of pepperoni pizza hangs in the air. Dad's probably passed out on the couch with that weird bible he's been reading. But the couch is riding solo. I pray he's asleep in his room 'cause I gotta get out of this tux and out of here ASAP.

I tug off my high tops and tiptoe toward my room, dodging the creaky spot in the floor, but stop when Dad's voice drifts from under his door along a sliver of yellow lamplight that slices the hallway carpet. He's still awake. He'll want a full report. But I gotta get to Mei's. Wake her up, tell her how I feel and hope she feels the same.

Maybe Dad's sleep talking. I hold my breath and listen before sneaking past his door but when he laughs and says, "No way—not even close," I stop.

He never uses actual words when he talks in his sleep. So…who's he talking to at 1:30 AM? Not a cop—he'd never laugh like that with another cop. I've never heard that laugh. I step to the wall around the corner from his room.

"I know," he sighs, his voice calmer, softer, not his usual in-your-face volume.

Normally, it's like his words are always being released from a pressure valve but not this time. Definitely not a cop. Not Lex. Not with that kinda sigh.

"I'm trying to figure out how to tell him, but I wanna get him through graduation before I drop this bomb on him, you know? It's always just been the two of us and I'm not sure how he'll take it. Glad he's headed to Stanford so he can hate me from there."

Whoa. My pulse pounds in my neck. He's talking about me. Or the me he thinks is going to Stanford. But why would I be mad at him? And who's on the other end of his freaking phone?

"I know, I know. Yeah. He's, like, the perfect kid and he'll get it eventually, but I just feel like I'm lying to him, you know? I made him promise he wouldn't get a girlfriend, and he hasn't. Thought it was a safe bet for both of us. But then you came along and completely blew my predictable, boring world apart."

Hold up.

Girlfriend?

The word screeches around the corner and slams into me, clogs my ears like mud shoved inside them so all I can hear is the word echoing. Dad's been lying to me. But for how long?

All the nights, the talks about girls messing me up. And he's got a freaking girlfriend?

My heart pounds up my throat with an army of angry words, my jaw clenched as I tune back into the conversation.

"I think you should come out the week after graduation," Dad says. "You can meet Marcus and I can stop sneaking around. Introduce my two favorite people." He laughs at something she says, his voice all smooth and full of smile. I wanna picture the girl on the other end but don't even know what Dad would look for. Thought women were STDs since he always lumps them in the same danger category. But he doesn't sound like he's talking to a disease; he sounds infected with words that belong to someone else. His voice is all soft and silky and I wanna barge into his room, but also don't because he's talking like he might be wearing lingerie or something.

"No, it's just..." He does a frustrated growl. "I'm ready for more, Kenna. Way more. Maybe a little less distance between us. See you more often. Like...maybe every day, in person...?" His voice slides into a smile like he's just hit a home run. "I'd even take being in the same state. Utah's too far away."

He's smiling through the phone to some girl in another state. I know the sound a voice makes when it's really into a girl—slower, smoother, like the words are candy you wanna bit into but don't so it'll last longer. I sounded just like that every time Mei smiled over the phone; her voice pumped through me until I was drunk on her, talking all sloppy and slow and—

"Yeah. I read some interesting verses tonight. I don't completely understand it all, but it makes me think." Pause. Swear word. "I've gotta go. Marcus'll be home any minute. Never missed curfew. This kid is definitely not me." He laughs, then sighs again. "Wish I could be missing my curfew with you right now, but...I'll call you tomorrow as soon as I can sneak away." He pauses again and his words float out of his room like germs I inhale that settle in me as nausea.

"Love you, too, baby."

Holy freak. 'Love'? *'Baby'*? I forget how to swallow and the lump in my throat stretches until I'm gonna choke. He's at love level? For how long? How long has he been pretending? And lying? Making me give up all the stuff I want because I feel sorry for him, and guilty, and wanna make him proud. I could've said yes to Stanford. Could have been with Mei. We'd still be together.

Dad's the one messing everything up, not Mei

I swerve around the corner, push open his door. His head jerks toward me on the pillow before he sits up, rubbing his hair.

"Hey, M.C. How'd it go?" He slides his hand over his phone on the bed like he can hide the conversation he just had.

"Apparently not long enough." I throw my thumb over my shoulder. "Want me to leave so you can finish talking to your girlfriend about what you should or shouldn't tell me?"

His Adam's apple bobs, and he stares at me for a couple irritated breaths, then closes his eyes and lets out a long sigh. "M.C., I…yeah." He swears and looks at me again. "We need to talk."

"You think? Sounds like we should've talked before the whole love thing happened with whoever was on the other end of your phone. I mean, I don't wanna point out the obvious, but you've practically nailed me to the floor to keep me from girls but aren't keeping your own rules." My words are hot, supercharged. "And what do you need to tell me besides you're in love with some woman in another state? Cause I'm all ears. Wide awake since I'm home on time so I didn't knock up Tavah. I heard everything except what someone else knows about me that I should know but don't. So what is it and who is she?"

He stares at me, then drops his eyes to the bed before looking up again. "She…is Kenna."

"Yeah, I heard. And?"

"Yeah." He nods to his comforter.

"And Kenna just magically appeared. Like tonight? Yesterday? Definitely not four years ago when you decided I should be a monk."

"No, M.C.…look." He slides to the end of his bed, gripping the mattress, digging his toes into the carpet as he watches them. "Corinne at work introduced us. Kenna's her sister. She lives in Utah."

"So you've never met her?"

"I have."

"Online? FaceTime? How? When?"

"She's come into town a few times and I—"

"And you lied. To me. Told me your were working or…?"

His jaw clenches, his pulse jumping in his neck. "Yeah." He nods slowly. "I did."

His confession is a nuclear bomb, and I'm running from the wave and the debris, bolting from the whole scene that just blew my world apart for the second time in two weeks. I haven't seen Mei because of Dad. We fought because of Dad. Snuck around because of him. Stressed and dodged and felt guilty. For nothing. I'm out of here. Going to Mei's, breaking her window if I have to. I'll do whatever I want from now on. Not sticking around here to take second place.

I rip my shirt buttons out of their holes, fling it on my desk before peeling off my tux pants, my legs sweaty from running, and shaky from the brain assault. I pull on fresh boxer briefs, yank on a t-shirt and shorts before jamming my feet into my Adidas. I throw my door open and slam past Dad, who's standing in the hall, arms crossed.

"Marcus, where are you going?"

"Call Kenna," I say to the front door as I throw it open. "Maybe she'll know."

CHAPTER 27

"This the place?"

My eyes fly open when the driver speaks, my head lurching from the headrest as my body screams back to life. Backseat. No hotel, no Nick. Dark lanterns criss-crossing above the street. I check the time: 1:18 AM. Six hours since I left Nick bleeding in the hotel room. Six hours since Su Ling rushed me out a back entrance of the hotel. Six hours since I called the police. Six hours is enough time for Nick to wake up and send people after me. Or my family. Or Marcus.

But…It's also enough time for him to get arrested.

I can't take any chances. I haul my voice up my throat, "Yes, thanks."

The driver scratches his arm. "Someone coming to meet you or…?"

Yes. Nick will be here if the police don't find him. I just need Guo Mama to help me figure out where to go. I dial her number, squeezing the phone so tightly my fingertips tingle. *I'm so sorry, I'm so sorry,*

"Xiao Mei?"

Tears fill my eyes but before I can respond, Guo Mama

shuffles to the shop door, phone at her ear. I disconnect the call and shrug out of the driver's jacket, handing it to him over the seat before grabbing my bag and throwing open the car door.

Guo Mama's eyes land on me and go from tired to afraid as I hold up my dress and stumble toward her. She thanks the driver before sweeping me inside and locking the door behind us.

My legs wobble, but her arms circle around me as she leads me through the store and into the breakroom. She pulls out a chair and holds onto me as I ease into it, then hurries back through the curtain and returns with a silk robe. She drapes it around me, before scurrying to the stove.

I pull the robe around me, letting the ripped dress slump to my lap while I stare at the linoleum, my mind unraveling as she works in silence. Every few seconds, she glances over her shoulder and a few minutes later, she takes my hands and wraps them around a steaming cup of tea.

"Drink. It will help."

I stare at the rippling black pool, then tip the cup, the liquid scalding my throat, warming me for the first time in days.

"I'm sorry to wake you. I didn't know where else to go."

"You did not wake me. I have been waiting to hear from you for hours."

My eyes hold hers, too many questions swirling in my head and jamming my throat to get words out, but Guo Mama answers. "Su Ling called your mama. Your mama called me."

"She knows?"

"Yes. She is waiting for my call." She closes her eyes. "Thank the gods you are here and safe, Xiao Mei." When she opens her eyes again, she studies me, her jaw set. "What happened? Actually, no." She waves her hand to dismiss her comment and closes her eyes for a few seconds. "Never mind. I know what, and I am so sorry."

I shake my head, then stop when it hurts. "I'm so, so sorry to put you in danger. I don't know where to go." The words scratch out of me. "I saw Su Ling in L.A. She helped me escape. I told the police where they can find her. Nick's there, too. But if they don't find him, he'll come for me."

"You are the one who told the police about Nick?"

I drop my face in my hands and shake my head. "I was too scared. I hope if they find her, they find him." Bleeding on the hotel bed.

Her hand rests on my shoulder. "I will help you find a safe place." She nods, her eyes searching my face. "But first, you need a warm shower. Then we can talk about where you will go."

CHAPTER 28

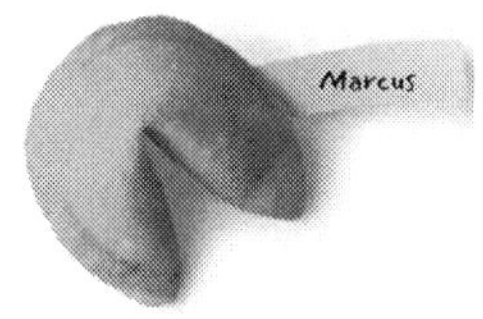

I skid around the corner and run past Guo's shop. A car idles at the curb, the driver's face lit by a phone screen. Guo's security gate's up, but I keep running until I'm standing below Mei's window.

I lean over and catch my breath, my heart pounding an internal bruise in a chest full of hot anger and desperation. My phone buzzes incessantly in my pocket so I pull it out. Four missed calls and a text from Dad: I'm sorry, M.C. Come home. Let's talk about this. You can't just run at 2 AM. If you don't come home, I'll come to you.

No. If he can go wherever he wants with whoever he wants, so can I. I drop my phone in my pocket and turn back to Mei's fire escape. Dad is not gonna ruin this more than he already has.

The ladder to her fire escape is still up but I'm so mad, I could probably scale the building. And if Nick's guys are around, I'll wreck them tonight.

I size up the garbage cans lined across the alley. If I stack them, I could grab the lowest rung. But when I dart toward them, the car in front of Guo's drives off and my inner alarm blares. Guo's shop should've been locked hours ago. And there's a light in the back, one in her upstairs window.

Visions of her lying unconscious skid across my mind, and I sprint to the door, but it's locked. I cup my hands around my eyes to look inside. The light's coming from her back room and I don't see any shadows prowling her shop, no Guo lying on the floor, but I dial her number, anyway.

The other end rustles after two rings. "Where are you, boy?"

"You okay, Guo? Why's your gate up?"

"You need to come, now."

"I'm right outside."

"Stay." The call ends and I stare at my phone, torn between going back to Mei's and staying here. Guo's obviously fine, but her voice wasn't.

My cold, worried thoughts about her mix with my dad-anger and slosh around in my stomach, hissing and steaming. Shoving my phone in my pocket, I rub my hands down my face while I scan the empty street. A crosswalk sign blinks on and off like my anger got inside it and messed with its wiring, too. What's Dad's problem? None of this had to happen. Yeah, I've been lying to him, too, but my lies didn't totally mess up his life. He still has his girl and whatever he wants. Because of him, I'm not going to Stanford, and I might never get Mei back. What else has he lied about? My mom? Maybe there's more to that whole story.

I swear under my breath and scan my apartment windows up the street, hands on my head. I'm not gonna stick around to find out what else he's keeping from me. Thirty minutes ago, I was afraid to leave him. Now...I don't wanna be anywhere near him. After I talk to Guo, I'm talking to Mei, and after that, I'll go to Johnny's. Email Stanford. Like Dad told his girlfriend: I'll hate him from there. If only I can still get in.

The shop door scrapes open, and I whirl around, scanning

Guo in her robe, her hair matted on one side. She reaches for me and pulls me through the door.

"What's going on, Guo…?" The mini fridge under the counter kicks on and hums, the cat clocks on the shelves tick, but she shakes her head and locks the deadbolt, pushing the button to lower the security gate.

I snap my head toward it, back to her. "Are you holding me hostage or something…?"

"I'm so glad you are here. So glad." Her red, puffy eyes close slowly then open again.

"Is everything okay…?"

"NO! Everything is not." Her words burst from her, and she bows her head, shoulders sinking. "Sorry. Not your fault. But now she must go away."

I frown. "Hold up. Who's leaving…?"

"Mei Li."

Her name is a force field that sends ripples through the shop as I slam into it, rattling my brain and my body. Feelings erupt, flinging questions and fear through my head until I'm swerving around Guo, shoving aside racks of robes to get to the light in the back faster. My chest has a jetpack in it, hurling me forward, my heart straining to beat me to her.

I rip aside the curtain covering the backroom entrance and scan the empty table, two abandoned teacups. Two empty chairs pulled away from it. I whirl around. "Where is she?"

Guo steps to me, her hand firmly on my arm as she looks up at me. "She is here, but…"

"But what? What's going on? Tell me." I search Guo's eyes for clues, but she pats my arm.

"She will not want you to see her like this."

My stomach clenches. "Like what?"

Guo takes a deep breath, sighs it out. Her shoulders slump, holding invisible weight. "She is very hurt, Marcus Miller."

"What did he do?" My voice is hard, fighting rage, and

her silence is all the answer I need. I wanna puke words and mental pictures. I wanna smash things. Break him into tiny pieces. "Where is she? Does she need a doctor? I need to get her out of here and—"

"No." Guo shakes her head. "No hospital. No doctor. No Ray, just you. Understand?" She holds up her finger. "She will be okay. I gave her something for the pain. If you care about Mei Li, you will do as I say. Tell me you understand." Her voice is low, but her eyes pin me.

No. I don't understand. At all. But I nod, afraid if I open my mouth, I'll yell or sob.

"She is upstairs in the shower."

Mei. Hurt. Upstairs.

"What do I do?" I ask, panic swooping over me. I have to see her, have to stop the pain, have to keep her here. This is my fault. If I'd just talked to her instead of freaking out that night at The Clubhouse, she never would've left. She never would've been near Nick. He never would've—

"What did he do to her?"

"Things he will never do again. I made arrangements for her to leave so she will be safe from everything."

"No." The word shoots out of me like a missile, attacking the thought of her leaving. "No way. She can't."

"She must. Things are not good here."

"But I'll keep her safe. She can stay at The Clubhouse. My dad can't say anything. I'm not letting her out of my sight again. And why won't someone call the cops? He can't just do this and—"

"The police will already be involved and that is another reason she must go away from here, but I will let her tell you why. She will not want you to see her like this, but she needs you right now. Go to her." She points a knobby finger toward the stairs that lead to her apartment over the shop.

I look at Guo, at her finger, at the stairs, back to her, then take the stairs two at a time, my heart struggling to break free.

But the locked bathroom door stops it short. I stare at the wood grain, my hands fisted at my side.

Water slaps tile on the other side of the door. Mei's on the other side with the water and the tile and…so close. Hurt. How bad? I lean my forehead against the door, hand on the locked knob I could break off.

I turn and slide down the wall, leaning my head back against it, hands clenched over my bent knees while I work to control my breathing and wait for the water to shut off. Squeeze my eyes shut. Listen. Wait.

Guo eases up the steps past me, walks through her bedroom door, and perches on the end of her bed, hands in her lap.

When a cry comes from the bathroom, my eyes snap open and I'm on my feet. "I need to get to her, Guo."

She hesitates, then nods and shuffles to her nightstand, pulling open the drawer and rummaging through it. She hands me a paperclip and I bend it, shove it in the lock until it pops, then slip inside the bathroom.

Mei's a sobbing smudge huddled in the corner on the other side of the frosted glass, and I choke down steam and fear to make room for my voice. "Mei?"

A fresh sob cuts through the spray and I curse, grab the handle, and fling open the shower door. Mei's on the tile floor, arms locked around her bent knees which are pulled to her chest, her black and blue body trembling.

"Please leave," she chokes, pulling herself into a tighter ball.

I drop to my knees in the shower, water pelting me, streaming over my head, down my neck. "I'm not leaving." I blink water and tears out of my eyes as I wrap my arms around her and hold her against me, resting my chin on her head.

Her breaths are shallow, her body shaking even in the scalding water. I reach to yank it off, then squeeze her tighter against me, my fingers flexing against her bare back, slick with water. I wanna punch a hole in the wall, but Guo Mama's soft voice deflates my rage.

"Marcus." She stands in the doorway, holding out a thick purple robe. If I reach for it, I let go of Mei huddled against me. If I pull away, I see everything—all of her. Everything I've fantasized about. But not like this—with signs of Nick all over her.

I clench my jaw and snatch the robe with one hand. Keep my eyes on Mei's face, while I slip the robe around her, then gently pull her arms from around her legs and slide them through the sleeves, swallowing as I fight to keep my eyes from sliding south of her face.

Once it's mostly around her, I gather her to my chest and lift her, carry her out of the shower, out of the bathroom, across the hall. The robe falls open and her bare chest burns a hole through my soaked t-shirt. I clench my jaw and lay her on the bed, pulling the robe across her body. But every time I blink, I see what's been done to her and anger boils inside me.

Instead of punching the wall or throwing something, I crawl onto the bed, lay in front of her, my lips pressed to her forehead while my head yells at me to throw something. Find Face Eater. Break him.

Mei stays curled in a ball, her eyes closed, hands covering her face to keep me out. I sweep her hair away and uncover a welt on her cheek like the one she had the night she came to The Clubhouse the first time. Blood has dried on her eyebrow and along her hairline. Her earlobe is torn, swollen and red.

My stomach crawls up my throat and I'm gonna puke, but instead, I run my hand across her forehead and down her face, avoiding the bruise. "Mei," I whisper. "Look at me. Please."

She turns her head away, exposing purple, finger-shaped bruises circling her throat. Like he tried to strangle her.

Shooting off the bed, I barely make it to the toilet before I lose it. Every emotion from tonight heaves out of me—the excitement and adrenaline from prom and Tavah, curiosity, hope, Dad's betrayal. Finding Mei like this. I vomit again, clutching the toilet for dear life. What did Nick do to her?

But I think I know, and the thought drops me to my knees. I lower my forehead to the fuzzy bathmat, wrap my hands behind my head and squeeze my eyes shut, trying to separate my anger from sadness. Nick will never get close to her again. I'll keep her with me. I don't care about Dad or Stanford or Kenna or anyone. I care about Mei, and if I have my way, Nick will be locked up, no matter what Guo says.

I haul myself to my feet. Talk myself into calm before washing my hands and searching Guo's cabinet for mouthwash. I swish it around, use a hand towel to wash my face, then toss it on the ground along with my wet t-shirt before going back to Mei and whatever happens next.

CHAPTER 29

I grip the edge of the mattress where I sit while Marcus stands in the open door, silent, shirtless, pale. I talk to my toes as they dig into the carpet. Loss, disgust, and shame bubble to my surface like oil on water, and I look to the ceiling, blinking to force it down. "You shouldn't be here."

Marcus hesitates in the doorway, then steps to the bed and kneels in front of me, taking my face gently between his hands.

"I'm not going anywhere, Mei. I just needed a minute. But I'm here—talk to me. Tell me what happened."

I've kept everything hidden, afraid of what my reality would do to him or me or us. But he's seen all of me now, and my will to keep him at a distance collapses under the weight of so many secrets. I exhale and words edge out of me in a whisper. "Nick happened."

Marcus's jaw tightens, and when I dare to look into his eyes, I watch a spark burst into a red-hot flame before he says, "Who is he to you?" His voice shakes and his hands press into the mattress on either side of me as his eyes hold mine.

"We've known each other since I was eight," I say to my hands in my lap, the words trembling out of me. "He was fifteen. I didn't realize until recently that he wanted more than friendship." The truth drops on Marcus, but I speak to drown the heaviness with more words. "I didn't know that everything he did for me and my family had strings attached." I shake my head, my face burning and throbbing from the pressure of so many admissions. "I thought he was just part of the family. But this past year, he started treating me differently. Buying me things. Taking me out. Using his connections to get me everything I wanted." Words ball in my throat, but I want them out of me. "Kissing me. Touching me. Demanding things I didn't want to give him. I didn't know how to say no." I close my eyes. "I just thought…"

What? What had I thought? Wasn't it obvious what he wanted? I circle my swollen throat with my hand, my voice a strangled whisper. "I should have run away months ago. Lin begged me not to go to L.A., but I had no choice." I shake my head, and Marcus is silent as I tell him everything that happened the night I left his house. How Nick threatened to hurt him. How he didn't take his eyes off me. Had me followed. How I wanted to contact Marcus but didn't dare. Seeing Su Ling at the party and how she saved my life.

Tears sting my eyes and I swipe at them, shaking my head, but Marcus leans his forehead against mine. "I'm here." His voice is low and tight but steady. "I'm never leaving you." He swallows hard but wraps his arms around me, holding me gently without saying a word. "Never, Mei. Nick's over. For good. He'll never hurt you again. He'll never get close enough."

"Marcus," I say into his neck, tightening my hold on him. "When I told you I wasn't safe, I wasn't lying. I don't belong in your world."

He pulls away, holding my face between his hands. "*You* don't belong in your world," he says, his voice gravel. "I want you in my world, Mei. Nothing else, nowhere else, no one else."

His words fill me, and I hold my breath to keep them inside, let them settle into the cracks and gaping wounds. "You don't know how much I wish that could be."

His hand cups the back of my head. "It can. All we gotta do is tell the police. Nick will be in custody. He won't—"

"I already called the police," I whisper. "I told them where to find Su Ling, and I hope they find Nick, too."

His eyes skitter over mine, collecting answers. "Then they're gonna lock him up. You're safe now. It's over."

His thumb runs across my cheek, but I shake my head and swallow. "And so are we."

He stills, his eyes searching mine. "What do you mean?"

I turn my head away from him, scanning Guo Mama's shelves of Chinese paperbacks before closing my eyes and letting the words that have traveled so far through me finally emerge. "I'm undocumented, Marcus. I'm not supposed to be here. In America."

Silence stretches between us, and I wait for it to snap, but the confusion on Marcus's face is too much.

"I'm not an American citizen. You wanted to know what Nick is to me? He's the only reason my family can be here. He's the reason we have the restaurant. Nick's baba helped us get out of Taiwan and before he died, he paid for the restaurant. The rest of the inheritance went to Nick. So my baba and Nick work together. He knows everything about us and could get us deported with one phone call." I close my eyes. "I don't even want to imagine what Baba will do to me if he finds out I called the police." I swallow and let out a shaky breath. "It's only a matter of time before we're forced to leave."

Marcus sits back on his heels, rubbing the back of his neck.

I blink back tears. "I thought I could figure out a way to be with you. But that was so stupid." My voice cracks and I cover my mouth. "Guo Mama's helping me disappear so Nick can't find me. There aren't a lot of options for me right now."

Marcus shoots forward, kneeling again, his hands cupping my face. "No," he says, squinting like my words hurt going in. He shakes his head slowly, opens his mouth, then closes it before pinning me with his eyes. "No."

I look down at my hands. "I don't have a choice, Marcus."

"No," he says again, pulling me up from the bed, wrapping me in his arms. "I'm not losing you again."

Reality presses down on me, and I close my eyes, my eyelashes brushing his chest. There really aren't choices. I've always known it and Marcus is figuring it out.

"I should never have let you onto my fire escape or written you notes or talked to you. I should never have let myself have any feelings for you because I knew it would all have to end at some point."

Cursing again, Marcus shakes his head and cradles the back of my head, smashing my cheek against his chest. "No. Nope." He lets go of me and steps back, rubbing his hands down his face, dropping them to his side. "We just…need some sleep. We'll figure this out tomorrow. I can't think straight right now." He pulls down the covers and helps me slide inside before sliding in after me, curling around me from behind like he can keep tomorrow from coming between us.

CHAPTER 30

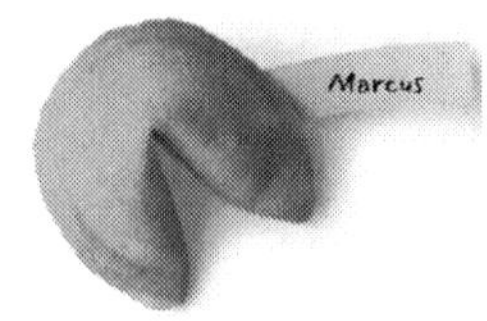

Mei's breathing is steady. Deep, even though I don't want it to take her too far from me. But I gotta think. Clear my head, sift through all the new info, so I ease away from her, instantly cold without her warm back against my chest.

I consider pulling my wet shirt on, then forget it and close the door behind me before taking the stairs down two at a time.

Guo sits at the table staring into her tea, her robe drooped around her, making her even smaller. She glances up, then pats the table and points to the chair across from her.

"Come here, boy."

I drop into the chair, my head still fuzzy from exhaustion. "This whole thing…" I put my elbows on the table, my head in my hands, and talk to the scarred wood. "What do I do, Guo?" I drop my hands and they slap the table as I look up. "I promised her I'd keep her from Nick but…how? What am I supposed to do about any of this?"

"She told you."

I close my eyes and nod. "Yeah."

"She has told you what she knows, yes, but there is more. So much more I cannot say."

I shake my head and open my eyes. "Then…if you can't tell me what it is, at least tell me what to do. I'll do it—whatever it is. Unless it's letting her go. Can't do that."

Guo watches me, hands folded on the table. "Mei Li cannot stay. It is too dangerous."

I blink. "But what if—"

Guo holds up her hand. "She cannot stay, Marcus. She must leave. This is all very tricky, but…I've been thinking, and…"

I stare at her, waiting. "And what?"

"She must leave San Francisco and you will not be together."

I frown, scan the kitchenette. "So that's it? That's what you've been thinking about?"

Guo hesitates. "Yes…but also…"

I lean into the table. "Help me out here, Guo."

"She could leave, and you could still be together."

I squint. "Like…how, if she leaves?" Her eyes spark and I tense my legs. "Not following…"

She places her hand on my arm, her knobby fingers like bent, dry twigs. "I called my brother in Seattle. He has a cottage where she can stay. There is room for two. Until we figure out how to keep her in America."

All feeling drains into my feet which want to run far from this conversation. "What are you saying?" I squint like I'm staring into an explosion. Of my brain.

"You heard me just fine but need time to think. It's a big decision. No easy solution."

"So…" I stare at the table like there's a map I can follow so I don't get lost in this conversation. "You're telling me I should go to Seattle with Mei."

Guo juts out her jaw. "I will not tell you to do anything. This is your decision. You do not have to go, but it is the only way to keep you together. I will not blame you if you choose not to, and we will figure out a way for you to communicate with Mei Li wherever she ends up. You just will not be together."

I stare at the table again until the wood grain blurs, then shove away from it and bolt toward the back door. "I need a minute. Or five hundred."

"Yes, take some time. And a shirt from the rack. You are half naked."

I grab an I Heart SF Chinatown t-shirt from the nearest shelf and tug it on. It's a little tight but I turn toward the door, then back to Guo. "This is crazy."

She nods slowly. "Every part of it, yes, but I am here for you. As if you were my own. Always. Whatever you decide. Understand?"

I step to her and gather her in my arms, her fuzzy robe sticking to my sweaty palms. "This is so messed up. I'm freaked out of my mind. But thanks for being my real mom." Right now, I need one especially since I'm not sure I have a dad anymore.

"Oh, you..." She squeezes my waist and swipes at tears before she steps back. "I'm so proud of you, and I will be here for you all the way. You and Mei Li are my xiǎo háizi." She smiles and nods. "Children."

Kissing the top of her head, I turn toward the door. "If Mei wakes up, tell her I'll be right back."

I'm up the alley in seconds, bent over, gripping my knees as I catch my breath. Holy freak. Did that conversation really just happen? Ten hours ago, I was leaving my apartment with Tavah. Two hours ago, I was running out of it to find Mei. And I found her, but...found so much more. Way too much.

I sprint to the corner. Watch the light turn from red to green to yellow, then red again. My brain cycles, too. Run with Mei? How? For how long? What would I tell Dad?

Would I tell him? My jaw tenses. No. I don't have to. He has Kenna. I could be with Mei.

But how? This would never work for a thousand reasons.

Pumping my legs harder, I round the corner, picturing Mei in the robe. Nothing underneath. Like…nothing. Just…all of her. Completely naked. Something I've dreamed of seeing, but not with Face Eater's stain smeared all over her.

I run faster, trying to leave thoughts behind, darting across streets, sprinting up hills, pushing my lungs to their limit all the way to Telegraph Hill. I try to catch my breath but can't, sprint up the steps when more thoughts catch up.

On step fifteen, I lean over the railing and puke in the bushes. Tastes like confusion, and leaves me dizzy, so I throw up again. This time, it's all my burning, oily anger toward Face Eater for what he's done to Mei and for forcing me to make an impossible decision. At Dad for lying and blowing up the one solid thing I thought I had.

I clutch my chest when a cold fear chaser follows. I lost Dad tonight. My solid ground. I can't lose Mei, too. What she told me and what Guo suggested changes everything. Except…nothing. At least not the way I feel about Mei.

I drop to the step, letting everything she told me soak in. I have to go with Mei. I want to. She finally told me everything. I'm in this with her already.

I sort through it until the sun peeks over the city below, then push myself to my feet, stretch the soreness from prom out of my legs. Prom seems so stupid now—people dressed up, pretending to be someone else. Me, trying to be someone else and feeling things for someone else while Mei was fighting off Nick. Or not able to fight him off. I hate that I don't know.

I bolt up the steps, sweating the fear and confusion out of me. We can figure this out because on step 116, I realize how much I need Mei. I couldn't handle being one street or an unanswered text or phone call away from her, so there's no way I could handle her being all the way across the world. No.

Things inside me that shriveled without her are popping back to life. When she was gone, I was, too. The way I feel about her is bigger than how I need her laugh or her smile or the way I want her body. Without her, the me I recognize doesn't exist and doesn't want to. It won't. So if she goes to Seattle, I go, too.

On step 300 I stop, hands on my hips as I squint into the morning sun. But I have college. Soccer. Med school. Right? All of that still matters?

My life was so planned out until today. Until I found out Dad's secret.

Now I don't have to stay in San Francisco. I could go with Mei.

I could go to Stanford.

I could take Mei with me. No one would look for her there. I'll keep her close and safe.

I drop to the step, elbows on my knees, hands clasped in front of me like I can squeeze the answer out of them.

Scenario #1: Get into Stanford. My scholarship includes a private dorm. Mei could stay there with me.

Probability of getting into Stanford: unknown

Scenario #2: Get a place near USF with Mei.

Probability of Nick hunting her down: 281%

Probability of Dad finding us and Mei getting deported: 99%

Probability of hurting Dad: 100%

Probability I don't care anymore: 3,000%

Scenario #3: Suck it up and tell Dad about Nick. Make him swear not to implicate Mei. Hide her at The Clubhouse until I figure out the whole Stanford thing.

Probability I won't be able to handle the look on Dad's face even though he's a liar, too: 98.9%. I saw his shocked/disappointed look when Jeff and I got busted by one of Dad's cop friends for trespassing in that abandoned building near Jeff's house. But this is way bigger. New levels of bigger.

Probability Dad will arrest Nick and lock him up:100%

Probability Nick could hurt Mei even in custody: 50%. He'll still have guys on the outside.

Probability of losing Mei: 100%

So…I need to get out of San Francisco. Unless…

Scenario #4: Forget it all and never see Mei again.

Probability I'll be wrecked/debilitated/paralyzed/good as dead: 1,713%

Somebody's getting hurt, no matter which scenario. Me? Dad? Mei? Maybe three for three, depending on my decision.

I draw a mental pie chart. Mei's a decisive 0%. I'm a solid 0%. Which leaves Dad all 100% of the hurt. Wouldn't have done it a few hours ago, but I'm willing now. I want Mei. He can have Kenna.

The only way I'll end up with Mei is to leave San Francisco with her.

Decision: Avoid Dad. Leave SF. Pray I get into Stanford.

But even if I do, I can't go until July. If I don't…we'll figure it out. Together. In Seattle.

Probability this is a stupid plan: 99.999998%.

But after seeing what Nick did to her, I'll do anything to protect her from him, and help her understand I'll never leave her or treat her that way. I'll be so careful with her. Give her nothing but respect. I'll never give her any reason to compare me to him. She once told me everyone wants to feel safe. She needs safe. I can be that for her.

I clench my jaw and look out over the bay. I'm not going home. I'll text Dad, tell him I'm staying at Johnny's for a few days to cool down. Mei and I will go to Seattle until I hear from Stanford. I'll use Meemaw's graduation money to get us through until then. $10,000 could help us start a life together.

I close my eyes. This could actually work. Not sure what'll

happen to Mei's family, but Mei and I will be together. She'll be safe, no deportation. Right? I don't know. Don't know anything about this stuff.

I swear and run my fingers through my hair. *What now, God?* I yell in my head. *What do I do with this? You brought Mei into my life, and it was the best idea you've ever had, but then... this. I know I haven't been the greatest human you ever created. I sometimes sleep in church, and I skipped the youth ministry humanitarian trip last summer. And I've been lying to my dad, but come on...a hint would be great about now. Tell me if I should do this. Promise I'll keep my hands to myself. Won't touch her if that's what she needs, because I'll never be like Nick. I wanna show her I really love her. And as for Dad, he'll obviously be fine. He can figure out his own mess. I need your help with this one. Just please, whatever you tell me to do, let me have Mei.*

I clasp my hands between my knees and stare at them, then growl and stand, running back down the steps. I zigzag through side streets to Chinatown, the flash flood of adrenaline drying up and leaving behind pain. I need to get back to Mei but need someone to tell me if this is right. God's not answering. For the first time in my life, I wish I had a mom. But I have Guo. Maybe she's God's big hint. Okay, but really...run away with Mei? We're freaking eighteen. Years of college. She wants culinary school. Maybe she wants a fresh start somewhere else. Maybe she'd find someone else. Maybe I would.

No. Nope. No other girls, no college, nothing will make me feel the way one smile from Mei does. She's mine. I wanna be hers in the forever kinda way. And if that means getting out of San Francisco together...

I swallow as the haze in my head clears. If I do this, Mei will know I want us all the time. Forever. Commit, like Dad said. Maybe if he'd taken his own advice, my mom would've stuck around. Maybe they'd still be together. Maybe he didn't love my mom enough, but after only eight weeks of knowing

Mei, I love her way more than enough. And I never wanna be where I was five hours ago—without her.

I take off down the hill, letting momentum throw me into my new direction. Leaving all my doubt and fear in my dust. Mei's name pounds through my head with every step—Mei, Mei, Mei. Me. Us.

I look both ways as I approach a street then sprint across it, not bothering to wait for the light to change and am rounding the corner when a siren blares once like someone's being pulled over. I glance over my shoulder as I pump up the hill but falter when the siren whoops again. From Dad's patrol car.

Jerking my focus back to the sidewalk ahead of me, I scan the street, places I could detour, disappear, but his car accelerates behind me and veers to the curb beside me. Dad throws the car door open and jumps out.

"Marcus, stop!"

My legs tighten, but I keep running, my hands in fists now.

"I'm telling you to stop as a cop, not your dad. Stop now or I'll arrest you."

"You can't arrest me for catching you in a lie," I yell over my shoulder, slowing as the hill gets steeper. "Go call Kenna." Pushing my legs harder, I grit my teeth and shove myself up the hill, faltering when the car revs behind me and screeches to a stop between me and the corner. Dad jumps out again and strides toward me, his face all business, no apology, no shame. His eyes burn through me.

"We can talk about our personal differences after you explain these." He flashes his phone screen toward me as he barrels closer. I stop, glued to the moment and the picture on his screen. Me. Mei. Walking and holding hands. I swallow, my blood screeching to a halt then draining from my face, pooling in my feet.

He jabs his screen, swipes, his eyes on me like metal bars.

"Have something you wanna tell me? Maybe why pictures of you with Mei Li Zhang are on my lead suspect's phone?"

My heart thuds in my throat, mouth dry. I cough, searching for air. Me on Mei's fire escape. Swipe. Mei in her beanie, walking into my apartment building. Swipe. Mei, Lin, me walking home from my soccer game.

Dad stops inches from me, so close I can smell his deodorant. "Go ahead—explain. I'm all ears."

My brain's static, only one word visible through the black and white: How?

"Talk. Or I'll take you to the precinct and make you talk."

He's using his cop voice, and it bounces around my head, stirs up the anger I just pounded down on my run. "You think I'm gonna tell you anything when you've been hiding everything from me?"

"This isn't about Kenna or me, this is about you and how you're involved with Nick Chao."

I bark a laugh. "I'm not involved with Nick, but I'm pretty involved with Mei Li Zhang. And P.S., nothing's ever been about me. It's been all about you and redoing your past through me. So I do one thing for myself and you wanna arrest me?"

He steps closer, gets in my face. "Marcus, you have no idea what you're messing with and who—"

"I told Stanford no." It rockets out of me, and I tense; I want the news to explode in his face and hurt as much as it did for me to decline my scholarship. "Because of you."

He squints. "You what?"

"I declined my scholarship. Because of you. Because I was afraid of leaving you here alone. Turns out, you won't be."

His eyes flash and I swear his face goes pale but his jaw tightens and he steps back. "We can discuss this later but right now, I need you off these streets, locked in The Clubhouse. I've been working this case for four years and know what kind of loser Nick Chao is." He holds up the phone, still laser-focused on me. "If you're involved with Mei Li, you're involved with Nick and if he knows about you, all his people know about you. You're walking around with a target on your back."

His words are pointed, like he shot them from his gun.

"Of all the girls you could've gotten messed up with, this was the messiest, and it has to end." He steps to the driver's side door and talks over the roof of his car. "Get in the car so I can drive you home. You need to stay in the apartment, understand?"

"I'm not going anywhere until you tell me why Nick cares I'm with Mei. What does any of this have to do with Mei or me?"

He leans against the car, aiming his words at me, point blank. "Nick's not the one you should be worried about, Marcus." He swears, closes his eyes, rubs his forehead, then turns his eyes on me again. "You're closer to this case than you even realize. Get in the car." His eyes push me back against an invisible wall, so I fling open the car door and drop into the seat.

He slides into the driver's side and talks to the windshield as he revs the car down the hill. "I need every detail of you and Mei Li and Nick. Before we get to The Clubhouse."

I scan the purple shadows bruising the buildings as the sun comes up, people waking up to a new day that doesn't include being implicated in criminal activity. I need to find the high I was riding before Dad showed up but unanswered questions and the threat of arrest stomps it out. I need to know how those pictures of Mei and me got on Nick's phone and why. Need to get out of San Francisco. With Mei. Forget graduation. They can mail my diploma. Forget Dad's threats. I've told him all he needs to know. Maybe too much. Definitely too much.

CHAPTER 31

Cold spreads up my back. My shivering points out the empty space behind me where Marcus was when I fell asleep. My eyes fly open to more darkness. It's inside my head, my chest, now all around me. It lifted when Marcus carried me from the shower. Darkness never stays in his presence. Maybe there was too much for him this time. I wouldn't blame him if he stayed away. He said he'd never leave me, but he thought he was talking to the old me.

I blink back tears because I don't want to add them to the darkness. I don't want to hear my own voice because its words pushed Marcus away. I grimace and roll over, grabbing my phone. 5:07 AM. The world is still spinning. I'm alive. I'm not in L.A.

I open my phone and search local news and don't have to scroll far before my eyes skitter across a headline: "*Missing Women Rescued from Sex Trafficking Ring in L.A.*" My breath catches on two words: *sex trafficking*. It spins and tries to catch what those words could have meant for me, but my mind blocks it. Clicking on the article link, I scan news about missing women being rescued from an upscale hotel in downtown L.A. My hand goes to my throat where, only hours ago, Nick's hands were wrapped around it in that same hotel.

I skim the article again. *Eighteen women rescued.* No names have been released to the public yet, but Su Ling has to be one of them. Would I have been the nineteenth missing woman if Su Ling hadn't saved me? What was Nick planning to do with me? Or any of them?

I search for his name. *Multiple suspects in custody.* No names. But Nick has to be one of them. And Xander. Chaz?

The fear and shame that Nick wrapped around me is suffocating, and I put my hand over my stomach, swallow hard. I stare at the ceiling fan and let it whirl my thoughts toward the moments before Su Ling showed up. Cold. Exposed. Rough—everything rough. Lips, hands, the bed under me, Nick's voice. Screams scraping up my throat. Twisting, kicking. Praying. Nick's demands.

I put my hands over my eyes to stop the scene from flying at me, tears slipping between my fingers to wash it away. My legs twitch, ready to run from the memories swooping around me, and I scramble off the bed, stand in the middle of the room, hand over my mouth so I don't scream or throw up.

My reflection in the mirror on the back of the door catches my eye and I turn toward it. Except for the bruises on my face and around my neck, I look the same; this robe hides everything. But I can feel the damage from the inside out.

My fingers tremble as I pull one end of the belt. The robe slips off my shoulders and drops to the floor, uncovering the red burns smearing my stomach where Nick dragged me across the carpet. I touch the swollen, finger-shaped bruises circling my neck, turn my back to the mirror and glance over my shoulder. Purple splotches stain my back, shoulders, thighs. Turning to face my reflection, I hold my breath as I connect the dots between blotches and bruises down my stomach, thighs, hips. I let out a painful breath, my mind digging a hole and throwing in the memories of last night as gratitude rushes through me. Nick has taken a lot, but Su Ling saved me from the worst.

A soft knock rattles the door and my heart sputters as I grab the robe and slide into it.

"Xiao Mei?" Guo Mama's voice is gentle and when I tell her to come in, she slips inside and hands me a cup of tea. "Drink this. Marcus will be back soon."

I ease onto the edge of the bed, hoping she's right, and take the cup in both hands, soaking in the warmth through my fingertips.

"I called my brother in Seattle," she says, the mattress dipping as she sits next to me and talks into the room, her hand resting on my knee. "Everything is set. You will stay in his backyard cottage until we decide where you go next. It is small, but nice."

I nod, but my head is fuzzy as I picture my next steps. Steps that will take me away from Marcus for good. I swallow the burn. "And I can never come back."

Guo slides a hand over mine and shakes her head. "No, Xiao Mei."

I nod too quickly, the movement shaking my whole body. Attempting to shake Marcus-thoughts out of it. Shake off the dread and pain. It has to be this way. Now. Because of Nick. I clench my jaw, force him out. "What will happen to my parents?"

Guo Mama shifts to face me, her tender eyes holding mine. "I do not know. They got themselves into this mess, they will have to get out. But you cannot come back. No matter what. Understand?"

My vision blurs as I stare at the tea swaying in the cup. I want to go back to before. I want to work in the restaurant and hang out with Lin and go to school and talk about boys. And keep the boy who lives around the corner only in my dreams so I wouldn't know what it's like to lose him. I should have stayed in my real life, so I would still have choices. I didn't think I had any until now, when they've all been taken away. I'm getting exactly what I chose. I've always wanted to leave home, just not like this. I should have faked sick and stayed home from L.A. Run away on my terms. But maybe trying to run from my life got me here.

I glance at Guo Mama who looks like she's aged ten years in the last four hours and force a smile. "Thank you for helping me. When do I leave?"

A rap at the door startles me and Guo Mama smiles, touches my cheek before shuffling to the door. Marcus would never knock. No one else would come to the shop this early. But when Guo Mama opens the door, Mama's standing on the other side of it.

Guo Mama touches Mama's shoulder and glances at me. "I will be downstairs," she says, hurrying out of the room.

Mama steps inside and closes the door behind her. She's wearing sweatpants and a jacket, her hair thrown up in a messy bun. She clutches a large manila envelope to her chest.

"What are you doing here?" My voice is a whisper, still untangling itself from shock.

"My Mei Li." Her voice cracks as she searches my face. "Guo Mama told me what happened. I'm so sorry."

A tear escapes, and I look down as it drops into my teacup, silence filling the space between us.

"She says you're leaving. That's good."

My eyes slide up to hers. "Good…?"

She shakes her head. "No. Not at all, but for the best. I am so proud of you, Mei Li. You have so much courage."

"I don't want courage—I want my life back but that won't happen now because I got scared and called the police."

Mama swallows, nods without looking away, her eyes glossy in the shadows. "I know, and I'm so glad you did and that you won't get your old life back. Now you can create a new, better one. Because you called the police, eighteen women are safe and Nick and many others have been arrested." She presses her lips together, her face pale. "There will be many more arrests, I'm certain, and I'm glad about that too."

My head snaps toward her. "How do you know that?"

"Xander called Chaz from jail. Chaz called me to tell me everything that is happening."

"Why would Chaz call you…?"

"Because there are many things I did not know were happening."

"But Chaz is involved. Why didn't he get arrested?"

"He's certain he will. And I'm certain the restaurant will close soon and we will be sent back to Taiwan." She looks at her feet. "I'm glad, because I want my life back too. I want nothing more to do with this one and I want you far away from it too."

I blink as the words pelt my head, a few soaking in. Arrests. Restaurant closing. Taiwan. It's not home anymore, but it's far from memories. From Nick. From things I want but can't have.

"I'll come with you," I blurt and Mama stares at me, then shakes her head.

"No, Mei Li."

"Why?" I whisper. "I have to leave, anyway. I might as well—"

"No." Mama says firmly, then takes a deep breath and sits on the bed beside me, careful not to touch me. "I've been sent to find you and bring you home immediately but if you ask me what I think you should do, I would tell you to listen very carefully to Guo Mama's plan."

"But what about Baba? What's he going to do?" My voice is horse.

"You owe that man nothing." She looks right at me for the first time in days. "He's not who either of us thought he was." She sets the envelope on my lap and stares into the room, tears trembling in the corner of her eyes before she turns to me and gives me a tight smile, her eyes searching my face.

"I must go. Do as Guo Mama says and you will be safe. I will find out how you are doing through her." Her voice breaks and she stands and walks toward the door, then stops, her back to me, hand on the knob. "When you read what's inside that envelope, please know I have no regrets because what I gave up brought you here and what you found here lets me know it was worth it. I love you." She glances over her shoulder, then opens the door.

I swallow the lump of tears suspended in my swollen throat and choke out, "Wait! You could come with me."

She steps back into the room, gripping the doorjamb. "I can't. But we will see each other again, I know it."

The stairs creak as she hurries down them, and I stare at the empty doorway, then blink my focus to the manila envelope. Picking it up like it might ignite any minute, I pry open the clasp and slide out the stack of papers and folders.

My passport and my CALC folder land on top and I stare at them. My notes…from Marcus. Notes I thought only Guo Mama, Marcus, and I knew about. They were hidden in my desk drawer…

My fingers hover over the pile before sweeping it aside to a stack of printed, stapled emails. Picking it up, I read the date: August 17, 2005. Scan the names: From Peter Mitchell to Huang, Jia Li. All from August, September, a few from October. I fan through them, my eyes skittering over page after page of emails between an eighteen-year-old Mama and a boy from Rhode Island, according to his first email, and when my eyes land on the word "pregnant", I close the folder as if I shouldn't know more, but a picture and a folded piece of paper falls out, floating to the floor.

I pick it up, my fingers trembling as I study the picture of a teenage boy with wavy, strawberry-blonde hair lying on a beach, smiling up at the camera, sunglasses reflecting the girl behind it. Frowning, I unfold the paper and scan the copy of a Facebook profile for Peter Mitchell, an older version of the same guy from the picture, standing on a rocky shoreline with three blond kids. I study his face, his lopsided smile. I don't recognize him, but I do recognize Mama's handwriting at the top of the page, and the message drops into my stomach in a cold, hard lump: *He doesn't know about you, but you should know about him.*

CHAPTER 32

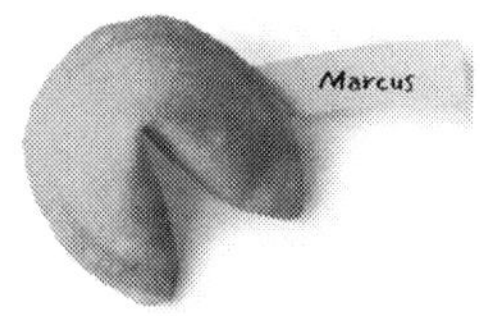

I give Dad maybe two sentences of information—how long I've been dating Mei and the thing Nick did to her that night in the alley. I leave out the thing he did to her last night or all the other times before. Or where she's at now and what she's told me about her situation because I just don't know where this is all headed. In exchange, Dad answers my question about what, exactly, Nick has done. Without telling me the top secret, for-cop-eyes-and-ears only stuff, he confirms that Nick is at the center of the missing women case but there are others.

Okay, so…according to Mei, she and her family are undocumented and supposedly here because of Nick, but is there more? Is she more involved with Nick than she's told me? Is she even who she says she is or is she trying to protect Nick and her family? The way she looks right now tells me otherwise, but I just don't know.

"I need you to think really hard about what you've told me and make sure it's everything because if something comes out later, you can forget college. So. One more time: is there anything you're not telling me that you should?" Dad checks over his shoulder and changes lanes, then turns the corner faster than any law-abiding cop should.

I don't even know what more to tell him because I don't know what I'm involved with at this point. I could tell him about getting jumped by Nick's guys. That Guo knows stuff, but it's all too heavy to drag up and out of my mouth so I shake my head. "That's it."

Dad's phone rings and he glances at the screen, then swears as he punches the button to answer. "Call you back in five." He ends the call and stares straight ahead. "I've got to get to the station so I'm going to drop you off at The Clubhouse and you're going to stay there and not answer the door, you understand? You cannot leave, no matter what, and you cannot talk to Mei Li. It's dangerous for both of you. No discussion, no exception."

I look out the window.

"Marcus?"

"Got it," I say through a clenched jaw.

"When I get home, we'll dig into everything else. All of it."

He veers to the curb and I'm out of the car, inside our building, taking the stairs two at a time as questions chase me up them. Is Dad just doing this because he found out I'm with Mei? Should I have told him what happened to her? Should I be with Mei? Is it safe for us to leave or will someone follow us? Should I leave with her?

I burst through The Clubhouse door, slam it behind me, and back against it, scanning the living room. This isn't home anymore. This is where Mei and I ended. Where I believed everything Dad said. I want to leave it all here and get out of San Francisco.

It's so quiet, the clock ticks in my head, reminding me how long I've been gone from Mei. I pull out my phone and dial Guo's number.

"Are you okay, boy?"

"Yeah. Just…so many things." I rub my forehead and close my eyes. "Can I ask you a question and will you give me an honest answer?"

"I always do."

"Is Mei involved with everything Nick was doing? Like, was she ever part of it? Or her family?"

"No, she is not. Neither is her mama but…" Guo pauses on the other end, and I tense. "I cannot say the same for her baba."

"Her dad's involved? Like how involved? Some kind of fall guy? Or Nick's henchman or something? What??"

"Or something."

I grip the phone and stare into the dark living room. So Mei's not involved but she's so close to the action.

"Does Mei know?"

"No. And it must stay that way until things are confirmed."

This phone can't even handle a secret this heavy. My hand aches. My throat. My head that's not sturdy enough to handle the realization that just plowed into it: even if I stay in San Francisco, I won't be with Mei. Stuff's going to happen to her family if her dad's really involved. We definitely have to leave, and we have to hide because this could be bad. All of it.

"You okay, boy?"

I push up through the layers of debris my life just made. "Yeah. So…do you think your brother would be okay with me staying at his place? And how soon can he be ready for us?"

"He is ready now. I already told him you would be coming with Mei Li. She will be ready as soon as you get here."

The call ends and I look at the phone, then dart into the kitchen and snag the lanyard with the motorcycle key on it and throw it over my head. Sprinting to my room, I pull my soccer bag from under my bed and empty it, shove clothes and hoodies inside along with an extra pair of Adidas. I snatch my wallet and Meemaw's graduation money, tossing it inside along with my passport, just in case. We might have to run a lot farther than we would have before I saw Dad.

Headed for the door, I pause, backtrack, and yank open my top dresser drawer. I grab Buddha and a couple books I haven't finished yet.

On my way past the kitchen, a note Dad left on the whiteboard on the fridge catches my eye. I missed it when I came home from prom since it was so dark but now, I see his message: *Wake me up when you get home*. Definitely didn't have to wake him up, and I wonder what my life would be like right now if he'd fallen asleep instead of talking to Kenna. Or hung up with her two minutes earlier. I wouldn't have known Dad's been lying. Wouldn't have run to Mei's. Wouldn't know about Mei's situation or any of this. I might have missed her. Never seen her again. Maybe I should be grateful for Kenna.

I wipe off Dad's message with the side of my hand and grab the dry erase marker.

"I left. My choice. I'll check in later."

I set the marker down and am out of The Clubhouse. Down the stairs, out the building, running through backstreets and dodging puddles in alleys. Every time I think of a shivering, bruised Mei in the shower, I run faster. Every time I think of the pictures on Dad's phone, I stumble. Anyone could be following me. They could jump me and lights out. Then again, I'd almost prefer that to seeing Dad again and explaining why I'm doing the exact opposite of what he told me to do.

My legs are cramping by the time I make it to Lex's house, sweat dripping in my eyes as I punch in his garage code, urge the door to move faster. Hope Lex really is with Dad.

When the door rises enough to duck under it, my eyes land on my bike and I straighten, stare at her. She's more beautiful than she looked in the pictures. I circle her, run my hands over her. Matte black body, chrome everywhere else. And a seat perfect for me with Mei right behind me.

Smiling for the first time in hours, I shove my bag in the seat compartment and slide onto the motorcycle, rubbing the handlebars. I'm totally in love. She's mine. And if I'm going by Ray Rules, I earned every last bolt.

I roll her out of the garage, punching the button to close the door, then slip the key in the ignition and ride toward freedom.

My hands ache from being clenched, gripping the handlebars like I can control my life if I just keep my grip tight enough. I squint against the heavy fog draped between buildings, my eyes stinging as I speed back toward Chinatown, taking corners way too fast, imagining Dad behind me any second.

Early morning buses rumble past and send ripples toward me, try to shake me off my bike. The whole world quakes beneath me. I accelerate, and a few minutes later, I turn so fast into the alley behind Guo's shop that I have to put my foot on the ground to keep the bike upright. Swearing, I steady it, veer behind a dumpster, then cut the engine and jump off.

Throwing open Guo's back door, I weave through the dark, around stacks of boxes, burst through the velvet curtain into Guo's kitchenette where she and Mei sit at the table.

Their heads snap up, Mei's hand on her chest before she closes her eyes and breathes my name. "You scared me."

"We have to go. Now. My dad knows about us. And Nick. There's…I'll explain later." My eyes meet hers. "I'm going to Seattle with you."

Emotions sweep across Mei's face, her eyes going from afraid to confused to hopeful to questioning while Guo watches silently.

"Marcus, no—you can't—"

"I'm going with you and we gotta go now."

She hesitates, her hand gripping the table's edge before she stands. "*Are you sure*?" she asks with her eyes.

I nod spastically. "*So sure*."

She presses her lips together, then swallows and turns toward a bag by the stairs. She's dressed, packed, shoes on. She was going to leave without me. I could have lost her, just like that. The way my heart folds over that thought to smother it is the only sign I need. I'm doing the right thing.

Guo's chair scrapes against the tile. "You will be safe there until we can figure out the next best thing. I will stay in contact. This is as it should be." She reaches up and pats my face.

I swallow and nod, glance at Guo who's staring at me.

"You are wondering what will happen to Mr. Ray, yes?"

"Yeah. Even though right now, I shouldn't care."

She puts her hand on my arm. "You love him, and he loves you. Everything will be okay. Magic 8 said so, and I will make sure." Guo opens her arms and wraps us both in a hug, her face against my chest as she talks. "Please be safe."

I lay my cheek on top of Guo's head as she speaks to Mei in Mandarin. My heart is racing. We've been here too long. Dad's gonna show up, stop us from leaving. Stop us from being together. Detonate my world again.

I lean down to kiss Guo on the cheek, then grab Mei's hand and her bag, not saying anything because there are too many emotions in the way.

Guo slips the address into Mei's hand, and I follow her out the door, pausing when Mei stops on the top step and stares at the motorcycle.

"You got it," she breathes, looking over her shoulder at me. "When did this happen…?"

"Incredibly long story and I'll tell you everything but right now, we gotta go." Darting around her, I drape her bag over the back of the motorcycle so it covers the temporary license plate, then take the helmet from the handlebars as Mei eases onto the seat.

I pause, gripping the helmet, because Mei is on my motorcycle. The only two things I want, right here. Twelve hours ago, I wouldn't have dared hope to see Mei again because it hurt too much. Now, she's here. It's us, together.

My heart beats in my throat as she takes the helmet from me, pulls it on, buckles it. Ready. Decided. I shove my sleeves up my arms to release heat trapped in my hoodie, but Mei grabs my arm, staring at THE END I drew in bold, black finality last night, then looks at me, searching.

"Why this…?"

Words throw themselves around my head, scattered and frantic. "When I didn't hear from you, I thought we were—"

She squeezes her eyes shut and shakes her head at my arm, then meets my eyes again. "Do you have a Sharpie?"

I slide the one I grabbed on the way out of The Clubhouse out of my pocket and she takes it, uncaps it, and scribbles out END, then writes BEGINNING under the black smudge on my arm.

Blinking away emotions, I tug her helmet strap toward me, my eyes locked on hers. "I love you," I breathe against her lips, and my mouth doesn't need a reintroduction to hers; I would never forget how she feels even if I'd never seen her again. Hers is telling me the same thing, and I give my mouth full permission to take us way past THE END and the old us and pull us to the other side of together where I'm staying for good.

A car parks at the end of the alley, and I pull back from Mei, glancing over her head. Not Dad, not a cop, but we have to get out of here before it is.

Sliding onto the seat in front of her, I crank the key and rev the engine, nodding at Guo standing in the back door before veering us around the dumpster and down the alley. Mei's arms wrap around me, holding us together while our old life crumbles behind us and we speed toward whatever comes next.

ACKNOWLEDGMENTS

And the Oscar goes to:

Director: Amy Michelle Carpenter
Editing: John Olsen
Production Design: Mary Gray
Visual Effects: Natisha Bethers with Asombra Studios
Best Picture: The entire Monster Ivy Team
Cinematography: Jake Allen

Honorable Mentions:

Thanks a million to…

Persistence, for being omnipresent since day one.

Hayley, Reba, Erykah and everyone on Instagram who has supported, encouraged, shared, and posted. Our book has taken flight across the interwebs thanks to you.

Whitney, for casually mentioning Monster Ivy over lunch at Storymakers. You were right about them!

Our beloved writers group, who has seen this book at its worst, messiest, most frustrating, brightest, and now at its completion and birth. A part of each of you is on the pages of this book.

Our friends, who have watched and cheered and consoled during this excruciatingly long process. You know who we really are.

Our families, who have witnessed incalculable hours of writing during the past fourteen years. There were probably many times you doubted this book would ever move off our computers, but never said so. Bennett, Miles, London, Liam, and MeiLi, thanks for being patient with us when our heads weren't exactly in the moment with you. Confession: the long walks we took you on as kids were excuses for us to plot and verbally write as we pushed double strollers uphill both ways. And to our husbands, Christopher and Jake, who never complained when we spent more time with imaginary people and in imaginary places than we did with you. We love you all more than this book. So...immeasurably.

To Heavenly Father and Jesus, who, despite Their immortality, were likely exhausted by our prayers. It's embarrassing how long it took us to figure out You always know best. We are ever grateful for Your infinite patience and listening ears. Our prayers will sound different moving forward, but never fear—You'll still hear from us. We have a lot of books to write.

ABOUT THE AUTHORS

Emily Cox is a fast-walking big thinker who believes in aliens, has a mostly-titanium face, and a rhyming maiden and married name (Box-Cox). She lives in Utah in a house of all boys.

Nicole Allen is a live-theater lover, crime podcast junkie, and the highly disputed funniest person in her family. She believes in karma but is skeptical about dinosaurs.

CONNECT

with us

STAY CONNECTED BY
JOINING OUR MAILING
LIST AND RECEIVING
UPDATES!

Made in United States
Troutdale, OR
01/30/2024